FEAR US

Broken Love Series

BOOK THREE

B.B. REID

Fear Us by B.B. Reid

ISBN-13:978-1540768513
ISBN-10: 1540768511

Second Edition 2016

Manuscript Analysis & Editing by
Rogena Mitchell-Jones, Literary Editor
Final Proofread by Ami Hadley
RMJ-Manuscript Service LLC
www.rogenamitchell.com

Cover Design by Amanda Simpson of Pixel Mischief Design.
Cover Photo by Paul Marinis and Jacob Lund from Shutterstock

Table of Contents

Dedication

Happy Birthday, Tae.
This one is for you.

LETTER TO KEENAN

Dear Keenan,

I hope by the end of this book you come back to us.

I miss the lighthearted you.

The one who would do anything for his friends and wore his heart on his sleeve.

Though we didn't like your cheating and lack of respect for women, we still loved you.

Love,
Beebs.

P.S. Don't let the darkness swallow you.

PROLOGUE

ELEVEN YEARS AGO
KEENAN

I KICKED THE basketball ball around the grass like I'd seen on TV. My father had asked what I wished to have for my birthday. I couldn't tell him my deepest wish without being locked away, so I requested a basketball. In the end, it was all spoiled by the revelation that he forgot to get a hoop. I could only bounce or kick the ball around, but even that small fortune wasn't allowed. Sometimes, I would bounce it anyway just so they would talk to me even if it were to scold.

Maybe today he would be nice, and we could get a hoop so he could show me how to play. It was already noon, and he wasn't gone, so maybe he would finally have time for me. I ran into the house with my new idea, hoping today would be the day. Excitement built with each step as I ran around the house as quietly as I could.

They never liked when I made noise. They would never get angry, but they would send me away to my room, and sometimes, they would forget about me. When I would get hungry enough, I would finally come out only to find a plate of food left waiting.

After searching the entire house, I finally found him in his office sleeping with his head down. He didn't wake when I walked in so I moved closer to stand beside him.

"Daddy." When he didn't answer, I tugged on his pant leg while clutching the ball to my chest.

"Keenan." My mother's voice drifted from the doorway. She sounded sad again today, but then she always sounded sad.

"Mama, will Daddy teach me how to play?" I held up the ball nervously.

The solemn look on her face had told me the answer before she spoke, but it wasn't the answer expected. "You know you're not supposed to be in here."

"I know, but I didn't know when he would come out."

"We've told you to keep out of sight and inside."

"But you won't let me play with it inside. Why did Daddy buy me this stupid thing if I can't play with it?"

"Keenan." This time it was a deep but drunken slur of my father to call my name. I turned away from my mother to see that he was now sitting up in his chair. Though his hair was ruffled and his clothing wrinkled, he still looked strong. He also looked annoyed judging by the blank look on his face. "Don't talk back to your mother.

"Will you play with me today?" I didn't intend to beg, but desperation had snuck in and now I was shaking with it. He blinked once—slowly as if clearing something before shaking his head.

"Go to your room."

Rejection stung, but it cut much deeper when it was

your parents who were constantly rejecting you.

"Why do you hate me?" I cried and threw the ball down. My temper had gotten the best of me, but it was just my hope for attention, even anger, but as always, I failed. He had already turned away and began typing on his computer as if he wasn't just passed out drunk after consuming the entire bottle lying next to his hand.

"Come," my mother called. She too had already turned away, expecting for me to follow. I turned back to plead with my dad once more but caught him staring after her. Pain filled his eyes just before they darkened.

"Go, Keenan." This time I obeyed and wondered if they would notice if I disappeared forever.

"Son?" Hope flared once again as I whirled around.

"Yes, Dad?"

"Don't come back in here and stay out of sight."

Defeated, I nodded and finally walked away with my head down.

Wanted.

That was my deepest wish.

To feel wanted.

By anyone who would care—even if for only a moment.

CHAPTER ONE

PROM NIGHT
KEENAN

I'M A FUCKING masochist. I steered my bike into the expansive driveway. I hadn't realized just how much it rang true until I shut off the engine and dismounted.

It's too late to turn back now.

The last remnants of daylight faded away, but I kept my shades on as a shield. The last thing I needed was for her to see just how much she hurt me. It was one of the vows I made to myself when I lay dying in a hospital.

Never let them see. Never let them close. Never let them in.

I would live by that from now on, but first, I had to give in one last time.

My feet pounded the steps leading to the front door. If I had to be honest, I was nervous as fuck. This was not how I pictured this night. I never pictured it much at all, but I always knew it would be with her. That was when I believed in the fairytale I'd been bitched into believing. My hand lifted, but I froze before I could knock, realizing I was being sucked back into the same bullshit.

I wasn't about to do this again.

I was already backing away, but before I could turn to leave, the door opened. Dash, dressed in a richly tailored dark gray suit, greeted me with first, surprise, and then a wary look before walking away, leaving the door open.

I stared through the open portal, taking in the extravagant foyer well aware of everyone's uneasiness.

When did I become the bad guy?

I sensed my brother's glare and the dangerous energy that traveled across the room. I would have returned it if *she* hadn't chosen that moment to walk in.

I experienced what they called tunnel vision as I drank her in. She looked too fucking perfect, and even now, I could feel my anger abating.

Hurting her had become second place to the need to bend her over the nearest flat surface and restate my claim.

But why should I have to restate my claim? She was already mine and should have fucking stayed that way.

But she didn't. She left me.

Can you imagine how much it fucking hurt to feel as if each breath you took might be your last but always using the little you had to beg the one person who claimed to love you unconditionally just to be there?

It fucked me up.

But most of all, it changed me.

And I hated her for it.

My conscience whispered to me that it wasn't right to blame her, but the darkening part of my heart wanted to rip her apart and destroy her completely—and I would.

She had no idea what was coming.

"Keenan... How—how are you?"

*****

There were moments when I believed surviving being shot and losing my lungs were a big mistake. I thought maybe I would have been better off by taking the plunge than spending the next sixty years or so wasting away.

It had been a few hours, and I managed to call myself every name in the book. There was no one at this moment who thought lower of me than myself.

Sheldon looked stunning.

Her hair had been glossed.

Her dress fit perfectly.

She looked ready for the fairytale night with a Prince Charming.

I had tried to ruin that by making her feel guilty. But of course, I couldn't stop there. I was dead set on hurting everyone in my life, starting with the one person who would ensure that I couldn't turn back.

"Keenan, why are you doing this?"

"Isn't it obvious?"

"Not to me," Lake whispered demurely. I fought the urge to laugh. Despite the bravado that she'd shown over the last few months, she was still a scared little mouse. And now, my brother had her in his grasp and he would eat her alive.

"I'm jealous."

"But why?"

"Because my brother doesn't deserve a happily ever after."

"You don't mean that."

"Why don't I?"

"Look, I know you're hurting, and it was a lot to

take in, but you have to remember Keiran was just a child. There is so much you don't know. If you would just talk to him—"

"My brother," I bit out, "had eleven years to tell me the truth."

"Keenan, he didn't know she was your mother. She was his mother, too." Her lips trembled on the last, and I wondered who she felt sorrier for—him or me?

"It doesn't really matter, does it? She's dead. Nothing is going to change that. I hardly even remember her… I would say Keiran is the lucky one. He never had to look into his mother's eyes every day and wonder why she didn't love you, why she wouldn't hug you, or what you did wrong. Most days, she barely acknowledged me. My father wasn't any better. I was alone for seven years. There was no laughter or warmth. The silence was almost frightening. I think I hated it the most. When she left and never came back, I never even shed a tear. I almost wished she had been cruel, and then maybe it wouldn't have meant as much that she left and never looked back."

"But you had Keiran. You had each other."

I shrugged. "Keiran was very much the same then as he is now—distant, moody, and violent. You were right that day you asked if I was afraid of him. I was for the longest time, and I guess I always was. He wanted nothing to do with me. I just wanted a friend."

"But you got through to him."

"Did I?"

"Your brother loves you, Keenan. He may not know how to show it in a healthy way, but it's true, and I know you love him."

"Neither one of us knows what love is. He'll hurt you, Lake. It's his nature to do so. He may think he wants this with you, but one day, he'll crack under the pressure."

"Is that what you did with Sheldon?"

I felt my shoulders lift, but couldn't fully process the weight resting upon them. "The idea of love leaves a bad taste."

"Sheldon didn't deserve what you did. Why did you sleep with that teacher? It's a bit ridiculous even for you. It's downright ludicrous."

"Does it matter now? It all worked out for the best." I took another swig of the bottle that was nearly empty now. Her eyes, full of reproach, looked from the bottle and back. I was still recovering from the lung transplant and wasn't supposed to be drinking, but no one could ever accuse me of giving a shit and be right.

"How can I make this right?"

I laughed despite the bitterness settling in the pit of my stomach. I needed an escape. I needed to hide. Hiding is what I was good at.

I lowered my head and let my next words float over the skin of her neck. "You can start by letting me kiss you."

She jumped and slapped her hands against my chest when I pushed closer against her. "Keenan! What are you doing?"

"Did you know that I had a crush on you in the ninth grade?" I asked, ignoring her struggles.

"You what?"

"It's true. I made the mistake of telling Keiran one day how pretty I thought you were."

"Well, what did he say?"

I let out a laugh but felt none of the humor. "He threatened to break every bone in my body if I ever talked to you. I thought he might have gotten over his vendetta against you and wanted you for himself."

"Well, we all know that wasn't true."

"Maybe not, but he always wanted you. He was just good at hiding it." I lowered my lips closer and her eyes nearly bugged out of her head.

"I—I think I should go."

"Am I making you nervous?" I smiled down at her and conveniently placed my arms next to her head, caging her in.

"What a stupid question. Of course, you are. This is wrong."

"At the risk of sounding cliché, can I just say doing wrong can feel so damn good?"

"You're right... You do sound like a cliché."

"You are too fucking sexy for words. Keiran doesn't know what he has yet, does he?"

The slam of the door interrupted her response, and I felt my resolve collapse at the icy chill of the presence behind me, and the low, threatening growl.

"I know exactly what I have. My only question is what the fuck are you doing touching her?"

"Keiran," Lake shouted nervously. "He, uh—I, um—"

"Lake, go upstairs and don't come down no matter what you hear." He never spared her a glance, but he didn't have to. She quickly slid from my grasp. She was no sooner out of sight when I had taken her place against the wall. Keiran's arm pinned me to the wall by my throat making breathing hard. "Do you want to die that much?"

His menacing voice was enough to make the average person cower and beg for mercy, but I had practically been raised by him. I threw my head into his and stunned him long enough to deliver a hard blow to his jaw. He quickly recovered and managed to hit me two times, once in the face and the other to my gut before I could get another hit in.

Keiran might have been stronger, but I was quicker.

We were each deadly in our own right.

We wouldn't stop until the other was dead.

I flipped Keiran over my shoulder and onto the coffee table. It broke under his weight, and he hit the ground hard. Unsteadily, he bounced back to his feet and delivered a severe kick to my chest, sending me crashing into the wall behind me.

Slowly, I slid back up the wall, my gaze locked with his. We waited only a heartbeat, but the time seemed to stretch into forever before we crashed into each other once more.

"Son of a bitch. Grab them before they kill each other," a frantic yet familiar voice shouted.

I was thrown backward and Keiran in the opposite direction. I recognized Dash through my blurry vision with his arms wrapped tight around Keiran's chest. He struggled to hold on but managed to keep him subdued.

"Keenan, man, pipe down before I put you out," Q growled. It was only then I realized I was struggling just as hard. My gaze was still trained on him, and my mind was still corrupted by the need to murder.

Neither one of us were recognizable to the other. Blood poured from our wounds. Everything in the vicinity was either broken or shattered.

Lake suddenly appeared and ran through the room, crying hysterically, throwing herself onto Keiran.

I had only one guess as to who called them.

"*My* girl, Keenan."

"My mother, *brother*."

It was the last words I would speak to him for a long time.

*****

I should have left town when I walked out of that house and away from my only family, but I was hell bent on a course to wreak havoc, which is how I ended up in Sheldon's bedroom. "Keenan, why are you doing this? This isn't you!"

"Yeah?" I stared down at her body splayed out for me as an offering I had just recently finished devouring. "You think you know me?"

"What?" She looked around disorientated. "Of course, I do," she whispered softly. I didn't like the way she gazed up at me with love in her eyes.

Her love was a lie.

Love was just that.

A lie.

"But you don't know me. You never did." She tried to lift up, but the belt wrapped around her neck and tied to the rails of her headboard stopped her movements. "I watched him do this to her one night."

"What?" I ignored the confusion in her eyes and continued.

"I wanted to see what he was doing to her. I wasn't looking for pleasure. I was curious. Just me trying to be a good guy. I actually thought I might have been willing to protect her if need be because she couldn't protect herself. But then she fucking took him. She actually decided to be with him thinking he could change, but he won't and she won't realize it until it's too late. She's already trapped."

I knew I sounded like a crazy person rambling, but anyone with eyes and a brain would know it was true. Keiran was not only dangerous. He was possessive, too.

"Keenan, please let me go."

"I always wondered what kind of desire he could get from someone he claimed to hate. Now I fucking know." The slump in her shoulders and the way her eyes rounded told me she knew exactly who I hated.

"You hate me?"

"What I feel for you goes far beyond hate. I needed you, Shelly, and you turned your back on me just like she did."

"I am not your mother, Keenan!"

"Oh, I know that. The difference between you and her was that I actually believed you loved me."

"I do!" she cried out and struggled against her bonds.

I gritted my teeth. My internal fight was threatening to surface. I needed to stay levelheaded. "Then prove it."

"How?"

"Run away with me."

Son of a bitch... That wasn't what I was supposed to say, but I wasn't going to take the words back either. With each second that passed, and the fear growing in her eyes, the idea began to sound better and better.

"What?"

"You're either going to run with me or run from me. Make your choice."

I held my breath and kept what I hoped was a blank expression while my stomach twisted to the point of pain. I couldn't put a word on what I was feeling.

"I do love you."

Hope. That's what I felt. I was glad I could still feel at all.

"So you'll come with me then?"

That was until she took it away.

"No, Keenan. I won't."

*****

The one person who could make me stay or who could make me feel whole again—if I ever was—turned me away. There was no way I could stay. She wanted to be free, and I would let her, but not before I made her a promise.

If I ever returned—if I ever saw her again—I would keep her—and I would make her sorry.

I risked coming back to my father's house because there was one thing I couldn't leave without. I had made it to the landing before I heard the lowered voices. My footsteps lightened as I crept closer to the bedroom door left slightly ajar.

"I know you're pissed, but you can't give up on him. He needs you now more than ever."

"Keenan is capable of taking care of himself. He had no issues helping himself to you a few hours ago."

"Do you really think that was about me? He's fucked up right now, but he wouldn't go that far. He wouldn't hurt you like that no matter how much he thinks he wants to. He thinks you're choosing me over him."

"What if I am? He's made his feelings about me clear."

"Just like you made your feelings clear for me all these years? But even then, you still felt something for me."

"What are you saying?"

"I'm saying you were good at running and you ran because you were confused."

"Confused or not, he tried to take what belongs to me."

"First, I'm not your property, Keiran. Second, he cannot take what I am not willing to give."

"It doesn't matter anymore anyway." I could hear the frustration in his tone and could picture him running his hands down his face in that way he did that said he was ready to kill something... or someone.

I knew the risk I was taking by coming onto Lake, but she had been wrong. If she had offered, I would have taken because it was about her. I was willing to go that far because I knew what she meant to Keiran. I wasn't a good person and tonight proved that.

I moved away and quietly entered my bedroom only to see a figure lying in the darkness. Light breathing filled the room, and I realized whoever it was must have been asleep. I crept slowly toward the sleeping form until I was standing at the head of my bed.

It was Di. The daughter of the man my brother—Keiran—sent to prison.

I shook her none too gently and waited for her eyes to pop open. When they did, a terror I hadn't expected flooded her expression when her gaze landed on me. She quickly backed away and then thrust her hands out to ward me off. I never moved from my spot, so I wondered what she could possibly be afraid of.

"Why are you in here?"

At the sound of my voice, her head tilted to the side in recognition though her eyes still appeared lost. "Keenan?"

Her husky voice sounded like sex, and I got the idea that she could be a phone sex operator, but then scratched it in my head before it could fully form. She was too sexy to be confined to a phone. A body like hers was made to be on display. Maybe that's why her father pimped her out. And I thought I was fucked up.

She brushed her dark hair out of her face and stared at me with her wide eyes and even wider lips. I considered fucking her for a moment but quickly nixed it. The scent and feel of Sheldon were both still evident on my cock, and strangely, I didn't want anything to taint that. At least until I took a shower.

"What are you doing back here?" she asked when I turned away.

"I live here."

"If Keiran sees you—"

I slammed the dresser drawer after retrieving what I came for and turned on her. "Don't categorize me with the spineless fucks who tremble at the sight of him. I'm not afraid of him."

"Obviously. You guys fucked each other up pretty good," she grinned.

"Later." I made for the door but, of course, she had to keep going.

"Wait," she whispered loudly. "You look like someone who is running away. Where are you going?"

"Away from here."

"Where is away?"

"I don't know yet."

"Can I come?"

"Are you serious? Fuck no."

"I can make it worth your while. You will need money. I have it, but it's at home. I just need you to get me there."

I had to admit I was intrigued. My eighteenth birthday had passed three months ago, and I'd yet to receive my inheritance. I sure as fuck wasn't about to sit around and wait for it like some spoiled rich kid. I wanted no ties or obligations to my family. "How much money are we talking?"

Her smile spread even wider. "Enough to live free."

Chapter Two

FOUR YEARS LATER
SHELDON

"PENCILS DOWN. TIME is up. Please turn in your testing materials and have a great summer, everyone."

The classroom came alive with students rushing to turn in tests and start their summer. I blew out what little breath was left in my lungs, shouldered my bag, and headed to the front where the tests were being turned in. Finals were officially over, and in two weeks, I graduate. Sometimes, I still can't believe it's been four years.

They say time flies when you're having fun.

It might have been true except these last four years had been anything but fun.

"So how do you think you did?" Cool lips pressed against my neck as my bag was taken from my shoulder and slung onto a broad shoulder covered in dark cotton.

Eric Spencer was the one who every girl with a romantic heart dreamed of as her Mr. Right.

Sandy brown hair tangled in riotous curls complemented the twinkling green eyes staring down at me. He had good ole boy written all over him.

His hard body was free of tattoos.

He came from a good, wholesome family.

He was kind, sweet, and romantic.

And most importantly, he had not a disloyal bone in his body.

We've dated for almost a year now and never had I suffered from jealousy or insecurity.

He was perfect.

Perfect and convenient.

"Hard to tell," I finally answered. "I can't remember answering any of the questions."

"That's okay. I know you did because I couldn't keep my eyes off of you."

"Hmmm... Was it really me or were you just trying to take a peek at my answers?" I joked as we left the classroom.

"Can you blame me? Not only are you beautiful, but you're smarter than me, too."

Once we reached the parking lot, I swung around to face him, planting my hand on his chest. "Flattery will get you everything."

He leaned in to whisper against my lips, "I'm counting on it." I let his lips press against mine and although I felt none of the searing intensity that I was introduced to at a much more tender age, I enjoyed it.

And why shouldn't I? He was sexy as hell.

He just wasn't the one I craved.

Don't take yourself down that dark path, Sheldon.

"Oh, no you don't." It was hard to tell whom the warning was really for, but I jumped away, disguising the uneasiness I felt with a playful grin and tilt of my lips. "I have to get home, stud."

After snagging my backpack from his shoulder, I

started for my car, needing to put distance between us.

"Any chance I might finally get that invite?"

Shit.

"You know I can't do that."

"All I know is what you tell me, and that isn't much. Please, Shelly—"

"Don't." When his frown deepened, I added, "I asked you not to call me that."

I didn't miss the confusion in his eyes before he continued. "If I can't come home with you, will you at least tell me why you insist on remaining such a mystery?"

"If I told you, then you wouldn't be half as interested in me as you are now." I lowered my sunglasses, checked my watch, and practically ran to get to my car.

I was late.

I fought through seven miles of traffic. The short distance took me twenty minutes due to everyone rushing home. There was a forecast for a thunderstorm tonight. Summer storms always proved to be the fiercest so I could understand the slight panic.

When I finally reached my destination, I hopped out of my car and rushed over the sidewalk to the entrance where the manager was closing the door for the night.

"Cindy, I am so sorry."

"Sheldon, I told you to take all the time you needed." She turned from locking the door with a wide smile gracing her lips. "So how did it go?"

"I'm not sure..."

I picked up my little dark haired bundle who pouted and said, "Mommy late," before kissing me on the cheek.

It was a move she made when she was upset with me but still wanted attention that reminded me so much of her father. I nibbled on her chubby cheeks, and once she was preoccupied playing with my hair, I turned back to the daycare manager.

"You're not sure?" She cocked her hip and rolled her eyes. Cindy was like the big sister I never had although no one would ever really believe we were biological sisters simply because she's African American. "What the hell does that mean, Sheldon? You have too much riding on graduating."

"Language, Cindy."

For a girl who spent her entire day with kids, she had a really bad habit of letting her words fly.The first time Kennedy brought home a bad word was the day I started potty training her. Promptly after making her deposit, she jumped to her feet, pointed to the kiddie potty and yelled 'shit.'

"Sorry. I'm sure you did well, but you have to lighten up a little. If you stress then so does Kennedy."

I didn't need to be reminded of the risks of upsetting her. I never stopped thinking about it. "Easier said than done."

"Have you thought about what I said?"

"No. I haven't and I don't need to. The answer is still no. It will *always* be no."

"Sheldon—"

"No. Cindy, even if I wanted to, I wouldn't know where to look. He's *gone*." I felt the tremble in my voice and judging by the look on Cindy's face, I know she heard it, too. I looked down at Kennedy, who now stared up at me with wonder and innocence in her eyes that I wouldn't want to take away because of her father's black heart. "And if I'm lucky he'll stay away."

* * * * *

FOUR YEARS AGO

My guts felt as if they were crawling up my spine as I knelt over the toilet. It wasn't fear of the unknown or even the violent retching that made my body tremble.

I knew exactly what was wrong with me.

It was ironic that I was at a wedding when I realized it. Lake's aunt and the private investigator she hired to uncover her sister's death had taken the plunge and married so soon after knowing each other.

"Sheldon?"

When I looked up, I was met with sparkling, turquoise gems staring back at me with worry etched all over picture-perfect features. I tried to answer and pretend everything was okay. I really did, but instead, I turned for another round of emptying my guts.

This couldn't be happening.

I denied and rationalized it over and over in my head, but each time I felt my stomach turn and my head swim, I came closer to admitting the reality of my fucked up truth. I didn't realize I was choking until I felt gentle hands pull me from the floor to sit on the couch. Who puts a couch in a bathroom anyway?

"Lake, I don't know what I'm going to do." She rubbed my back and waited patiently for me to continue. It was the only thing I could think to say. I didn't realize how upset I'd made her until I heard her own sniffle and realized she was crying with me.

"Tell me what's wrong so I can help you."

Her panic sparked my own again. "Oh, God, Lake... he left."

She visibly relaxed although she still wore a worried look. "It's going to be okay, Sheldon. I'm sure he's okay."

"It's not that," I whispered low. My fear amped

with each passing second. Once the words were out, I wouldn't be able to take them back. It would become real.

"What do you mean? What is it?"

I needed this to be a dream. I shook my head before turning to look her in the eyes. "I'm—

The door burst open before I could finish, and Keiran stormed in looking pissed. I hadn't realized just how much time had passed and the lingering threat that had almost gotten them both killed.

He spotted Lake sitting on the chair.

If I didn't admit it now, I may never.

He headed straight for her.

My gaze locked with his, and I let the truth free.

It stopped him in his tracks.

"I'm pregnant."

*****

PRESENT

Twenty minutes later, I walked into our modest two-bedroom apartment that contrasted greatly with the luxury I had grown up in. The best part was I didn't care because it was mine—ours.

I set Kennedy down, who immediately toddled off for trouble in parts unknown. I had strict instructions for her to stay out of the bathroom and kitchen, but just in case my little, hardheaded tornado chose not to listen, I kept gates in the entryways.

Her toys were kept in a bin in the living room so I knew where her first stop would be. I had maybe an hour to prepare dinner before she would be on the move again, so I usually waited until she tired herself out and put her down for the night before doing homework or studying.

We had a routine that worked for us. There were some bad days as a single mother and a baby cheated out of a parent, but we loved each other through it. It was enough because it had to be.

Besides, Kennedy wasn't lacking from love. I had more than enough help when I needed it. Her existence changed more than just my life, and I'll never forget the day I found out I was pregnant. It was the first time I think anything had made Keiran Masters afraid.

Instead of starting dinner, I followed her into the living room and watched her from the entry.

"Mama. Toons."

The sound of my little girl's voice snatched me from memory lane. Her dark eyes, much like her father, stared up at me.

When I didn't move fast enough, she lifted the remote from the coffee table, turned and said, "Mama, I watch toons now," while pressing any and every button.

I studied her as she frowned in concentration, watching for any sign of absence or upset.

Every day, she became more independent and fiercely so. I knew helping her would only upset her, so I waited patiently while she figured it out. It didn't take long for my little genius to find a suitable channel, and when she did, I left her alone to fix dinner.

Adapting to motherhood was rocky in the beginning, and when I'd finally adjusted and found a rhythm, it was snatched away. Kennedy was diagnosed as an epileptic a year ago. The first time she had a seizure was the scariest seconds of my life. Even though the episode didn't last long, I rushed her to the hospital that night, not knowing how or why, and I died each second that past. Because of her tender age, the doctors chose to keep her overnight but were prepared to call it an isolated incident.

That was until not twenty-four hours later, she suffered another seizure. A couple of tests confirmed the doctors' fears that it was epilepsy.

I remember thinking how she was too young.

Too innocent and undeserving.

Feeling helpless while she suffered twisted me inside out and ripped me apart. Every day, I worried that somehow simply caring for her wouldn't be enough, and for the second time, I would lose the love of my life.

A year ago, I thought I was prepared to leave Keenan behind in my memories, but when I thought I was losing Kennedy, I sought him out. I reopened the wound for the sake of the life we created. For a moment, I believed he had the right to know even though it was his decision to leave. But when I couldn't find him, and I began to realize he was gone forever, the wound healed differently.

I hated him for everything he forced me through for love. In the end, what hurt the most was he got to be the one to leave and I was left holding the shattered pieces.

When dinner was finished, I spooned her favorite meal of mac and cheese into a bowl with franks cut into small pieces.

"Kennedy, I made your favorite!"

I waited with a smile. In no time, she appeared at the gate and flashed a toothy grin. "Franks?" She shouted excitedly causing her r to sound like a w.

My cell rang just as I opened the gate. I sat her in the chair and pushed the bowl of mac and franks in front of her before picking up.

"Hey, Lake."

"Don't hey me. How did it go?"

I feigned irritation and sighed, "Do you know, the

more you're with him, the ruder you get?"

I would never have imagined the woman Lake Monroe is today was the same timid, naive girl who was bullied mercilessly by her now boyfriend.

Four years ago, no one knew the reason behind the deep hatred Keiran Masters felt for her. He had been the king of Bainbridge and had no problem using his power to ridicule and cripple her social life and self-esteem for ten years before it all changed for love.

Even though love had softened his rough edges, he could still be a scary motherfucker. I used to worry for Lake because people didn't just change overnight, but so far, I haven't seen signs she might be unhappy.

"Fess up and quit stalling. I can't trust my future kids to some quack."

She began murmuring to someone in the background before I could respond. It must have been Keiran because I heard kissing followed by a loud slap and giggling.

"Do you two need some time alone?

"Huh? Oh, sorry. So did it go well?"

"I won't really know for sure for another week. You know this."

"But do you think you did well?"

"Lake, what is this about?"

"What do you mean?"

"I mean, why are you suddenly so interested in my grades?"

"Do I need a specific reason to be interested?"

My eyes narrowed although she couldn't see me. Something was up. "Put Keiran on the phone."

"I don't understand why—"

"Lake," I growled.

The next second a deep voice filtered through the phone. "What's up?"

"You tell me. Lake's fishing. What's going on?"

I knew if there was anyone who wouldn't insult my intelligence by beating around the bush or pretending, it would be Keiran.

"I'm going after him."

Not even a few deep breaths could calm the turbulent storm in my head. I tried to tell myself it would be just like every other time. Keenan was never coming back. He promised me so the night he left.

"Keiran, don't you think it's time to give that up?"

"I found him, Sheldon."

My pulse quickened, and my heart skipped a beat.

"You told me you would stop looking," I snapped. Did he really find him? I had a million questions I wanted to ask, and yet I knew better than to give into the possibilities, but my heart had different ideas.

"I told you this was the last time," he defended.

"And so you just happened to get lucky?" There must have been a million rocks Keenan had hidden under.

"He's my fucking brother, Sheldon." His voice dropped threatening, but then almost at the same moment, he added softly, "I probably would have never given up."

"Why do you care so much? He hates you and don't you remember what he tried to do to Lake?"

"It's not something I'll forget anytime soon. What's your point?"

"He could be dangerous, Keiran. It's been four years. We don't know him anymore."

"I'm not turning my back on my brother."

"It's funny because it's exactly what he's done to you."

"How long do you think your excuse for him would be enough for Kennedy? One day, she's going to ask real questions."

"She's doing just fine without him."

"That isn't your decision to make. She needs her father."

"You're wrong, Keiran. It is my decision to make, and she doesn't need that coward." I hung up without waiting for a response. Let him be on the receiving end of rude behavior for once.

I double-checked to make sure Kennedy was okay before heading for my bedroom.

Once inside, I closed and locked the door, ran to my bed, and screamed my frustration into the pillow.

How could he do this?

No one knew what bringing Keenan back here would mean.

Chapter Three

FOUR YEARS AGO

PROM WAS EVERYTHING I thought it would be and nothing like I wanted. All night, I was surrounded by friends. There was laughter, music, dancing. The colorful lights and ornaments had lit up the gymnasium. Everything should have been perfect, but it all had felt so wrong.

If it weren't for Willow, I wouldn't have even bothered, but according to her, I needed to make a statement. I had been fully prepared to play dress up and enjoy the night. I had even looked forward to witnessing Keiran slow dance. It was supposed to have been amusing, but when he gently led Lake to the dance floor and took her into his arms, it only served to remind me of all that I had lost from love. I could tell he was nervous, but the way he stared into her eyes and her at him—as if they were the only two people in the world, seemed to help him through it.

They had been together for all of two minutes while Keenan and I had been together for two years yet, somehow, their bond seemed truer. I think it was at that moment I began to resent the idea of love.

There was a saying that love doesn't love anyone.

Whoever said that was a fucking genius.

I walked inside the house alone after being driven home from prom by Keiran and Lake. My parents were away on a business trip, so the house was quiet and dark. I didn't want to be alone, but there was no one available to call. Willow unexpectedly had to leave prom early after a rather angry phone call from her mom. All she managed to say before leaving was that she had to get home right away. Dash surprisingly offered to take her, and even more surprisingly, she went without a fuss.

I had high hopes that those two would quit fighting the inevitable. It was a hope I didn't bother to keep secret.

I made my way into the kitchen and snagged one of my dad's beers. I preferred something much stronger, but eventually, my parents became smarter after catching us stealing the drinks for the fifth time. They now changed the combination to the cellar every week.

Memories of a simpler time, when love was simple and new, invaded my conscience, and suddenly, I wished for those days again.

I wasted no time shedding my dress and heels. My favorite pajamas were spread out on the bed so I grabbed them and headed for the en suite bathroom for a much-needed soak.

My last thoughts, before I succumbed to sleep, were if I might have been better off never going to the prom.

Some time later, cold air greeted my skin as my body was lifted from the even colder water. I was fighting the disorientation left over from sleep and the hands that were carrying me.

"No," I protested while not entirely sure what I was fighting.

"I see you haven't gotten over telling me no yet."

The deep voice registered at the same time as the shock of having him here. "Keenan?"

He didn't bother to answer as he carried me out of the bathroom and into my bedroom, but I witnessed the hardening of his jaw. I also saw all the bruises.

"What happened to you?" I shrieked and shivered from the cold. "Wait, I need a towel."

The impact of my body hitting my bedsheets was the only answer, and when I managed to turn over, I had to fight off an even colder chill.

Keenan radiated anger, and I knew I played a huge part in it. He still wanted me to be someone I couldn't anymore. It wasn't the betrayal he accused me of—it was survival. He had my heart and always would, but if I continued to be with him, he would steal my very existence.

"I've seen all you have to offer. You don't need a towel."

"Yes, but I was wet, and now I am wet and cold."

A slow grin appeared and a quick rub of his chin followed by, "I promise to warm you up soon enough," was all I needed to give in to fear.

"And how do you plan to do that?" I asked unnecessarily. We both knew what he came for. The only question was whether or not I would give in. I met Keenan's stare and had the strange feeling the choice wouldn't be mine to make.

"Later. We have things to discuss."

"Things?"

He turned his back and walked silently to the window to place his hands on the glass. His head hung low, and when I peered through the dark, I could see his shoulders rise and fall with his deep breaths.

"Why?" The single worded question spoken brokenly would be forever etched in my memory. There were so many answers to that single question, but there was only one I think he needed to know.

"Because you hurt me... for the last time," I added. This wasn't like all the other times he'd hurt me, and I took him back.

"So it's that easy for you, huh?"

"Easy?" I was off the bed in a flash, dragging the sheet with me to ward off the chill and preserve some modesty. "You think this is easy?"

"I really don't care if it is or not. Discussing our breakup is low on the list of things I want to do to you right now."

"Then why are you here, Keenan?"

"I want to know why you don't want me anymore."

I clenched my hands around the sheets to keep from reaching out to him. I wanted to touch and comfort him, but then I realized this was how he was always able to get me to go back before.

"It's not you I don't want," I whispered before allowing my voice to harden along with my resolve. "It's the emotional baggage I have to carry by being with you, and the fact that you slept with my teacher along with every girl in Six Forks."

"Fine." He whirled around to face me with frustration lining his features. "I fucked her. I fucked her and many other faceless girls. I can't tell you why when I can't even remember their names."

"You need to leave, Keenan. We're over. Forever."

It was like a dark shadow clouded his eyes as he stalked closer. I was locked in his possession long before he touched me. My body lifted until I was on my toes as he tightened his hands around my arms. "I'm not going anywhere." He took my lips in a brutal kiss that was painful in more ways than one. My sheet was ripped from my body and left to float to the floor. "And neither are you."

*****

PRESENT

"Mama. Up." I felt the blankets lift from my face and peeked with one eye to see a conspiratorial grin beaming brighter than the morning sun.

"So what is it this morning?" I grumbled as I struggled to awaken fully. "My shoes? The wall?"

"I made bubbles, Mama."

"What?" She jumped down and ran off into the master bathroom. It was the only door I didn't keep gated having thought it was safe. "Kennedy Sophia Chambers. If you did what I think you did, you're in big trouble, little girl."

When I heard the unmistakable sound of water splashing, I rushed into the bedroom. I tripped twice while attempting to untangle my feet from the sheets. My heart was racing for the few seconds it took me to make it into the bathroom.

"Mama. Look!" Kennedy was standing safe, sound, and proud next to the large garden tub. Amidst the bubbles were various toys and dolls floating. Some had even sunk to the bottom. It wasn't the toys, however causing the pounding near my temple. Nearly the entire bathroom floor was covered in sudsy water, among other things.

"Kennedy, what did I tell you about the bathroom?"

Her smile slowly faded as she tucked her hands behind her back. She may be young, but she was extremely adept at sensing moods and from the tone of my voice, there was no question that I wasn't happy.

"But mama, there wasn't a gate."

"You know my rules, and you could have been hurt."

"How?" she placed her hands on her hips. "Bubbles are nice."

"Oh? Should we call your uncles and ask them?"

Her eyes had widened before she yelled, "You wouldn't!"

"Oh, I would," I whispered and winked for good measure. "Now, I want you to go to your room and think about what you did, and maybe I won't call them."

She wasted no time stomping off with an attitude. It was pitiful how much better Keiran and Dash were at disciplining her yet she worshiped the ground they walked on.

Dash, unfortunately, had just left for Germany and wasn't scheduled to fly back for another couple of months. He was learning how to run the family business and so Keiran would pick up the slack in disciplining Kennedy.

I may not have been lacking in the parenting department, but the extra help always came in handy, and Kennedy responded better to her uncles.

Since I was done with school and only had graduation left, I mentally planned an entire day for us to pig out on snacks with a slew of Disney movies for company until I remembered Kennedy had an eye doctor appointment. My kid had been squinting enough times lately for me to worry that her eyesight was poor.

"Hey, brat!" I called to her from my bedroom.

"Yes, Mother?"

"Oh, so now I'm mother?" I knew what her game

was. When she was upset with me, she called me mother instead of mama.

"We have somewhere to be. Can you get dressed for *mama*?" I stressed the word for emphasis.

A stretch of silence greeted me before she begrudgingly answered with, "I suppose." It came out more like 'pose' but it made me laugh all the same. I shook my head and admitted to myself that sometimes I couldn't believe she was really mine. She was a piece of work, which I fully blamed her sperm donor for it.

Somewhere where my conscious lived, I knew it wasn't entirely his fault he wasn't here for her, but the scorned woman in me disagreed. He made the decision to run away whether or not he knew what that night had created.

My parents had been away, and Dash never came home, so Keenan had been free and all too willing to bend me to his will repeatedly throughout the night. I couldn't even remember ever using protection. He had taken me hard and unapologetically. It was brutal in more ways than one, and like a fool, I let him take out his frustrations and hatred between my thighs. But still, the only thing I regretted about that night was losing him forever after, but it had been *my* choice.

"Mama, can I wear my new leggings?" Kennedy's voice brought me back to the present and called attention to the heated flush spreading over my skin. Nothing about that night was right or even could be called sane, but it never failed to warm me in places that hadn't been touched... or claimed... in four years.

"That depends," I teased as I pulled out a pair of jeans and a t-shirt, "will you need help putting them on?"

"Mommy, Uncle Keke said I was a big girl so I can do it by myself," she fussed.

"I was just asking. Don't get your panties in a bunch," I muttered under my breath. I had to be careful of what I said around her. She paid attention and repeated almost everything she heard.

Not wanting to leave her alone for too long, I cleaned up the bathroom and showered as quickly as possible and dressed even quicker. The days of lingering showers and meticulous outfit selections were long over. Besides being so young, she could have a seizure at any moment.

Every second I was afraid for my daughter.

I lived for her, yet she terrified me.

I wondered if this was what true love really felt like.

After Kennedy had been dressed and fed, we headed thirty minutes into town to the family optometrist belting out lyrics along with Katy Perry.

Coming back to Six Forks always made me nervous. After finding out about Kennedy, my relationship with my parents had become strained for many reasons. My parents had never fully supported my dreams to become a fashion model, and until the day they found out I was pregnant, they held high hopes that they could talk me into a more respectable profession. One that required a four-year degree.

In a way, my parents got their wish, but not in a way they'd ever imagined.

Dash was disappointed in me and barely spoke to me throughout most of my pregnancy. He had helped Keiran search high and low for Keenan though I'm sure his motives were far more sinister. It was the first time in a long time Dash and I had been at odds with each other. Eventually, the fear and loss of love had begun to weigh on my emotions until I began to consider abortion.

But my fears and my final decision changed the day

I heard my baby's heartbeat. Keiran had all but kidnapped me and dragged me to the doctor when I told him my decision. But it wasn't to the nearest clinic. He had taken me to an OBGYN minus an appointment and intimidated the flustered, elderly doctor into giving me an ultrasound. Thankfully, he had the conscience to wait outside, but it didn't matter anyway.

The manipulative bastard had done the trick.

I wanted my baby.

I just didn't realize how much until I found out how very much alive she was.

After that, Keiran stuck by my side as much as possible along with Lake, who, thankfully, had a gentler touch when it came to persuasion. If it weren't for her, Keiran would have driven me insane. I would never understand how she dealt with his controlling and bossy tendencies on a daily basis.

Beyond his shortcomings, I had learned something about him during those nine months and the following years that a decade of school with him hadn't shown me.

Keiran had a heart.

A heart with bleeding holes, but a heart nonetheless.

My change in perspective mixed with unbalanced emotions might have had something to do with my pregnancy, but either way, I was grateful for him. One could even say we were friends… sort of.

* * * * *

The visit to the optometrist ended with Kennedy being fitted for a pair of eyeglasses. Her vision had suffered only a minor decrease, but she was in danger of becoming severely nearsighted. Of course, this wasn't much of an issue for Ken once she was able to pick out purple eyeglasses with glitter.

We'd just pulled up to a stoplight when Kennedy said, "Mama, I want ice cream."

"Ken, it's ten in the morning. It's not time for ice cream yet."

"But, Mama, an ice cream a day keeps the doctor away."

"You know that's an apple, right?"

She lowered her kiddie shades, pursed her lips, and peeked at me over the top. "Not today."

"Okay, so which one of your uncles is responsible for this? You know what? Scratch that."

I knew who was responsible. It was amazing how much of an influence a complete stranger was on her, but she was every bit of her father. Conning and sweet-talking was her specialty.

"Auntie Lake said I'm just like my daddy, but I told her I never met my daddy. How come, Mommy?"

The car jerked to a stop, and I realized my foot was trying to force the brake pedal through the floorboard. Car horns blared and angry drivers cursed as they swerved to avoid hitting my car.

I am going to kill Lake.

Maybe I was just hearing things?

Kennedy's speech was still developing, and sometimes, even I could have a hard time understanding her. Sometimes she misunderstood words and used them wrong.

Could that be it?

Kennedy had never asked about her father before because I had never brought him up. I knew it wasn't right, but I could never bring myself to talk about him. I figured I had a little more time before she started asking questions.

But I guess time really didn't wait for anyone. Another hard lesson I had to learn because of him. I didn't want to blame him for everything that had gone wrong, but it was kind of hard when he wasn't here to defend himself.

I pulled over into the gas station because this wasn't a conversation I could have while driving. Do I tell her the truth or a lie? A quick look in the rearview mirror told me this wasn't just a random question.

God, she's only three.

It wasn't supposed to be time. I parked and took a deep breath before I turned to the back seat to face her. "Ken, your father is—"

I stopped short when I noticed an extremely large man, wearing all black in the middle of summer, hunched over and peering into the car window where my daughter sat. She silently stared back as her body tensed.

"Who the fuck are you?" I screamed though the windows were closed.

When his hand reached for the door handle I scrambled to hit the lock button which was when I noticed a second man, equally dressed in black, standing next to my door with a handgun pointed directly at my head in the middle of broad daylight.

"If you so much as bat a fucking eyelash, I will blow your brain through your ears, got me?"

"Mommy!"

"Kennedy!" Ignoring the warning, I whipped around to see my daughter fighting the large gnarly hands lifting her out of her car seat. "Take your hands off my daughter!"

Everything happened fast.

Too fast.

And the worse part was I didn't even know *why*. I

screamed for help, but nothing came.

Not the sound of my voice or a good Samaritan.

Only pain.

The last thing I remembered was the ringing of my ears drowning out my daughter's screams for me.

CHAPTER FOUR

KEENAN

"KEEP YOUR ASS still, Lacy." *Or was it Lucy?*

"I can't," she whined and wiggled her ass. "It hurts."

I suppressed the temptation to shove her off my table and instead, pressed the needle deeper into her skin. Her hiss of pain was music to my ears, and even now, I could feel my dick hardening.

There were two types of people when it came to pain. Those who received it and those who gifted it.

Let's just say, I've become one generous motherfucker.

"Still," I ordered again, this time lower and deeper, letting her know I was serious, "or get the fuck off my table."

She murmured an apology and managed to keep still while I finished up the last of the large butterfly tattoo, stereotypical of women who failed to realize when it had gotten old. Normally, I would have turned her away, but the desperate need for a distraction called for desperate measures.

"Five-hundred," I ordered after wrapping up her tat. "Pay up and get out."

A tattoo as easy as hers wouldn't cost nearly as much as I was charging, but I was in that kind of mood.

She made a small pout but wisely, didn't argue. She knew better than that. The reputation I'd built up over the last four years preceded me.

"Don't worry. I left you a little extra ass candy."

"Really?" she squealed. The stupid bitch actually turned, hoping to see her tattoo. Fucking airheads.

"Listen, Lucy—"

"Lacy."

"I have shit to do and you're holding me up." I snapped my fingers for the money, ready to toss her out on the street with or without the money.

"Oh, um..."

I peered down at her and felt my jaw clench. "Fucking A. You don't have the money, do you?"

"Not—not quite that much."

"How... much?"

"Two."

"Leave the money on the table and get out. Don't come back." I was already turning away, expecting her to be gone sooner rather than later."

"Oh, wait! I know."

You have no fucking idea.

I kept moving to my back office with her on my heels. My mood only darkened when I sat behind the large mahogany desk, and she followed me to her knees.

"Last chance. Leave," I warned.

"But don't you want me to pay you first?" She ran her hands up my legs and even with my jeans separating us, my body ran cold. "I've got something better than money," she purred.

"Oh, yeah?" I ran my fingers through her hair. "What's that?"

"Let me show you," she replied as she attempted to unbuckle my belt. My hands stopped her as I leaned forward.

"You want to suck?" She licked her lips and dropped her head forward, but my hand suddenly in her hair stopped her as I used her hair as a leash. "I asked you a fucking question."

"Yes. I want to suck."

I let my smile take over my features, which seemed to bring her ease. "Well, then suck you shall. But it won't be my dick."

"You want me to suck someone else?"

I suppressed the urge to shake my head. These Hollywood sluts have little shame.

"I want you to stick those pouty little lips," I pointed to where the pipe stuck out from the wall, "on that rusty pipe over there."

"What?"

"Now. Suck that pipe, Lacy. Make it feel good."

"But I could get sick," she whined.

"I simply don't give a fuck. I gave you the chance to leave." When she continued to hesitate, I lost the last bit of patience I had. "Do it or I make you, and I can't guarantee you'll still have all your teeth when I'm through."

She stood to her feet and crossed the room to the pipe. I watched her long enough to see her lower to her knees before picking up my cell. When the voice on the other end spoke, I wasted no time digging in her ass. "What did I tell you about sending your slut bucket friends to my shop and promising them a discount?"

"Isn't that like the pot calling the kettle black?"

"Come again?"

"If anyone is a slut, it's you... King Slut."

I sat back in my desk chair feeling more annoyed with each second that passed… "Where did you hear this?"

"During my recent short but pleasurable stay in the lovely town of Six Forks."

"I haven't been there in four years, Di."

"Yes, but apparently, you're a legend because the ladies still curse your very existence *and* your dick."

"Well, maybe it's time I stop sending you there. I pay you to get useful information, not gossip."

"Isn't it the same thing?'

"Depends on who you're talking to." I held my breath, waiting, as only the sound of her breathing passed through the phone.

"I didn't see him."

"Of course not. He's probably still being a studious college twat for his little princess."

"Keiran? A twat? Studying?"

"You don't know him so don't pretend you do."

"So why did you send me back to that hot ass place if you knew he wouldn't be there?"

"I didn't tell you to stop sucking," I barked to the blonde when she lifted her head.

"My jaw hurts."

"Are you seriously getting a blow job while you're talking to me?"

"Doesn't matter. I'm done talking." Before I could end the call, I heard her shout to wait. "What?"

"It was for her, wasn't it?

"And if it was?"

"I would have to say I'm curious why? I mean it's obvious you still love her judging by the large sketch on your office wall. Kind of sweet but a little obsessive."

"I guess I had a moment of weakness. It's a common trait for sluts." I hung up the phone and closed my eyes before opening them. My gaze traveled to the sketch I drew of Sheldon the night I took her virginity. She was fast asleep, and even after the things I'd done to her body, she still somehow looked pure.

I reflected on the last four years, and for the millionth time, I wondered about all that I might have missed. Was she still the same? Was she better or worse?

Was I?

Not for the first time, I wondered if the life I led was worth anything. My only other option had been to continue living the life I had before leaving. Eighteen years was a long time to live a lie. I couldn't sacrifice more time to it.

One might think that if you spent your life living for the wrong reason, then there was no point in living at all.

I had my chance to die, but I was too much of a coward to take it.

Now I'm forced to live another lie.

But this time is different.

This time it would be my own.

I looked over at the blonde who looked near to passing out. "Get out."

*****

A few hours and a couple of appointments later I stepped out of my shop and locked up for the night.

I opened Broken Ink shortly after I grew bored of being holed up, and I was convinced my brother wasn't hot on my trail.

Di convinced me to let her tag along after telling me all about the money her father had stashed away in their home. It took careful thinking, but after pulling the caper, we walked away with a fifty-fifty split.

Since I didn't graduate due to my lengthy stay in the hospital, I settled for a GED and later, a license for the shop.

In the beginning, business was nonexistent. In a big city, it paid to have connections, and the only customers gracing my shop back then were friends of Di. I never thought that doing cheap tats for her friends would pay off until I hit the jackpot by doing some very serious ink for an aspiring band who hit it big six months later. It worked out for me that part of their sex appeal came from the hardcore tats that had all of California and even people out of state rushing to my shop. The boom in business made me forget the reality that I was running because none of these people knew me.

I gave them all a fake story and even more of a fake name, and while I knew my cover wasn't airtight, it worked so long as I didn't give anyone a reason to dig.

But it wasn't them I was worried about. It was everyone I left behind. Knowing my brother, he would look for me because of who he is, but after what I'd done the night I left, I wouldn't bet on it unless it was to kill me.

He was a vengeful person and no one knew that better than his former pet turned girlfriend.

She was the reason he would come after me if he ever did because four years wasn't nearly long enough for him to forget what I had done. I wondered what he would do if he knew Lake wasn't the only one I'd hurt that night? Keiran had never been the knight in shining armor, but even then, I could see the change that Lake had caused in him.

Instead of happiness for my brother and a girl I once called a friend, all I felt was envy and anger. I once believed in my own way that love might have been real until it was shattered the night I met my real father and found out my brother, who I knew as my cousin all my life, killed my mother. Our mother.

Love faded that day.

And when Sheldon turned her back on me, it died completely.

My phone pinged with an incoming text message. It was a Friday night so I already knew what the message held without looking at it. Another invite to a party guaranteed to end with fucked up life choices being made.

And like always, I'd accept without ever answering the invitation.

And why not? I was free to do so. I didn't have to answer to anyone. I didn't have to care what anyone thought.

And even more tempting, I didn't have to feel guilty for hurting anyone but myself.

Most of the people who frequented these parties were either escaping pain or looking for it. I was just another body in a world full of sin that didn't fit in either category.

The text message, when I finally read it, held an address and nothing else. It didn't take long for the hosts, or whoever extended the invitation, to catch on to the fact that I would never respond, so after a while, they would only send an address.

If I showed, I showed. If I didn't... well, I always did.

Being alone was never good for long. I'd had enough of that growing up. I craved contact. I needed attention. I demanded to be noticed.

I laughed silently first, and then out loud when I remembered on more than one occasion Lake saying that I was an attention whore. She saw right through me, so I had no choice but to befriend her. I didn't anticipate actually caring about her. I didn't show it the last time I saw her, but I never really wanted to hurt her. Just my brother.

I may seek attention, but that didn't mean it filled the void. It was more like a temporary fix that I quickly became addicted to—it was part of the reason I was still searching.

I hopped on my bike, and when it roared to life, I sped off for a night of darkness and sin.

*****

The address took me to a seedier part of town that even the cops gave a wide berth. It was a wonder how many of the city's elite would be caught dead in a place like this, mixing with scum. I toed the line between the two classes.

A row of houses, each in worse shape than the one before it, were littered with partygoers coming and going. I picked one to park my bike in front of.

"Chris! Welcome to the party, man!"

The voice came from my left, and by the time I dismounted, he was on me. Keith was a big time dealer who liked to host parties to scout out potential clientele and competition.

There was more than one occasion when a party ended badly due to a shootout or a druggie overdosing. In fact, it was the very type of situation that resulted in our friendship three years ago. I saved him from a few stick-up kids, and he repaid me by sending me fresh clientele and invitations to his parties.

More often than not, I would bring my business here and do a few tats for extra cash—not that I really needed it.

"What's up, bro? You got the party started without

me?" I teased as we slapped hands. He strategically managed to push a beer in my other hand. I wasn't usually the beer drinking type, but these days, I began to care less and less.

"We always get the party started without you. You show up when you feel like it. If we waited for you, it would be time to end it before it ever got started."

"Haven't you ever heard that a true party doesn't stop?"

"Yeah, well, it would be kind of hard not to stop when everyone is passed out drunk from booze and buzz."

"So why out here? This isn't your usual kind of spot."

"Man, the pigs have been sniffing around my shit so I had to change it up. Besides, I've been hearing about a smaller dealer around these parts that wanted to take my spot."

"You know one day your shit is going to catch you by the collar, right?"

"And when it does, at least I'll be able to say I lived my life the way I chose. How many people do you know who can say that besides me and you?"

"If you say so, man," I agreed half-heartedly. In truth, Keith was dying. His path of self-destruction would lead him to one of two places—the grave or prison. But was I any better? I may not indulge, but I was no better than the rest because I *chose* this life.

Di had warned me just about every day how easy it was to get sucked into the fast life, but what she didn't know was I never do anything I didn't want anymore.

The last time I did, it cost me everything.

At least now, if I woke up tomorrow and decided I wanted a completely different path, I would take that road, but until then, I lived for today and today only.

"So what brought you by tonight?" Keith asked, forcing my attention back to him. "Bitches, booze, or buzz?"

"Boredom."

"Ah." He'd gone quiet as he looked over the party and sipped on his beer. After three years of friendship, he knew not to push the issue. It was common knowledge that I never indulged at these parties beyond alcohol.

I was content to stand here and people watch for the rest of the night until Keith's crew staggered over with their groupies in tow.

A chorus of drunken greetings from the guys and sexy smiles meant to seduce from the girls interrupted the silence. Keith snapped his fingers at someone I couldn't see, and not long after, lawn chairs were brought over. I was handed one and wasted no time kicking back.

"Chris, man, your hands are looking a little empty," Ryder, Keith's right hand, said. "Katy, go sit on his lap."

The redhead massaging his shoulders promptly skipped over to me with a wide grin as if he had just given her a million dollars rather than passed her around like the slut she was. I never aspired to have that kind of power, but it was always amusing to watch.

"Hi, I'm Katy," she offered unnecessarily as she lowered herself on my lap. She subtly lifted her skirt so her ass, clad in only a thong, rested directly on my dick.

"So I've heard." My voice came out strained as my dick rose against my will to cuddle between her ass cheeks.

I slowly took in her appearance and found everything about her fuckable, from her size D breasts to the soft skin of her thighs.

My cock was ready to fuck.

When I leaned forward and simultaneously wrapped my arm around her waist, she tossed her hair and smiled at me over her shoulder.

"Katy, was it?" I whispered in her ear.

CHAPTER FIVE

KEENAN

"WAKE UP."

I growled at the feminine voice that pulled me from the deep sleep that I didn't want to end. I was afflicted with the same dream I had every damn night since the day I left home.

A yawn involuntarily escaped before I could even open my eyes. I could taste the booze on my tongue and felt the muscle strain from too little sleep. When I finally opened my eyes, I was met with an angry pair staring back down at me. Before I could order her to get out, ice-cold water hit me in the face.

"Fuck!" I roared. "What the fuck? I was awake, you crazy bitch!"

"Oops. My mistake." Di shook the bottle of water she was holding and grinned down at me sweetly. She was dressed in workout gear from head to toe as sweat glistened on her skin. Sunlight shone through the window, and I could just make out her nipples through the thin shirt.

"You work out without a bra?"

"I don't wear bras much period. They are uncomfortable and a waste of money. Are you seriously just now noticing?"

"Yes. I don't find you all that attractive. " Instead of huffing and puffing like many girls would have done, she rolled her eyes and tipped her head back for a sip of water.

I used her distraction as an opportunity to make my move. Her yelp of surprise was quickly muffled by the blanket I had only just discarded.

"Keenan!" she shrieked in outrage. She managed to push up on her hands, but I was already flipping her over to her back. My knee came in between her thighs, and I used it to spread her wide before settling between them.

Once I was anchored, I took the time to take in her fierce expression as she glared up at me. She continued to fight even though we both knew her chance of dislodging me was zero to none.

"Settle down," I ordered.

"Get off of me."

"Isn't this what you wanted?" I let my voice drop low and even, in a way that said I was ready to fuck. I could tell she noticed from the startled look in her eyes. My hips pressed against her sex and the gasp that left her lips was full of surprise. I felt my cock harden to my surprise.

Maybe I shouldn't have turned that girl away last night.

"Are you kidding me?" she spat.

"Why else would you bring your ass in my bedroom if not to fuck?"

"You weren't answering your phone."

"Maybe it was because I was sleeping," I said slowly, letting my irritation be known.

"And the reason for all this is because?"

"To let you know that if you come in here again, uninvited, we *will* fuck."

"Once a whore, always a whore," she mocked.

"Are you angry because I'm stronger than you or angry because you secretly want me?"

"Neither, asshole. Now get off of me."

This time, I lifted off her and reached for my shirt at the end of the bed. Di bounced to her feet with a huff while shooting daggers at me.

"What are you doing here?" I asked without meeting her glare. She had no right to be upset after barging into my space uninvited. I lived alone in a high-rise apartment right in the middle of Los Angles. Whenever I stepped outside, I was likely to cross paths with an actor or lead singer in a rock band, and even that failed to excite me.

Di moved into a similar, though smaller apartment, a few floors down, after refusing to live in her father's house, which she dubbed a gilded whorehouse.

After we had stolen the money from his hideaway in the house, we played around with the idea of torching the place until I remembered that my whole purpose of moving was to keep a low profile.

That night was also the night Di and I almost fucked on a bed covered with money we tossed around after getting shitfaced. We'd come dangerously close but seemed to simultaneously come to our senses for different reasons that may have not been so different.

We never talked about it and never made another move like it again. Our partnership had grown into a friendship when we realized neither of us had many people left that we could trust.

I stepped into the bathroom without waiting for an

answer, knowing she would only follow. She seriously needed to work on boundaries. I briefly wondered what Keiran would have done had it been him having to deal with her shit.

I laughed when I figured he probably would have snapped her neck by now. When the thought settled, amusement had been replaced by the grim reality of who my brother was and how it brought me here. Away from my home, my friends… everything I'd ever known including Sheldon.

And she haunted me day and night.

"I got a call from a client saying you never showed for your first appointment."

"What time is it?"

"One in the afternoon."

"What time was my appointment?"

"Seriously? You don't even remember?"

I grabbed the toothpaste and coated my brush. "Can you answer a simple fucking question without asking a question?"

"You went to a party last night, didn't you? With that lowlife drug scum?"

"That's another question, but can I ask *you* something? When the hell did you become so fucking stuck up your own ass?"

"Right around the time my father went to prison and stopped selling me like a whore."

"So you're saying you need some ass?"

"Can you please think with your brain and not your dick for at least once in your life?"

"I've got to take a piss. Are we through here?" I nudged her from the doorway and slammed the door before she could answer.

My need to urinate wasn't as bad as the need to hide my reaction to her judgment of me. It wasn't anything I wasn't used to or haven't earned. Despite it all, it still made me want to put my fist through a wall.

"Should I tell your client to reschedule?" she yelled through the door.

"Tell them to either reschedule or fuck off," I yelled back as I stepped into the shower and let the cold spray wash away the unwanted feelings.

* * * * *

Since I missed my first appointment, and after checking my calendar, realized I didn't have another for a couple of hours, I took my bike in to get serviced. This bike, Di, and the clothes on my back were the only thing I took with me when I left Six Forks.

I told myself the reason I held onto the old bike wasn't because Sheldon and my names were keyed on the side. The memory of how it ended up there wasn't the hearts and flowers story anyone might assume. She actually keyed it there after the third time I was caught cheating. It read—*Keenan & Sheldon forever*.

She carved it there right before dumping my ass. Getting her back took a lot of groveling, and it wasn't until she left me for good that I realized she should have left me a long time ago.

And if I really loved her... I would have let her go a long time ago.

If I were wise, I would never step foot in Six Forks again. If she were lucky, she would never have to lay eyes on me again. I played with the idea of having my bike repainted for what felt like the millionth time, and each time I would bring my bike in, I bitched out and cursed myself the entire way home.

Every once in a while, I would send Di back to Six Forks as my spy. I never knew exactly what I was looking for, and Di never asked questions for the most part. Everyone had gone away for college including Keiran. Di was able to find out that Keiran, Lake, and Dash were all studying at the same college. Sheldon apparently chose to stay local and went to the university in the neighboring city.

I wasn't surprised given her dream to be a model, which didn't really require a degree. I figured her father strong-armed her into college. And why did that disappoint me?

I shouldn't care.

Her future was no longer meant for mine, and the reminder only served to bring the rage to boiling pitch inside me. I remembered how I left things with her. How I blamed her and hated her for leaving me.

When I needed her most, she cast me aside.

I'm responsible for many wrongs in our relationship, but one thing I'd never done was abandon her. Fucking that teacher was one of the lowest points in my life, but the lowest was begging her to be with me.

I wouldn't be begging again.

If I ever saw her again, I would take what was owed to me. She had just better hope our paths never crossed again. It was the last thing I said to her.

I was so deep in my thoughts, I hadn't realized the owner of the shop was standing in front of me, watching me curiously.

"Say, man. Have you given more thought to getting your bike repainted? I guess by the look on your face the little lady who carved that artwork on your bike is no longer in the picture."

"You could say that," I said slowly to hide the rage growing in the pit of my stomach. It was the same vicious cycle that occurred every time she was brought up, and I was forced to remember her treachery.

One day, the need had even taken over my good sense, and I had been halfway back to Six Forks to drag the backstabbing bitch back to my bed whether she was willing or not. An emergency phone call from Di saying she had been in a car accident turned me around.

It wasn't until I returned to find her sitting by the poolside sipping a margarita that I realized it had been a trick to get me back here. The asshole had actually handed me a drink, smartly followed by, "You're welcome."

After the boys had finished my bike, I headed to the shop. My next appointment wasn't for another hour, so I planned to spend the time freestyling new designs for my scrapbook.

However, my plans flew out the window because, no sooner had I settled in my chair with my favorite scrapbook, the shop door flew open, slamming into the wall and cracking the glass.

An overly muscled guy in his early thirties, dressed in a plaid shirt with a bushy red beard approached me with three more following behind.

The look on his face and the fact that he broke my door told me he wasn't here for a tattoo or social call.

I didn't need to worry about appearing unfazed by the potential threat. My 'give a fuck' had taken a vacation a long time ago and never bothered to come back.

"Hey! You Chris?"

"Depends on why you're asking."

Chris Johnson was the name I adopted when I came to California. Di thought I should have gone with something less boring but boring was unassuming. A common name gave me less chance of being caught if anyone ever became curious enough. There had to be thousands of Chris Johnsons in the world, which allowed me to blend with the crowd.

"A few days ago, you tattooed a girl and made her suck a rusty pipe *after* you tattooed 'whore' on her backside," the big redhead spoke again.

I made a point to let my gaze travel over the man whose intimidation tactics were a little outdated. "I got to say you look great since the last time I saw you although a little different."

"She was my baby sister, you little shit."

"And so I suppose you're here for a tattoo?"

"I ain't here for no fucking tattoo, boy. I'm here for a body."

"Sorry," I said without a hint of fear or emotion. "I don't seem to have one in stock, but if you come back later, I might have a few laid out for you."

That was a lie but giving the impression I was a ruthless killer would call the bluff of a lesser enemy.

It was something I picked up from Keiran although the difference between him and me was he actually *was* a killer.

I never realized how much his influence had not only affected me but also kept me alive for the past four years. I didn't mix with the right crew because I was no longer interested in doing the right thing.

"Later isn't going to work for me," he yelled unnecessarily. Spit flew from his mouth as he talked. His skin was now a deep red, and I couldn't help but think of those fat, red sausage links that split open when you boil them too long. "I'll take yours instead."

The three men who had yet to speak all drew on me as I continued to sit with my sketchbook in hand. I had my own piece taped under my chair for insurance just in case a client ever got a little froggy, but something, or rather someone who caught my eye made me rethink my next move.

"You got anything to say now, pretty boy?"

"Aww, shucks. You think I'm pretty?" I mocked with a fake country twang.

"Enough, Keenan," the deep voice of my big, bad brother boomed behind the unsuspecting men.

Before they could blink, the gun, equipped with a silencer, blew out the back of each man's head in quick succession.

When the last body fell, I was left with the only person I had ever feared. His dark eyes were as cold as I remembered as he stared me down. I had to remind myself it was a long time ago. I became an entirely new animal since discovering how fucked up he really is.

"How did you find me?"

"Is that the first thing you say to someone you haven't seen in four fucking years?"

"Were you expecting a hug and a kiss on the cheek, or did you forget the fact that I would sooner kill you than shake your hand?"

"If you ever feel the need to take it there, Keenan, just let me know..."

I waved him off. "Say whatever you came to say and leave."

"I didn't come here for polite conversation over tea. It's time to go home, and I'm your escort."

Laughter bubbled inside my gut until it spilled over.

"Nothing has changed, I see. You still seem to think the world is supposed to bend for Keiran fucking Masters. Well, I'm not following blindly behind you anymore. I lead myself."

"You sound like a female. Have you been talking to Lake?" He blew out a heavy breath and growled. "Fuck it. Here are your options–you can walk on your own two feet..." He paused and the next second, I was staring down the barrel of his gun as he aimed it directly at my head, "or I can make you."

"So you really did kill her?" I asked, meeting his hard gaze dead on. If he was willing to kill me, what chance did my mother have with him, even at such a tender age? Sometimes I wondered if she ever begged and if he really didn't know who she was when he killed her as Lake had claimed.

"Yes," he answered without question, but the falter in his stare let me know that he wasn't completely out of touch with his feelings.

Maybe Lake had softened him up. It was time to test that theory.

"And now you want to kill me?"

"Want is incorrect for what I'm feeling, little brother. I *should* kill you." I watched his grip tighten and his eyes darken to nearly black orbs filled with rage.

"Go ahead. It's not like I'm hanging around for anything in particular."

"Yes, you are. You just don't know it yet, and I refuse to let her do without any longer because you're a coward."

I shot out of my chair and stalked close until my chest was pressed against the barrel of the gun.

"Since when do you care so much?" I growled from deep within the very chest that was seconds—or one wrong word—from being blown away.

I assumed he could only be speaking of Sheldon. The girl who I gave my heart to all those years ago. She had finally decided to let me go after I stomped all over hers for the last time.

"Since I had to pick up after you. You have no idea what you left behind, but you're about to find out."

The threat hung in the air between us as we watched each other in silence, letting our eyes say what our mouths wouldn't. Keiran had never been one to hold back so for him to do so now must have meant this was big.

I simply concentrated on trying not to care. Curiosity killed the cat, after all.

"What am I supposed to do about this mess? I have a client who will be here in less than an hour."

I changed the subject to avoid Keiran getting the look in his eyes again whenever his mood turned deadly. Despite having seen a dead body before, I still freaked out a little inside at the sight of the corpses lying at our feet. Keiran, however, barely batted an eyelash.

"We need to dump the bodies."

"How? It's broad fucking daylight." Fortunately, nothing else was around due to the economy and the high price of office space.

"First, call and cancel all your appointments and lock this place down," he ordered. "I'll take the bodies to the back."

*****

It took the rest of the day to dispose of the bodies and clean up the shop.

We waited for the cover of darkness before making our move. I thanked my lucky stars I had skipped breakfast that morning, because whatever I'd have eaten would have been lost when it was time to dump the bodies.

Or rather, the *body parts*.

"You can go now," I huffed when he continued to hang around after we returned to my apartment.

Neither one of us had spoken since dumping the four men.

"You know that's not going to happen."

He looked around the apartment with a scowl on his face. I was never really here outside of sleeping and showering so the place was clean.

The upscale design was certainly nothing to frown on.

"Do you have a problem with my place?" I lowered to sit on the black leather couch where I kept a nine hidden under the cushions.

"Doesn't matter. Are you ready to say goodbye to it?"

"I'm not going anywhere."

I whipped the gun from under the cushion. Keiran looked from me to the gun without a hint of fear as if he had anticipated my move.

The smirk on his face made me want to shoot first and ask questions later.

The problem was he actually believed I *wouldn't* shoot.

"That was a bitch move. You're better than that. I *taught* you better than that."

"All you managed to teach me was how to get through life by fucking people over and using their weaknesses against them. Yeah, you taught me so much."

"We were never good people, Keenan. What did you expect? We were doomed from the moment we were born. I may have been a killer, but at least I'm not a fucking coward."

"So not wanting to turn out more like you makes me a coward?"

"No."

He stalked closer as he spoke, maybe hoping to intimidate me, but I didn't back down as expected. After all, it was he who had taught me how to make people fear me rather than me to fear anyone.

"Running away from your responsibilities makes you a coward. You left them behind and didn't look back."

"Them?"

I was sure confusion was written all over my expression, but the loud vibration of his phone distracted him.

Deep, angry lines formed along his forehand as he stared down at his phone. He was so engrossed in his phone that he completely forgot about the gun pointed at his head.

When the infamous vein appeared on his forehead, I finally lowered my arm. He angrily punched at the screen before bringing the phone to his ear.

"Keiran!" I could hear what sounded like Lake scream over the phone.

"What's going on?" All that could be heard over the line was the sound of Lake crying. She was saying something, but I could barely understand her and when Keiran cursed into the phone, I knew his patience had run out.

"Fuck, baby. Stop crying and tell me who hurt you."

"Not me," I heard her groan. "It's Sheldon."

My heart rate tripled and then quadrupled its pace when I heard Sheldon's name. She was hurt?

I didn't realize my fist was balled and my nails were digging deep into my skin until I felt the first drop of blood.

I didn't hear the rest of the conversation, and by the time I cleared the murderous rage clogging my senses, Keiran had ended the call.

"What's wrong with Sheldon?"

"Keenan..."

"Fucking tell me or I really will kill you."

The gun shook in my hand as I watched him take a deep breath and scrub his hand down his face in a clear sign of agitation. “She’s been shot. She—”

My fist connected with his face before I even realized I had moved.

Chapter Six

SHELDON

"YOU DIDN'T HAVE to call him."

My voice trembled with the many emotions I was currently feeling. The physical pain was nothing compared to the feeling of being completely helpless.

"Are you kidding me? Do you know how much shit he is going to give me for waiting as long as I did? You were shot in the head and unconscious for almost twenty-four hours. He's going to kill me!"

"You and I both know Keiran is too selfish to deprive himself of you, and I wasn't shot *in* the head. It grazed me."

"Sheldon, Kennedy is missing. We need to tell him. The sooner, the better."

"She's right, honey. If anyone knows who was behind her kidnapping, it would be him," John spoke up. He only just arrived a few hours ago. Lake had to call him when she couldn't get in touch with Keiran. Fortunately, I regained consciousness in time to stop—no beg—her from calling him before I'd spoken with the police.

We all knew what would happen when Keiran found out Kennedy was gone. He just might kill me along with the bastards who took her.

If she was ever found.

"Oh, God." Sobs forced their way through me as I thought of the monsters that had stolen Keiran when he was an infant. Lake rushed over and started rubbing my back. I knew she was just as scared as I was though she was better at hiding it.

I and everyone else were deadly sure the kidnapping was related to Keiran's past somehow. Who else would attempt a random, careless kidnapping in broad daylight unless there was something big to gain?

Mitch.

It had to be him. He'd done it once with his own son. There was no reason to believe he wouldn't do it to Kennedy. He'd once again managed to escape and stay hidden for four long years.

Keiran never stopped searching even though we all believed he was likely dead after owing so much debt with no way to pay.

Panic ensued as my imagination ran rampant with thoughts of where my baby might be and if she was okay or suffering for reasons that she couldn't understand.

Every second she was gone I died a little more inside.

And to make matters worse, the father of my child could be returning with Keiran, and he had no idea she even existed. I closed my eyes and said a silent prayer that Keiran hadn't caught up with him before the phone call. It might have been selfish, but I would do anything to protect my child.

"Are you sure you told the police everything you

knew?" Lake asked for the umpteenth time.

"I'm sure. It all happened so fast so there wasn't much to remember." But what I could remember, very vividly, was the screams of my daughter as she was being forced away from me.

The bullet, luckily, had only grazed the left side of my head, but it was enough to render me unconscious. The doctor assured me the wound wouldn't scar, but cosmetics was the last thing I was worried about. I had told him just as much.

Keiran had just taken off yesterday morning for California to bring Keenan home and had been unreachable while everyone scrambled to find Kennedy.

The few witnesses who stepped forward said she had been taken into a black van with missing plates. My only guess would be that they couldn't have gone far without the risk of being pulled over. It was all I could hope for.

"How long—" I stopped to clear my throat and swallow down panic. "How long until he gets here?"

"Eight or nine hours, maybe?" Her voice trembled while nervousness was sketched all over her face. "Your parents have called Dash, and he's on his way from Germany as we speak."

I stifled a curse and managed to keep a straight face. My parent's reaction was bad, but Dash's would be one hundred times worse.

My parents had done nothing but blame me for losing Kennedy along with grilling me over my activities. They hated that I moved away with Kennedy although it was only thirty minutes away. They accused me time and again of punishing them by taking her from them.

Never mind that I was in college just as they had always wanted. They believed my need to be completely independent was selfish due to having her so young. I was depriving her of her heritage, my father would say.

From the moment Kennedy took her first breath, she had only been without one thing and that was her father. Even so, she was loved as if she had two parents instead of one.

Lake would always say that maybe they were upset I proved them wrong and I had shown them a teen pregnancy didn't always have to end in disaster.

* * * * *

No sooner than I had ended my phone call with Dash, Keiran burst through the door with a stormy expression. I could tell by his unkempt hair that he had been running his fingers through it. His jaw was locked and he looked ready to battle any and everything that stood in his way.

It was the last thought I had before my mind drew a complete blank. Following behind Keiran was the only person who ever made my heart race and break simultaneously.

It seemed that God had once again ignored my prayers because here was Keenan Masters, my first love, my first heartbreak, and the father of my missing child, standing before me.

I could tell instantly, without ever speaking a word, he was nothing like the boy I fell in love with. This person who had returned to me four years later was a cold shell of him.

There should have been some profound method of dealing with the day you come face to face with love again. Even one that had been as broken as ours had.

He looked at me with disinterest from his perch by the door. His Mohawk was gone and replaced by a head full of dark hair that still kept its spiky texture. His jaw had lost its boyish youthfulness and he had grown hard. His lips were still plump and perfectly kissable. His eyelashes were long giving his eyes deceptively playful character. Dressed in his signature dark clothing, I could still see that his body was now covered in tattoos. They peeked from his short shirtsleeves, and I had to admit, even those appeared dangerous.

"How are you feeling?"

The sound of Keiran's gruff voice broke me from the trance I had currently been entrapped in. Keenan's stare was more than a little disturbing. With one look, he communicated how much he would like to hurt me, but this time with his bare hands. Even after four years, I could still read him.

"A little sore, but the doctor said I should be discharged in the morning as long as I take it easy."

I agreed even though I knew taking it easy wasn't an option. How could anyone think I could ever rest knowing my daughter was out there alone and unprotected? I mentally prepared myself for the battle that would disrupt once Keiran found out Kennedy was missing.

"Please, Keiran, you have to get me out of here now." I decided once we were somewhere more private, I could tell him. Twenty-four hours had already passed and the police had already warned me the first forty-eight were the most critical.

He didn't seem to hear me as he looked around the hospital room. "Where's Kennedy? Who is watching her? Was she hurt?" Keiran fired off questions faster than I could answer them. Lake paled as she backed into the corner furthest away from him.

"I—I have to tell you—"

"Who's Kennedy?" Keenan asked with disinterest.

Before I could answer, the door burst open as my

parents and two men I didn't recognize filed in. They were dressed casually in dark jeans and collared shirts, but the serious looks on their faces said their appearance would be anything but casual.

"Sheldon, these are the men we hired to find Kennedy," my father stated.

"Yes, ma'am. I'm Greg and this is Vick," the longhaired blond introduced his partner and himself. "We will be assisting the police offline to find your daughter." The disinterest in his tone made me wonder how invested in this case he really was. His unkempt attire and scruffy beard were anything but professional. His partner was even worse. It looked as if he had just finished rolling in the dirt. These weren't the usual men my father hired whenever he needed something taken care of.

"What the fuck do you mean *find*?" Keiran bellowed.

"Daughter?" Keenan choked. I could hear the anger and judgment in his voice as if he had the right after coming back into my life uninvited.

If I thought the brothers were intimidating before, it was nothing compared to the sight of them both glaring at me now.

"You haven't told them yet?" my mother questioned.

"N—no. I was just going to before you guys interrupted."

"Oh, dear."

"Someone had better start talking in the next two seconds," Keiran threatened.

"Two men took Kennedy yesterday morning after her eye doctor appointment. A man had appeared out of nowhere and opened her car door when we were parked at a gas station. I was shot trying to stop them from taking her. I have no idea who they were or why they took her—"

"That's why we are here, ma'am," the detective interrupted. We need a complete list of friends, acquaintances, extended family members, neighbors, and anyone down to the mailman who may have come in contact with the child before the abduction."

"How the fuck could you let this happen?" Keiran began to pace angrily, ignoring the investigators questions.

I never got the chance to respond because Lake had flown out the corner and into Keiran's face. "She didn't *let* anything happen, Keiran." She stabbed him in his chest with an angry finger, backing him against the wall. "Look at her. Look at where she is. I think it's obvious she did all she could to save Kennedy. This is her *child* we're talking about. She isn't to blame here, so quit it because you're not helping."

"Why didn't you tell me this shit before?"

"Because I wanted you home safe. You and I both know you would have gone berserk and Kennedy needs you now." She looked over at Keenan with disgust. "She needs both of you."

Keenan's brow lifted, but thankfully, he didn't question her statement. Either he still had no idea who Kennedy was to him or he was bastard enough not to care. I secretly hoped it was the former.

"Kids, we really need to get started if we want to bring Kennedy home soon," Mr. Chambers interrupted.

The lead investigator cleared his throat and pulled out a notepad and pen. "Yes. Let's first start with her age. How old is she?"

"Are you fucking kidding me?" Keiran barked. "Let me put it this way... she's too fucking young to survive on her own. Would it matter if she was older or younger?"

"Look, kid, I've been doing this long enough to know what I'm doing. Your ruckus and bad attitude are what will get this little girl killed."

Oh, shit.

Keiran was on him before he could finish. Before anyone could know what would happen, Keiran brought one of the hospital chairs down on the investigator's head and proceeded to beat him over the head repeatedly until he was a crumpled mess in the corner of the room.

It took every hand to pull him away. Surprisingly, it was Keenan who managed to subdue him well enough to keep Keiran from killing the man.

My attention was diverted by a nurse entering the room to see about all the commotion and quickly dashed back out likely to call for help or the police or both.

"Keiran!" Lake yelled. She was crying hysterically. I hadn't realized how fast my own heart was beating until the machine I was hooked up to started to sound. My hands clutched the sheets while I willed my trembling to stop.

If Keiran reacted this strongly for Kennedy when she was only his niece, how would Keenan react when he found out she was his daughter?

It took another few moments for me to realize that everyone but my mom had exited the room. Vick had just managed to pick up his unconscious partner and carry him out of the room.

"Where did everyone go?"

"Your father and John took Keiran to cool down. Keenan and Lake followed after them."

"This is bad. Who are those guys? They don't work for dad."

"No, but your dad's men are tied up with something else, and these were the only investigators we could find on short notice."

"Something else? That's it? Dad only uses the best. Are you saying my daughter—your granddaughter—isn't more important?"

"It's not like that, Sheldon." My mother's lips tightened in anger. Her perfected features seemed distorted and almost ugly as she glared down at me.

"Let me guess... business?" It was always business. Business always came before us unless there was legal trouble they needed to clean up. We couldn't and shouldn't ever tarnish the family image.

"How dare you speak to me this way."

"Whatever, mother. I get it. My daughter may not have her grandparents on her side, but she has me..." I paused when a thought hit me like a Mack truck. "Would you prefer it if she were never found? Would her disappearance salvage the family name and image?"

"Sheldon Chambers, where is this coming from?"

"You and Dad have made no attempts to keep secret that you hate Kennedy for being illegitimate."

"I don't hate my grandchild. How dare you!"

"No, but you resent her. You hate me for having her."

"We always wanted better for you, Sheldon. I never supported you dating that boy, and then you insult us further by having his child. His family members are nothing more than common criminals hiding behind their stolen wealth. If you ask me, they should just let their family line die with those young boys."

"You are a piece of work, Mom. Does Dad feel this way as well?"

"Of course. Your Dad and I have worked hard to give you and Dasher the best life has to offer. Then you spit in our faces by choosing trash."

"So why bother to help Keiran when he managed to get in trouble?"

"Because if we didn't, then your brother, as naively loyal as he is, would have done so himself. We couldn't risk our name being entangled in his mess."

"You cannot continue to choose our life for us. You have no right."

"We have every right, Sheldon. As long as you carry our name, you will act accordingly."

The low, dangerous growl from the door stopped me from really letting her have it. "Well, maybe it's time she stopped carrying your name."

I sunk back into the pillows, wishing I could just disappear. I chewed on my lip in anguish, wondering how much he heard.

"And whose should she carry?" my mother scoffed. "Yours?"

"It would serve her right," Keenan replied with a smirk.

What the hell did he mean by that?

"I don't think so." My mother watched him as if he were little more than a bug she would like to crush under her expensive pumps.

"It's funny that you look at me as if I'm trash, but your daughter is the one to have a kid out of wedlock."

Pain shot through my chest while my stomach twisted in knots at the demeaning way he spoke of me. I knew his comment was meant as much for me as it was for my mother.

"I'm almost sorry I missed your desperate attempt to salvage your royal ass of a name."

My mom and Keenan had always been polite with each other in the past. I had even believed for a long time that they approved of him despite our rocky relationship. It wasn't until I'd gotten pregnant and Keenan took off that they had been open about their dislike.

I needed to diffuse this situation and fast. "Keenan, stop. Mom—"

"You seem to be severely misinformed if you think you can look down on my daughter when it was you who got her in trouble."

Oh, fuck.

Already, I could see the wheels turning in Keenan's head as he pieced together exactly what my mom was saying.

"Mom, now is not the time. Keenan, there is something I have to tell you, but it can't be now. Not here."

"Come again?" Keenan demanded, ignoring my plea.

"Kennedy is three years old. Do the math."

CHAPTER SEVEN

KEENAN

"SHE'S ONLY THREE," the troll emphasized as if I were a moron.

In a way, I guess I was if I didn't figure it out from the start. If Melissa's attempt was to knock me on my ass, she succeeded.

Three.

Three years.

Three *fucking* years old.

I wouldn't even insult my intelligence by doing the math.

Kennedy was mine.

Mine.

And this bitch had hidden her from me.

I knew I was the one to run away, but I didn't need to question if Sheldon would have ever told me. I could tell by the glances she was casting, the nervous stutter, and her pale complexion.

She didn't want me to know.

Did I even want to know?

When I agreed to return home, I planned for it to only be temporary. I would have done anything not to ever see Sheldon and had every intention of slipping away the first chance I got and disappearing for another four years.

I never expected to return home to face her as the mother of my child. My *missing* child.

Two men filed in the room while I was struggling to find the words to unfuck this fucked up situation.

This time it was two detectives from the FBI who were here to question Sheldon. I wondered if they might have found something if they were back this soon.

I listened carefully while Sheldon went over details with the detectives, but the rigidness of her spine told me she was very much aware of me. Even now, she watched me from the corner of her eye.

To fuck with her, I moved closer to the bed and let my hand drift down to grip the railing. Her small gasp was barely audible, but I caught it. I reveled in the idea of making her uncomfortable. Involuntarily, I envisioned restraining her to the rails and making her beg for forgiveness and mercy. When my cock twitched, I mentally scolded myself. Now was not the time, but soon it would be. It was the only promise, other than finding the daughter I never got to know.

I had warned her, and now I could make good on the promise I made four years ago. I didn't realize until this moment that it was exactly what I had wanted. I just needed the perfect alibi.

"She's mine?" I told myself I would wait until I caught her alone, but it flew out of the window along with my restraint.

I didn't realize she was crying until her head whipped around. Her amber eyes were filled with pain and fear, and for the first time, I felt remorse.

And I didn't like it one fucking bit.

I didn't give myself time to think or rationalize. I gripped the back of her neck to keep her from escaping, and right there in front of the detectives, I licked her tears, starting from the corner of her lip.

I repeated my torture on the other side of her face and enjoyed her gasp of breath and the desperate way she gripped my arms.

Was it to keep me close for more or to push me away?

It didn't really matter because, from this moment forward, she would be mine to do with how I pleased.

"Keenan—"

"Before you say anything, I want you to know that whatever excuse or bullshit argument you are about to throw at me won't matter." I dropped my lips to her ear to ensure that only she would hear me. "Do you remember what I promised you?"

To my surprise, she nodded slowly though her eyes flashed with a bit of anger. Well, tough shit. I was angry, too.

The detective who had asked the majority of the questions chose that moment to interrupt. "Excuse me, but are you a relative?"

I ripped my eyes away from Sheldon's long enough to answer the bushy-faced detective. "No." Subtly, I gripped her neck tighter and demanded, "Why don't you tell the nice detectives who I am."

If looks could kill, I would have died multiple deaths in the short span of time it took her to answer. "He's—" She stopped to take a deep, shuddery breath. "He's her father."

Atta girl.

Now that we got that out of the way, I could concentrate on making her pay for stealing my seed and keeping her from me.

"And were you present at the time of the incident?"

"When my daughter was taken from her mother? No." I made sure to meet Sheldon's stare before continuing with my answer. "I wasn't aware that she existed at the time of the *incident*."

How textbook could these people get?

"Ms. Chambers, once again, we will need a complete list of relatives and acquaintances. This is our first time hearing about a father. There could be a connection."

Did this motherfucker just imply that I had something to do with it?

"That's because he ran away before she was born." Melissa's voice managed to break the connection as we both seemed to jump apart.

"What's the matter? Did you get a curl out of place?"

"That's enough, you two," Sheldon scolded. Her grimace of pain, as she clutched her head, was enough to make me stand down for now. The only thing I wanted causing her pain was me. First, I had to be the one to nurse her back to health.

"There has been a small development. One of the traffic cameras near the gas station your daughter was taken from captured a photo of a black van speeding through a red light."

"And you think it was the people who took her?"

"Same time. Same place. The van didn't have any plates for us to track so it could be a while before we have something concrete."

"And while you're here, who is out looking for her?"

"We have our best men as well as the state and local police force combing the city for her."

"And what if they aren't in the city?" I pressed, letting my aggravation show.

His gaze turned scrutinizing as we stared each other down. "We would search the nearest areas first to rule out a possible family abduction."

"Such as?"

"A disgruntled parent who decided to take the law into their own hands and remove the child from her legal home because they were unhappy with their parental rights."

"Oh, yeah?" I knew what he was implying. "And what if they simply wanted to punish the other parent? That's why I would do it."

Sheldon's indrawn breath filled the room. I watched her from the corner of my eye while keeping the detectives under my hard gaze.

"Keenan?"

"Are you confessing?"

"Are you an idiot? I only found out about my daughter twenty minutes ago."

"We have to cover all angles. It's our job to be thorough."

"Your job is to find my daughter."

"Your daughter?" Sheldon snapped. "She's not your daughter. You may have contributed to her biological makeup, but she doesn't belong to you."

The detectives left wearing smirks on their faces. I waited until the door was completely shut before following behind to lock the door.

"Would you like to repeat that?" I kept my tone even and spoke slowly, giving myself time to rethink my next move.

"You cannot just come back and lay claim to my daughter as if you have any rights."

I finally turned away from the door, and with only

one look, she began to back against the pillows as I stalked her.

Self-consciously, she wrapped her hands around her middle, but I wouldn't let her hide. Not this time. I swiftly wrapped my hand around her chin and lifted her face so I could look into her eyes.

"So are you saying it wasn't my cock that filled your pussy with come? It wasn't my seed that grew inside you? It wasn't me you saw each time you looked in her eyes?"

"No. I'm not saying that at all. What I am saying is that it wasn't you who watched her grow inside me. It wasn't you who watched her come into this world. It wasn't you who helped teach her the first words she spoke. I'm her mother, but I'm also the only father she's ever known. She doesn't need you. We don't need you."

"That may be, but I'm here now, bitch, and I'm not going anywhere."

I may have walked away from her before, but there was no way I could or would do it again. It was the threat—no the promise—I made to her the night I left her tied to her bed for her parents to find her.

Lake burst through the door with a look filled with dread just as Sheldon was ready to retort. Her chest heaved up and down as if she'd just run a mile rather than come from the waiting just outside the door.

"They're arresting him!"

*****

Everything erupted in chaos at once, and for the umpteenth time in my life, I watched my brother as he was led away in handcuffs.

Everyone in the vicinity stopped to the watch the scene unfold. Doctors, nurses, and patients all seemed to forget what they were doing as the town's bad boy was read his rights. Keiran went peacefully, and even more surprisingly, it was Lake and John who yelled endless obscenities and insults. Never mind that Keiran had likely put a man in the hospital because of his violent rage.

The Chambers were in the far corner and already Sheldon's father was on his phone, no doubt calling his lawyer to bail Keiran out. I watched him make eye contact with John, the man I believed for eighteen years was my father. Some unspoken communication passed between them, and then they were heading for the elevator behind the officers with Keiran in tow.

Lake stepped forward to lay a comforting hand on Keiran's arm.

"Stay the fuck away from me," he growled at her. Hatred and anger flashed in his eyes, and I could tell it surprised and hurt her the way she stepped back.

I smiled when I realized that everything wasn't perfect in happily ever after land. I always wondered.

The hall cleared after the elevator doors closed, and I stood there staring at the empty space, wondering what I should do next.

"What's going on?" Sheldon asked from her room door.

"Shouldn't you be in bed?"

She lifted an eyebrow and propped a hand on her hip. "Shouldn't you be running?"

I stepped into her space until my hips were pressed against hers and curled a finger around a glossy lock.

To a passing bystander, it would look like a simple embrace between lovers and not the assertion of power it was.

"I hope you have as much mouth when I have you alone and naked."

"We're alone now," she challenged. "But you won't be getting me naked, ever."

"What I'm going to do to you won't bear having witnesses. Nothing will give me more pleasure than punishing you past your limits. I'm going to make you scream for me, Shelly, and when you do, you'll be begging."

Just like you made me beg.

She rolled her eyes and scoffed. "You sound like your brother."

"I am my brother."

The grittiness in my tone was unrecognizable even to me. The proof of my claim lay in what I helped him do not twenty-four hours ago.

"I'm going to hurt you, Sheldon, and not just where it cuts deepest." I touched her collarbone and then trailed a finger down her chest while cursing the gown for keeping me from touching her completely.

"So do you actually expect to just pick up where we left off?"

"Second chances can be deadly, but I set you free once. Now you're mine."

"I won't love you again, Keenan. It's not something I can survive a second time."

I laughed because I didn't know how else to react. We had unfinished business, but the only thing I felt for her was anger and lust. Love didn't have any place here.

"I don't want your love. I just want you." I didn't realize how true it was until I'd spoken the words.

"Isn't that the same thing?"

"Not anymore," I whispered reluctantly.

She made a show of hiding it, but I didn't miss the anguish that flashed in her eyes before they turned into cold, angry flecks of amber.

"Stay away from me, Keenan... and *my* daughter."

"I'm going to find our daughter, so get well, Sheldon. I'll see you both soon."

I disarmed her and stole her breath simultaneously as I sealed her lips with mine and fuck me if she didn't still taste as good as ever.

I was going to make it my mission to ruin that.

CHAPTER EIGHT

SHELDON

IT'S BEEN A week since I've heard from or seen Keenan, and I still felt his kiss as if he were standing here kissing me senseless at this moment. A huge, frightened part of me hoped he had changed his mind, gave up, and went back to whatever hole he crawled out of—or knowing Keiran, he had been forcefully persuaded from hiding.

The knowledge reminded me that Keenan's being here was his fault anyway. If he hadn't insisted on finding him, I wouldn't be so terrified of myself.

Only angry was more like it because despite what my mouth said, my heart still beat for him. I knew it the moment I laid eyes on him again—that everything about us may have changed, but my feelings remained.

The thought of him still owning any part of me was enough to drive me insane.

I felt as if I were dying inside but living again at the same time.

But I was no longer a naïve teenager. I was also a

mother who had a child to protect, and I'd been through too much to give in again.

Sometime over the last four years, it became less about his affair with a teacher and more about the fact that he ran away and left me with the broken pieces of our love.

"I can't believe how long this is taking," Dash growled as he paced back and forth. I sat on the couch in my living room, feeling like a scolded child awaiting punishment.

Keiran still had not been released from jail and the investigation was going nowhere. We have been combing every street, alleyway, and sometimes going as far as breaking into places that look abandoned in search of Kennedy.

I helped with the search despite everyone's protest. The doctor had ordered me to take it easy because, although the bullet had only grazed my temple, any trauma to the left side of the brain could affect my vision, speech, and mobility of my right side.

Our only hope now was that Keiran could lead us to who had taken her. Bail was denied and visitation was limited when the private investigator pressed charges. He had been pretty adamant about burying Keiran after suffering a small skull fracture but an even bigger blow to his ego.

Graduation was in a week, which also meant Keiran would miss his graduation. Lake was devastated and had been camped out with me since his arrest. She said she couldn't bear flying back to Arizona and leaving him behind despite the way he treated her during his arrest, so we've been using each other for comfort.

For the first time in a long time, I thought about Willow and what she would say or do if she were here. It's been three years since I've spoken with her and even longer since I last saw her. I told myself I wouldn't be, but I was hurt when she decided to leave us all behind. She cut off all contact and even stayed away from Six Forks.

Dash never spoke a word about her, but I knew it had to hurt him twice as much as it did me. Call it twin intuition.

Lake had confessed to ruining their friendship forever when she made the decision to follow Keiran to Arizona. Despite Keiran's record, Arizona had offered both Keiran and Dash an athletic scholarship among Duke, Wisconsin, and Kentucky. However, Keiran had been prepared to turn them all down when Lake told Keiran that attending college with Willow had been their plan ever since they were little girls. Nebraska was where they would have studied for their humanities degree together—Willow in textiles and fashion, Lake in education.

Somehow, Lake had convinced Keiran that a long distance relationship would work and that she couldn't be the cause of Keiran giving up his dream, and so they attended separate colleges.

True to new love, long distance lasted for a semester and then Lake transferred to Arizona, which Willow had taken hard, especially after Willow's mother disowned her for sticking with her decision to pursue a fashion degree. Her mother wouldn't approve of a career she believed didn't offer a future or security.

Lake, Keiran, and Dash had gone in search of Willow after an entire semester without contact to find she was no longer attending the school in Nebraska. When we realized she had not returned home, worry grew into anger. It was as if she just disappeared.

"Sheldon... Sheldon!"

Dash's voice penetrated my thoughts, and I was

snatched back to the present.

"Can you please stop shouting my name?"

"Your daughter is missing and so is your *baby daddy*," Dash sneered. "Are you really sitting here day dreaming?"

"No one is more aware that my daughter is missing than I am!" I was off the couch and in his face. I had never hated someone as much as I did my twin just now. I shared a womb with him, but I'd never felt more disconnected from him than I had the last four years.

Ever since Willow had disappeared, he'd turned into a bastard. He was hard and cold and relentless. Despite all his efforts, he managed to become our father, only worse. I'd never known my father to be anything other than a hard man, but Dash had once been easy-going, charming, and easy to talk to.

"I have no idea who took her and why. I don't know if she's been fed or if she's warm at night. I can't even sleep because all I can hear is her screaming for me. I can't eat because just the idea of what she's going through makes me sick. I want to die, Dash."

My cries were drowned in his chest after pulling me close. I clung to him despite our differences.

"I'm sorry, okay?"

I nodded because speaking was impossible. I'm not sure how long we stood there, but when we finally pulled apart, the entire front of his dress shirt was soaked with my tears.

I laughed, and when he looked at me curiously, I pointed to his shirt.

His face twisted as he took in his shirt, which no doubt cost more than my rent. "Great, now I'm covered in snot."

"It looks good on you. I hear it's all the rage in Paris."

"Oh, yeah? How am I supposed to catch women with my sister's boogers all over me?"

His joke made me panice and I could no longer keep from asking the question I held in all these years. "Dash?"

"Yeah?"

"Why don't you find her?"

Just like that, his expression transformed from playful to serious. "Because she doesn't want to be found… and she doesn't want me."

"But how will you ever know for sure if you don't go after her?" My question seemed to make him hesitant as he rubbed the back of his neck in the way he did when he was nervous. "I have to tell you something. I'm—"

A knock on my door interrupted whatever he had been ready to say. I went to open the door and found Keenan standing on the other side with a guy I recognized but whose name I couldn't remember. His blond, wavy hair and bright blue eyes gave him a polished, college look, and I wondered if I'd gone to school with him. Maybe he was in a fraternity.

"Are you going to let us in or continue to drool over Jesse?"

Jesse! He was the tech geek that had Lake befriended in high school. He attended our school only briefly before moving again. He came around again when Lake decided to play detective and uncover Keiran's past.

"What are you doing here?"

"We're here to help find rugrat." Quentin, who I hadn't noticed standing just behind Jesse, answered before shouldering his way past Keenan and Jesse and into the apartment.

"May I?" Jesse seemed to be the only male with manners.

I wordlessly gestured for him to enter. He flashed me a polite smile before entering but not before casting a sympathetic glance my way.

And then there was one...

"Where have you been?" The question had flown out before I knew that I would even ask it. I wanted to take it back, but the self-satisfied smirk on his face made it too late.

"Honey, I'm home," Keenan singsonged. He wrapped an arm around my waist before picking me up to move me aside and enter the apartment.

As soon as he set me on my feet, I dug my nails into his skin, forcing him to let me go. "Our daughter has been missing for a week and you spend that time having a high school reunion?"

"So now she's *our* daughter?"

I heard my hand impact the right side of his face before I ever felt the sting in my own hand. I took a timorous step back when his expression shifted from shock to amusement. Even so, I could see the deception in his gaze. His smile said he was amused, but his eyes promised retribution.

"You're going to pay for that later," he whispered so low I almost hadn't caught it.

"Get away from my sister and explain where the fuck you've been for the last week."

For the first time in four years, I was thankful for my brother's presence and interference. This time it was I who wore a smug look.

"It's nice to see you too, Dash," Keenan replied seemingly unfazed. He walked deeper into my apartment, giving it a once over.

"Keenan," Dash growled in warning.

"While you all were checking alleys and holding vigils, I was searching for the man I *know* has Kennedy."

"You don't think we've tried that? That the FBI hasn't tried that? We've covered every angle. We've tried to find Mitch if he even can be found. With all his debts, he's likely dead by now."

"Or he was just waiting for the perfect opportunity," Quentin added. "I don't think we should sleep on Mitch until we are absolutely certain.

"He's right." Lake emerged from Kennedy's bedroom where she had been sleeping. "Besides... we haven't checked *every* angle."

Her and Jesse seemed to have some kind of silent conversation going on.

"Camden," Jesse blurted.

"Who is Camden?" Keenan asked.

"Camden isn't a person. It's a place. It's where your grandparents live and where your father came from."

"And you know this how?"

"When Keiran blackmailed me, I did some digging. Jesse and I came across very little, but what we did uncover was obviously meant to stay hidden. Mitch's parents. Your grandparent's," Lake directed to Keenan, "are still alive, and I believe they are still living in Camden."

"So we go there," Dash stated. "How far?"

"A couple of hours?"

My heart skipped a beat at the possibility that my daughter was close even if she was currently in the hands of some of the world's most vicious people.

"There is only one question. Why would my grandparents take Kennedy? I've never even met them. They've never shown interest in us so why her?"

Was it jealousy I detected in Keenan's voice? Our daughter might have been kidnapped by these people and he was jealous?

"I know it doesn't make much sense, but it's the only angle we've got left. It can't hurt."

"It doesn't matter. I want my daughter back. I don't care if we have to search the pope's house. We're going. Do you have an address?"

"No, but that's where I come in," Jesse stated, stepping forward. It was only then I noticed a duffle in his right hand. "Just give me twenty-four hours tops."

"Twenty-four hours? But it's already been a week. She could be—"

"Don't say it," Keenan ordered. He was so close that his breath fanned across my skin causing me to shiver. *When did he move so close?* "It won't help anything, and we need to stay focused."

He gripped the back of my neck with a tight squeeze, silencing my smart retort. It was a move no one else seemed to notice as the others had formed a plan on how to get Kennedy back.

My gaze fell on a picture of her I took last summer during her first trip to the beach. She had been in love with the water. I could still hear the sound of her tinkling laughter as she pointed at the surfers and yelled, "My turn," at the top of her lungs. She never forgot that trip and almost every day she'd asked for the beach. I had planned to take her again after graduation.

I didn't realize I was hyperventilating until I was being lifted in strong arms and carried away from the worried gazes.

"I got her, man," Keenan gruffly stated. Dash had probably stood to come to my rescue just as an older brother should.

But when Keenan managed to get me in my bedroom and lay me down on the bed, I wondered how good of a brother he actually was.

I sat up quickly and looked around as if my bedroom was a foreign place. “Why am I in here?”

“You were having a panic attack.”

“I’m fine now.”

“Are you sure?” His concern surprised me. A week ago, he had sung a different tune and now he was helping me?

“I’d like to be alone.” That was only partially true. Alone was the last thing I needed right now, but neither did I want to be in his company. I couldn’t stand the silence and the void the empty apartment created without Kennedy.

“Done.”

When he walked out and slowly shut my bedroom door behind him, I was relieved and partly amazed at how easy it was to get rid of him. I lay back against the pillows and closed my eyes.

Maybe he had gotten over his anger.

CHAPTER NINE

KEENAN

I'VE BEEN PLANNING for this moment all week long. After two days of searching for Kennedy high and low, I had to rethink my strategy. With Keiran in jail once again, I called up Quentin for intel on the organization that enslaved them both fourteen years ago. Four years ago, they were completely eradicated, and the major players, as well as many of the minor players, were now serving hard time in prison. That didn't leave many answers left.

Mitch was the likely bet on who took Kennedy and why.

He was after money, and since he couldn't possibly claim any money with both of her parents alive, it left only one solution.

He would sell her.

But to who?

The leader of the child enslavement ring was murdered in prison shortly after his arrest.

Everyone was currently huddled around the dining

table, peering over Jesse's shoulder who was already typing away on his computer that looked like it shouldn't belong in an ordinary citizen's possession.

Quentin had suggested we enlist his help based on the work he did for Keiran years ago. Apparently, he was a wiz with a laptop and internet connection. He was currently an intelligence contractor working for large corporations and the military to help find and bury information.

After high school, Quentin had enrolled straight in the Army and completed two tours in four years. He always seemed to be on the go as if he was running from someone or something. I guess we all had demons though I wouldn't doubt that his were more fucked up than mine were.

"How's she doing?"

"She's fine. She's lying down to rest and thinks everyone should give her some space."

"Everyone or just you?" Dash asked.

"Do you want to say what you have to say so you can finally get your panties out of a bunch?"

"Motherfucker, I don't want to say anything to you, but what I do want is to beat you into an early grave for what you did to my sister."

"What happened between me and her is none of your business, and your sister can take care of herself. Actually, I take that back. Clearly she can't, but no worries... Daddy's home."

No sooner had I spoke the words Dash was on me. His fist nearly broke my jaw on impact, and I crashed into the wall behind me but quickly recovered. I battled with whether or not to return the favor and effectively ruin our friendship forever, but when he caught my jaw again, I threw caution to the wind.

I pushed forward and used his momentum with my

strength to flip him over my shoulder, sending him crashing into the wall behind me. When I twisted around, he was already on his feet. Looking at him, no one would ever guess he was becoming one of this country's most powerful businessmen, but I was ready for him.

Dash's next move was thwarted by Quentin putting him in a headlock. Jesse had stepped forward between the two of us, and I had just noticed Lake's hand on my arm.

"What the hell is going on here?" Sheldon yelled from her bedroom door. Her face was contorted with fury as she took a look around the room. When her gaze landed on a large dent in the wall, she bound forward. When she stood in front of me, she poked her finger in my chest. "Where the hell do you get off on trashing my apartment?"

"You should ask your brother. He started it."

"News flash—you aren't sixteen anymore, and you cannot just fight in my apartment. What if someone calls the police? We are supposed to be looking for my daughter, not picking fights. Whatever issues you two have with each other needs to wait until Kennedy is home safe."

"Watch your tone, girl. I'm here, aren't I? If you were a good mother, she wouldn't have been taken in the first place."

"Keenan!" This time it was Lake to raise her voice.

Where the hell had that come from?

I didn't want to mean it, but I would be lying if I said I didn't. Somewhere out there, my daughter, whom I'd never met, was out there suffering because her mother didn't protect her, and not only that, but she didn't fight hard enough. She gave up.

"You have no idea what kind of mother I am to

her."

"And whose fault is that?"

"Bro," Quentin interjected as he came between us. "Now is not the time. We're so close to finding rugrat. You two can fight over who's the better parent when we get her back.

Sheldon stepped back and disappeared into the kitchenette where she grabbed a bottle of water from the fridge and chugged it.

When she finished, I watched her plentiful chest heave up and down from exertion before ripping my gaze away to face Dash. He glared from the other side of the apartment while Jesse stood in front of him. Did he think he was protecting him or me?

Dash's duty was to his sister, and if it were mine, I would have reacted the same. Even so... if he insisted on standing between Sheldon and me, I was prepared to do what was necessary.

"There's this older boy at school who keeps picking on me. Today, he took my lunch and I was hungry all day because I was too afraid to tell. What should I do?"

"You kill."

"Kill?"

"Yes. You hurt them before they hurt you."

I heard Keiran's voice in my head from when I was eleven and he was twelve. He had just gone to junior high that year, leaving me alone. I had never had to fend for myself before because I'd always had Keiran by my side, but that was the year I learned.

After he had told me what to do, he taught me how to use a knife and showed me the gun he mysteriously had hidden in the backyard. Whenever my father wasn't home, we'd practice with the knife on snakes or whatever we could find.

But all that changed the day Keiran had dared me

to use the knife for real. I'd come home with a black eye courtesy of Tommy. Keiran had said it was time to teach him a lesson, and at school that next day, I did.

I didn't kill him, but after he'd gone home with his face mutilated, his parents no longer deemed the area a safe place to live.

I made sure he would never talk before deciding not to kill him. Unlike Keiran, I couldn't kill as easily, but it was safe to say we weren't all that different after all.

"I think I'm going to take off," I announced unnecessarily because I had nothing else to give.

Once her apartment door closed behind me, I placed a phone call.

"Get everything ready."

Once I gave the order, I ended the call.

* * * * *

"Don't look so surprised to see me, brother. I wouldn't be here if I didn't need your help." I took a seat in the plastic orange visiting chair, facing Keiran.

"I figured as much. I'm just surprised you're here at all."

"Well, the daughter I never knew I had is missing. I feel a certain obligation to stay."

"And after she's found?"

"Look, I'm just taking this one fucked up situation at a time. I can't see that far into the future," I lied.

"You would leave behind your kid?"

"She's been doing okay so far without me." My words came out bitter, which was unexpected. The thought of leaving them behind again made my blood run cold, but I wouldn't allow my feelings to ruin me again.

This time I would be the one doing the ruining.

"She could do better if she had you."

"Why are you so sure about that?"

"Because you know what it's like to be without a father."

I wasn't expecting his response and wondered when Keiran had become so insightful.

"That won't be a problem if we don't find her soon."

"I don't think it was anyone from the organization. Most of them were arrested and the rest have likely scattered to unknown parts. It's Mitch. It has to be, and if it is him, then there is a great chance Kennedy is still alive."

"Why do you say that?"

"Because he'll try to use her for ransom."

"What would make him think we have the money?"

"Because we've inherited the second portion of our inheritance."

"How much?"

"A whopping ten million each."

"He's going to want it all."

"And we're going to give it to him right before I kill him."

"My daughter, my kill."

"You've never killed anyone before."

"I think it's as good a time as any to start."

Keiran didn't respond. Instead, he held my stare as if trying to read me. After a few moments of intense silence, I broke it.

"What if he sold her?"

"He won't."

"And you are sure of this how?"

"Because what he can get for ransom from us is a thousand times more than what he will get for selling her. The girls don't sell for much."

"This is my fucking daughter we are talking about," I growled. I didn't like the casual way he spoke of bartering her as if she were a fucking goat.

"And this is real life. If you can't handle what I'm saying, what makes you think you could kill him when the time comes? Because it will come, Keenan. He isn't walking away again and I'm not walking on the right side of the law this time."

I nodded my head in agreement. Mitch had many reasons to die. My mother and my daughter had suffered at his hands… and my brother.

I could see the worry and fear that Keiran tried to hide with a hard visage. He was fighting himself to be a protector.

"Did Quentin tell you about Camden?"

"He did, but I wondered what was taking you so long to tell me yourself."

"Because nothing's changed."

"I never said it had."

An uncomfortable silence fell between us once again as we both became lost in our thoughts. A part of me wished I'd never come on to Lake and yet a part of me wished I'd been successful. I also wish I knew which part was stronger.

"So, what was that at the hospital?" I knew I wouldn't have to elaborate given the way he hung his head and took a deep breath before meeting my stare again.

"I fucked up."

"No shit. I thought things were good between you two."

"They are… they were. It's not her. It's me. I fucked up in California."

"What did you do?"

"Those men I killed. I promised Lake I wouldn't

murder again. I convinced her I had put the past behind me, but clearly, I haven't. I don't even know how to tell her."

"Are you afraid she'll leave?"

He laughed though a dark look clouded his features. "No."

"Because you wouldn't let her?"

"I couldn't even if I tried."

"Is your guilt the reason why you pushed her away?"

"Partly, yeah. That and because I blame her for Kennedy not being home yet."

"Why would it be her fault?"

"Because if I didn't care so much about disappointing her, I might have found her by now."

"That's insane."

"No more than you blaming Sheldon for losing Kennedy."

"Who told you about that? Dash?"

"Q. He told me about the fight, and I know what you're thinking."

"You don't know what I'm thinking.

"I practically raised you. All those thoughts and feelings in your head I planted there just as they did me. You're going to kill him if he stands in the way."

"Dash's future is entirely up to him. Sheldon and Ken are mine. They don't walk away unless I allow it."

"Dash is our friend, Keenan."

"Since when did you ever care about anything other than getting your way? It was you who taught me by any means necessary."

"Yes, but I also didn't run away for four years and come back and expect everyone to just fall in line."

"Not everyone. Just Sheldon and my kid. And you forget... I didn't come back. You brought me here, and now you'll bear the consequences. You all will."

I stood and left without another word or a backward glance.

* * * * *

"Hey, boss."

"Stop calling me that."

"Well, stop being so bossy if you don't want to be the boss."

I pinched the bridge of my nose and prayed for patience. Sometimes I felt like Di was a pain in the ass on purpose.

"Did you do what I asked, *Diana*?" I used her full name, knowing how much she hated it though she never said why. I never cared enough to ask.

"Yes, I did, boss man, so when should I expect you?"

"However long it takes to find her."

"I can't believe you have a kid."

Yeah, me either.

"It serves you right that it's a girl, though."

"And you say that because?"

"Because the players always get a little girl. You'll be beating the boys away with a bat when she's older." She shouted over the phone as if she had just found a pot of gold.

"Will you fucking stop yelling?" I was two seconds away from hanging up on her.

"I'm sorry, baby doll."

"Don't call me baby doll."

"Why not? It fits you because you're pretty."

"I'm... what?" I meant it to sound more menacing. Instead, it came out as a shriek.

"I bet the poor, insecure little boy inside you is

grateful for my compliment even if the douche isn't."

"Why do you refer to me as two different people? And I'm not insecure."

"Oh, but you are." She fell silent for a moment before blurting out, "Is that why you're such a slut?"

I hung up on her.

It took everything not to make the phone a permanent part of my old bedroom wall. Instead, I clutched the phone tight, willing my anger away. I thought I would be used to her by now but had to admit that Di knew where to hit when she wanted to. She always claimed to be a good people reader, but I'd always believed it to be complete bullshit. She just never knew when to shut up.

I wasn't the least bit insecure.

Why would I be?

I'd never had a problem catching the attention of a woman before. They would always flock to me and I would accept them because...

My ringing cell phone snapped me out of my wandering thoughts, and when I checked the caller ID, I debated not answering, but I knew I couldn't do that to her again.

A week ago, Di had completely freaked out when she realized I had disappeared, either assuming I was dead or I had ditched her, but once she found out Keiran was behind it, the jokes haven't stopped rolling in since—

"Does he have you chained in the basement?"

"Would I be on this call if I were?"

"It's possible. He's got a soft spot for you, you know."

"No, he doesn't. He tolerates me."

"Well, he hasn't cut off your hand for touching his girl yet, so I guess toleration will work" She snickered.

I knew I shouldn't have told her about that, but one thing I realized over the years was that Di was easy to talk to. It's too bad Sheldon never liked her. Maybe that was why I kept Di so close all these years. We could have parted ways a long time ago but never did. It was my own little pound of flesh.

"What?" I barked into the phone.

"I'm sorry, okay? I know how you feel about being a slut."

"Di..."

"I meant being *called* a slut."

My only response was almost unintelligible, but it was all she would get. Neither of us had ever been good at apologies, and if I were, the last four years would have gone a lot different.

"Just keep everything in place and stay out of trouble." With that, I hung up and jammed my phone in my jeans pocket.

I headed back downstairs where I had left Quentin and Jesse. Jesse had been up all night digging for simple information that someone had gone through a lot of trouble to bury and keep buried.

"I found an address," Jesse hollered as if I weren't just three feet away. The table littered with Red Bulls might have had something to do with his high energy. "Camden is pretty big for a town. It's bigger than this place, but I found the place. It looks like it sits on its own land. There is no one around for miles."

"How the hell do you know all this? We've never even been to this place." Quentin asked a little harsher than necessary. The vibe between the two of them was too strange for two people who had only met once, but like everything else, I kept my head low. I wasn't planning to stick around.

"Satellite. I hacked into one that had slack security

and pinpointed the location. We're getting live video feed of the house now. It's pretty big, and it's completely isolated. It's the perfect place to hide someone."

"Have you seen any movement?"

"Not yet. If they are smart, they will keep their heads low so it could be a while before we can confirm anyone is even there."

"We don't have a while. Text me the address, stay on the radar, and keep me posted on any activity. If a bird shits on the roof, I want to know about it. I'm going out there."

"I'm going with you," Quentin announced. I nodded once but was already on my way out the door.

*****

The house was exactly how Jesse described it. Along with the address, I had him send me pictures of the house and surrounding area, so we were able to pick out a scouting spot before ever reaching the house.

Quentin convinced me to wait a couple of hours to survey the area to see if anyone was coming or going, but after forty-five minutes of nothing, I was tempted to ditch the plan and charge in with guns blazing.

It's amazing how much I was willing to risk and how far I was willing to go for someone I'd never met.

"Keenan, your phone has been going off the last five minutes. You going to get that?"

I looked on the dash of Keiran's car just in time to see the screen light darken. By the time I picked it up, the phone was ringing again.

"Yeah?" I answered while keeping my eyes trained on the house.

Sheldon's frantic voice caused my heart to feel as if it were being ripped from my chest. I could barely hear her babbling over the pounding of my heart.

"Slow down, baby. What's wrong?"

I was torn.

Torn between staying and saving my daughter or racing to comfort my high school sweetheart. I had to steel myself against the onslaught of emotions and remember that love wasn't part of the equation.

"I came home and found a note asking for money or Kennedy will die."

"Fuck!" I banged my fist against the steering wheel, forgetting that Sheldon was on the phone.

"What's going on?"

"Someone delivered a ransom note."

A knock on my window interrupted whatever Quentin had been about to say. We both had our guns drawn quickly, but the driver's car door was opened, and I was yanked out before I could pull the trigger.

Chapter Ten

KEENAN

"WHAT THE FUCK are you doing here, son?"

I brushed away my father's—no, John's hands and took a step back. "You seem to have selective memory. I'm not your son."

"Have you always been this stupid or just today?"

"I don't have time for this." I turned back to the car, but he yanked me up by my shirt and slammed me against the side of the car.

"Then you make time, and for the record, you little shit, I don't care what biology says. You're my son. Question it again and I will kill you myself."

I saw the truth in his eyes along with anger and the anguish even though I didn't want to. "How did you find me?"

He had been missing for the last week and chose now of all times to show up.

"I found a kid in my home doing something that didn't look the least bit legal. Do you know something about that?"

"He's helping me find my kid."

"What makes you think she's here?"

"It's the only place we haven't looked."

"You shouldn't be here. It's not safe."

"It's not the best time to start caring, *Dad.* If she's in there, I need to get her."

"How did you find this place?"

"Is it true?" I asked, ignoring his question. I knew he knew what I was asking. I wanted to know if his parents, my grandparents, had been living right here all this time. I'd never met them, and John had never spoken of them.

"It doesn't matter. You have no business here. You don't belong here."

"You've got it partially right. I don't belong anywhere." I realized four years ago, but time changed a lot, and I eventually learned not to give a shit.

"Are we doing this?" Q asked, coming around the car. John kept his eyes on me.

"Yeah, we're doing this." The tension in his shoulders increased. "But not today."

One thing I liked about Q was he didn't ask questions.

We made the drive back in half the time when I sped all the way to Sheldon's apartment. If there was now a ransom note, it could mean finding Kennedy safely rather than shooting blindly in the dark.

I didn't care much for what would happen to me, but Kennedy didn't deserve to die because of her mother and me.

"Where is it?" I asked as soon as I was through her apartment door.

Lake had her arms wrapped around a trembling Sheldon as they huddled on the couch. I made it a point to avoid looking in her eyes or going near her and not being able to comfort her.

It's not that I couldn't.

I just wouldn't.

Lake seemed to pick up on my inner turmoil because she plucked the note from the floor where it lay by Sheldon's feet and brought it to me. She quickly turned back to Sheldon but not before glaring.

I had the feeling she was beginning to think less of me these days—that is if she could think any less of me. In high school, I had made it a point to be her friend when it became obvious to me that she had nothing to do with framing my brother even when he refused to see it.

I shook off thoughts of another time that I no longer allowed to exist anymore, not even as a memory. It had all been a lie.

The notepaper crinkled in my hand reminding me of the present—

WHAT ARE YOU WILLING TO DO FOR HER?

"It's not Mitch's handwriting," Lake offered emotionlessly as soon as I was done reading. I turned the noted over, searching for more, but there was nothing else.

"How the hell is that possible?" I hadn't realized I'd spoken the words aloud until I felt the rumble in my chest rise with each word. Mitch was the only person who made sense. If not Mitch, then who?

"I believe I know the answer to your question," John said, stepping forward.

* * * * *

I had no time for this. After four hours, I was more impatient than ever. I was in a race against time and losing meant my daughter's life.

John had led Sheldon and me out west. He had insisted we drive together, but I insisted harder that we drive separately, and when Sheldon attempted to drive herself, I put an end to that, too. If being near me unhinged her as much as I thought it did, then it would be exactly what I would do.

Lake, Quentin, and Jesse stayed behind. Quentin and Lake offered to pick up the search while Jesse kept watch on the house in Camden. Each of us attempted to convince Lake to stay behind knowing Keiran wouldn't like her putting herself in danger, but her anger towards him made her pigheaded.

My anger towards my brother wouldn't allow me to care.

"What is this?" I asked when we pulled up to a building that resembled a hospital. The sign we passed read Summit Rehabilitation for Cancer Survivors.

John hadn't given much explanation for the reason for this trip across state. "Just trust me," was all he bothered to give.

I didn't trust anyone, least of all him.

A blast of cool air hit as soon as the automatic doors slid open, allowing entrance into the facility. Sheldon had managed to remain silent, but I could tell she was feeling as anxious as I was. We approached the large receptionist's desk where three women who looked like nurses bustled around each other in some sort of harmonized frenzy.

"Good evening, Mr. Masters," a nurse close to John's age greeted. "I'm sure you are aware that visiting hours are almost over."

"It's nice to see you again, Suzy." John's monotonous greeting was as empty as his expression though his eyes seemed to bore into her. "This won't take long," he half-heartedly assured.

The nurse didn't respond but, instead, pursed her lips in disapproval. I read the sign on the desk and realized that visiting hours weren't over for another thirty minutes so what was her problem? When John moved away without another word, I decided it wasn't important. His heavy footsteps led us down a long hallway. He took a quick right and came to a stop at the first door down the corridor.

Sheldon still had yet to say anything but continued to check her phone repeatedly.

Time was running out.

The chance of a victim of kidnapping being found alive or at all after the first twenty-four hours was slim. Kennedy had been missing for over a week now.

"Look, son, when I open this door, I want you to keep your cool."

"Who the hell is in there, and what do they have to do with my daughter?"

John didn't bother to answer. After giving me a stern look, which I ignored, he turned the knob and entered slowly. I stepped inside and looked around cautiously before my eyes settled on a figure that appeared to be sleeping.

Five seconds was all it took for me to realize who it was that I was seeing. He was hooked up to a machine with many wires running in and out of his body. His form was no longer as large as I remembered. Instead, he looked frail and weak.

A compassionate person would have seen a man who needed healing.

All I saw was an opportunity.

I didn't realize I was charging until my father locked me in a chokehold. Sheldon stood in the corner appearing shocked and more than a little frightened. An accidental glance in the mirror next to the bed revealed just how savage and dangerous I must have appeared to her.

"Keep your head, son. He can't hurt you."

"But I can hurt him."

What did this mean? Here lay Mitch, who barely looked able to walk much less kidnap or orchestrate a kidnapping.

"You've been keeping him here?" I roared. "You're protecting this motherfucker?"

Sheldon's gasp drew my gaze to her, but the sight of Mitch's eyes open wide and staring at me stopped me.

"Oh, my God," Sheldon cried. She bent over in half and used her arms to clutch at her stomach as she began to dry heave.

The primal desire to protect reared its misguided head, but I ignored my instincts and focused on the shit unraveling in front of me.

This situation had just graduated from bad to seriously fucked up. If Mitch didn't have our daughter, then it could mean anyone with nothing to gain by keeping her alive was responsible.

The memory of the ransom note, even though it wasn't much of one, was the only thing keeping me sane at this point. Kennedy had to still be alive. I just needed to figure out what the note meant.

"I'm not protecting him, but he is my brother. I didn't have any other choice."

"You always have a choice, John, or did you just forget he had my mother killed by his own son?"

"Believe me. I haven't forgotten. I never forget. It's all I can think about every minute of every day."

"So how did you find him?"

"I didn't. He came to me."

"When?" I didn't bother keeping the disgust from my voice. All the anger and hatred building quietly inside forced its way to the surface.

"About a year after you disappeared and Keiran left for college."

"This is so fucked up." I hadn't realized I was pacing until I bumped into Sheldon. I peered down at her shivering form, but my heart was just as cold as my mood. "Move," I barked down at her. Surprisingly, she moved without a word, but if looks could kill...

"Keenan, I need you to promise me one thing."

"Are you serious? Why would I do that?"

"Because I'm asking you to. I know I have no right to ask you for anything, but I need you with me on this."

"What?" I growled through my clenched teeth.

"Your brother. He, uh..." When John's face paled, I knew. I fucking knew.

"Son of a bitch..." My gaze traveled back to Mitch, who continued to stare. "He doesn't know he's here, does he?"

"No, and if he ever finds out—"

"He'll fucking slaughter this motherfucker."

*****

I promised John I wouldn't tell Keiran where Mitch was, but what he didn't know was that I had my own reasons. I'd finally found a way to get my pound of flesh from one Keiran Masters. I, like anyone, knew Mitch was the only demon Keiran had been unable to exorcise, and as long as he remained unfound, Keiran would never be able to lay those demons to rest.

Mitch would die soon anyway, and Keiran would be none the wiser. John would likely never tell Keiran of his part in keeping Mitch hidden for the last three years because Keiran wouldn't see it as anything less than betrayal.

If I weren't so set on a course for revenge fueled by hatred, I would have literally skipped from the facility.

After all Mitch had done, it was cancer that would kill him.

Even though the facility's name indicated it was for cancer survivors, it also serviced patients who essentially came to die after every treatment and medical theory failed.

The ride back was filled with tension and silence. Sheldon and I had retreated into our own thoughts. She could have been a porcelain doll the way she sat all stiff and silent. Her eyes were trained forward as she stared mindlessly out the window.

"You need to stop sulking."

What the fuck? Even to myself, I sounded like a heartless asshole, but it was too late to take it back. I decided to see where this would go.

"Excuse me?"

"You're fucking sulking," I repeated.

"This may be hard for you to grasp, but my three-year-old daughter has been missing for a week, and I just found out the only person who could have been a suspect had nothing to do with it. Mitch was a dream compared to the nightmare I'm living in at the moment."

"I don't think anything could possibly be worse than the unscrupulous greed of a man who once sold his own child for gambling money."

"That didn't help."

"It wasn't meant to." I took the risk of taking my eyes off the road to face her. Her face was drawn tight and her fingernails dug into her jeans. I'd forgotten how good the pain of her nails digging into my back felt, but I promised myself I would have that feeling again soon.

"Keiran should have never brought you back." She

whispered it so low, had I not been playing close attention to her, I wouldn't have heard it.

"No, he shouldn't have, but he did, and I won't be going anywhere, baby, so get used to me. I'm a different animal now... so don't fuck with me."

"What do you want from me?" Her voice had risen so high and unexpectedly that I swerved before quickly righting the car.

"I want you to tell me about her."

"That's it?" I could tell she wasn't expecting my answer, and I didn't miss the wariness in her voice. She had every need to be suspicious.

"For now."

She was silent for a few heartbeats before finally asking, "What do you want to know?"

I blew out air in frustration because I really didn't know. "Anything. What color are her eyes? What kind of food does she like? What's her favorite color?"

"Well... she has my eyes and your hair. She likes anything that is covered in ice cream... even meat." I tried to stop it, but I couldn't fight the smile similar to the one Sheldon currently wore as she spoke about Kennedy.

"Her favorite color is blue. She hates anything to do with pink. She's obsessed with the Ninja Turtles. Michelangelo is her favorite."

"Did you teach her that?"

"What?"

"To like Mikey?"

"I know he's your favorite, but no, I didn't teach her about any of them. She naturally gravitated to him. I tried to get her into Dora, but she hates it."

"That's my girl."

Sheldon stiffened at my statement, but I shrugged it off. The more she spoke of Kennedy, who I noticed she affectionately called Ken, the more I realized how alike my daughter and I was.

The realization further cemented Sheldon's future. I could almost taste the pain I would cause her. My fingers gripped the steering wheel, the leather creaking under my hands as I imagined it was her throat.

My cock also stirred to life thinking about the moment I could begin to make her pay. I would make her pay more times than one before I ended it all.

"Keenan?" she called, breaking me from my fantasies.

"Yeah?"

"I have to find her soon. Kennedy's condition is too delicate. I don't know what they will do if she—" Sheldon choked on her words, and when she started to cry, my tension kicked into high gear.

"What do you mean? What condition?"

She took a deep breath, which seemed to calm her before continuing. "Since she was two, she's suffered from seizures. The doctors haven't been able to find a cause since she's never suffered a brain injury."

"Epilepsy?" When she nodded, I brought my fist down on the dash, cracking the surface and pressed down on the gas, speeding all the way back to Six Forks.

CHAPTER ELEVEN

VICK

"BOSS, THE CAR took off."

"The place is compromised. Move to location two when it's safe but keep eyes out for them in case they come back before."

"And if it does?"

"You handle it."

The line went dead before he could ask for further instructions. The man cursed while silently wishing he'd never agreed to this job. Kidnapping kids was new to him, but it was a job, and one that paid well, though he now wished he'd asked for more.

The day he snatched the kid, she had some sort of episode that scared the hell out of him.

He almost dumped the kid off anonymously to the nearest hospital, but his partner convinced him not to by reminding him how much money was at stake.

Luckily, whatever it was didn't seem to last long so they chalked it up to a reaction from being kidnapped, but when it happened a second and third time, we starting drugging her.

He looked over to the monitor where he could watch her sleep off the drugs. She was so still that he wondered if she might actually be dead.

He wanted to stop drugging her, thinking her little body couldn't handle so much of it, but his partner didn't think it was worth the trouble.

"What's the word?" Freddy asked, zipping up his pants as he emerged from the bathroom.

"We have to move, but he also gave the OK to take care of them if they come back."

"What the fuck does that mean? We can't kill them."

"Your guess is as good as mine."

"Do you think we should go with Plan B? We don't have much time left before they become suspicious."

"I told Greg it was a bad idea taking two jobs. We can't complete them all."

"No, but they both pay," Freddy grinned.

"He's going to get us killed."

"He's going to get us paid. This family is as rich as they are fucked up. Just look at this house. All of this and no one even bothers to live here. If they are going to just waste money, why shouldn't we help ourselves to it?"

"I don't know, man—"

"Think big, Vick. Besides, with Greg in the hospital, we get a bigger cut."

"I can't believe he just bashed his head with a chair."

The warnings we received about Keiran Masters did nothing to prepare us for seeing him in action.

He secretly envied the younger man who was able to invoke so much fear with just his presence.

When he spoke, everyone in the room tensed. Even

his family and friends feared him.

As he recalled the cold, dark eyes from the hospital that promised death, he wondered what it would be like to have that much power.

*****

KEENAN

"Do you have anything on the house?" I asked as soon as we were through the door. Sheldon insisted on returning to her apartment, but I was having none of it. I dragged her back to my father's house. Lake and Quentin were back from searching for Kennedy while Jesse still kept eyes on the house in Camden.

"It was so quick I'm not even sure if it happened, but the curtain there..." Jesse pointed to a window on the lower level of the house, "it moved just after you left. Could have been a draft or—"

"Or the people who took my daughter?"

"You really think it could have been your grandparents?"

"I don't know, but I now know it wasn't Mitch."

"How?" Quentin asked.

"He's dead," I blurted. It was the only believable lie. If Q knew about Mitch, he wouldn't hesitate to tell Keiran because that's where his loyalty was.

I wanted to silently warn Sheldon from telling just in case, but Q watched me too closely as if trying to read me. "Fuck," he barked. "Keiran isn't going to like this."

"I'm pretty sure it's all Keiran would have wanted."

"Only if it had been by his hands."

I needed to change the subject and fast. I hadn't

had time to concoct a proper story to tell anyone about the impromptu trip. After Sheldon had told me about Kennedy's condition, it was all I could think about. "It doesn't matter now. It's done."

He hesitated only a second longer than necessary before asking, "So what makes you think your grandparents even know about her, and why would they take her?"

I struggled in my head with a reason for why they could be guilty but couldn't find one no matter how hard I tried. I ran my fingers to the end of my hair and tugged with frustration.

"Are they even still alive?" Sheldon asked.

"I don't know. I never suspected them, but I was hoping something or someone in that house could have told me something."

"It would almost be too easy if it were someone you knew," Jesse remarked.

A thought popped into my head that I couldn't shake, and before I realized my feet had even moved, my hands were on Sheldon, pinning her against the wall. "I'm going to ask you this only once so have your brain advise your mouth not to lie to me."

"Let me go," she growled. If I weren't very near to murdering her, I would find her pout cute.

"Keenan, have you lost your mind?" Lake yelled.

"Dude," Q chimed in.

I blocked them all out. I couldn't see anything but the fantasy of Sheldon's life draining from her eyes as my brain began to form images one after the other.

"Have you had another motherfucker around my kid?"

The audible hitch in her breath and the guilt that flashed in her eyes did nothing to stop my growing rage. "What do you mean?" she stammered.

"You bitch." I released her neck and took a step back. "Who is he?"

"Who is who?" she screamed. "There's no one!"

"That's not what your eyes just said."

"So now you're a fucking mind reader?"

"No. I'm *your* fucking mind reader. Shelly, don't play with me," I warned.

"You have no right to question my love life."

Love? Was she in love?

Fuck that. I'd stop her heart with my bare hands before I allowed her give it to anyone else.

I turned to face the other occupants in the room who stood by shell-shocked. Quentin held on tight to Lake's arm while she continuously tried to tug from his grasp.

"Get the fuck out."

I watched them all scramble while my heart pounded against my chest. Q shut the door, but not before giving me a warning look, one I wouldn't be heeding.

When I turned back, Sheldon was gone. My feet moved swiftly around the first floor as I searched high and low for her. I didn't bother to call after her knowing she wouldn't answer.

She had many places to hide but nowhere to run.

The thought of the chase made my cock harden until it was practically beating against my jeans with anticipation.

Chapter Twelve

SHELDON

I HID IN Keiran's old room of all places. I don't know why I ran. There was nowhere for me to hide, but I thought maybe if I stayed out of sight long enough, it would give him enough time to calm down.

I'd never seen Keenan with a temper like he'd had today.

I was even more surprised at my reaction to him.

I couldn't, in all conscience believe when my body trembled at the sight and sound of him it was only in fear. My body betrayed me each time he looked at me. His eyes seemed to send me a message that I couldn't yet decipher, but I knew it held a promise that I wasn't sure I would want him to keep.

"Shelly, open the door." The smooth tone of his voice belied the predator he was.

"I can't do that." I willed my shaking hands to stop along with the sweat running to the end of my fingertips.

"I would prefer it to breaking down this door, and I

know you would too, so be a good girl and let me in. You don't need to hide."

"I'm not hiding. I wanted away from you."

"Because you're guilty?"

"Because what I do during my spare time is none of your business. Look, these past few days have been stressful. I think we need some time apart."

"We've spent enough time apart, and I promise you won't live another day without me." I heard the apparent threat and shivered from the cold promise. I found myself crying despite my promise not to weaken.

"You're just like him." It was terrifying how much like Keiran Keenan had become.

"I'm nothing like him. I'm much worse. Now open the fucking door." A loud bang against the door made me jump clear across the room before I could answer.

"Keenan, stop!" I was delirious as I begged at the top of my lungs. The door splintered and heaved under the force of his blows. "Please, just let me go."

"You will always be someone I want, Shelly..." I hadn't realized Keenan gained entry until his hands were in my hair and the other had gripped my chin. "...so what fucking makes you think I will ever let you go again?"

"Because we can't do this."

"We can do anything we want when I demand it, and right now, I want you to kiss me."

"What?"

"Prove to me there is no one else—that there has never been anyone else, or I promise you will not walk out of here alive.

When I continued to hesitate, his arms dropped around my waist to crush me against him. When I tried to back away, he tightened his arms until I cried out from the pain. I felt his cock harden against my stomach and stared at him in disbelief.

"Are you getting off on this?"

"Yeah," his gravelly voice confirmed. "I am."

"Keenan, what happened to you?"

"You broke my heart," he answered matter of factly. Despite his arms binding me to him, I felt my knees weaken. I had to clutch his chest to stop the feeling of falling.

"You broke mine, too."

He had made a rough sound in his throat before he growled, "Quit stalling, or I'll find another way to shut you up. I'm not in a forgiving mood, Shelly. You won't be able to take me."

The warning in his eyes made me finally lift my lips to his. I was surprised at how much I really wanted to kiss him even if it was for a lie.

The way he watched me, even after my lips touched his, was unnerving, so I closed my eyes and sunk into the sin. I kept the kiss soft and slow so as to not give him any more of myself than needed, but it only lasted three seconds.

His teeth sunk down onto my lip causing me to gasp. He used the opportunity to deepen the kiss, drawing out my tongue, and when he began to suck on me, my body heated to fever pitch.

I could only hope he got what he needed because I was no longer in control.

When he picked me up and wrapped my legs around his waist, I didn't fight him. I felt him carry me off but was too afraid to look.

Without warning, he yanked my legs from around his waist and I stumbled back before righting myself. I took a quick look around and realized we were now in the bathroom.

"Shower. I'll find you something to sleep in."

"I need to go, Keenan. Lake will wonder where I am."

"You're not leaving." It was all he said before disappearing.

If he thought he could bark orders and I'd obey, he was sorely mistaken. I waited long enough until I was sure he'd be gone and took a step for the door. He'd left it open, and I figured if I were quick enough, I could slip past and out of the house before he returned.

I made a silent dash down the hall, confidence building with each step. I just had to get down the stairs and I'd be home free.

I'd just made it to the landing when I heard it. It was a sound so faint, but I knew he was there.

"Keenan?" I called without turning.

"You don't listen well, do you?"

Before I could offer a response, his hand was on my elbow, gently tugging as he led me back to the bathroom. I watched his face for a sign—anything but the silent way he moved. When we entered the bathroom, he let go of my elbow and indicated with a nod of his head to sit, and wisely, I did.

I didn't need his confirmation that I fucked up. His silence ironically said it all. But when he left the bathroom once more, I relaxed.

Maybe I should have just taken the shower and convinced him to take me home afterward. Anything was better than slowly becoming unhinged. My nerves were frazzled, and my confidence had long withered away with his first touch.

Keenan finally returned minutes later carrying a royal blue shirt in his hand, one I instantly recognized as his t-shirt. I slept in that shirt every night, but when he left four years ago, I left it behind. It should have still been in my old room, buried with all the other memories of him I'd left behind, so how did he get it?

"How did you get that?"

"Easy. Your parents are away a lot."

"You broke into their home?"

The impatient look he shot me made me sit back like a coward. "Spare the melodramatic bullshit. It's a little late to care now, don't you think?"

"Why wouldn't I care? It's wrong."

"You didn't think it was wrong when we were together. I know you remember all those nights I'd climb up the stairs and fuck daddy's little princess's pussy senseless while he slept down the hall dreaming of empires to crush."

"That was a different time."

"You're right, it was." He said nothing else as he moved for the shower. I'd been so engrossed in the past that I hadn't noticed the hex key he carried in his hand.

"What are you doing with that?"

He ignored me and fiddled with the shower handle while I watched in confusion. Is the shower broken? If so, why was he so set on me taking a shower?

The shower handle eventually slid off when he tugged on it revealing a small stem. He slowly turned the stem counterclockwise, each turn making a clicking sound.

When he was done turning it, he slid the handle back on and tightened the screw using the hex key once more.

Pocketing the tool, he turned to face me with a blank expression. "Undress."

This time I slowly obeyed. His gaze never wavered as my clothes slid from my body. Surprisingly, he didn't look at my body but kept his eyes trained with mine. I didn't know whether to be thankful or feel inadequate.

When the last item was shed, he took my hand and

led me into the shower. I half expected him to undress and join me, but he simply turned the handle towards the sign that read hot.

"Aren't you going to close the door?"

"You have eight minutes."

"Do you really think timing me and standing guard is necessary? I think I can handle personal hygiene on my own... By the way, this water is kind of hot. Is the water heater broken?"

"Who is he?"

My head was under the spray, but because of the increasing temperature of the water, I ducked my head from under the water just in time to hear him.

"I told you there is no one." I absently reached to turn down the temperature of the water, but his hand on my wrist stopped me. "Let go. The water is too hot."

"You now have about four minutes to tell me the truth. Who is he?"

If I wasn't so distracted by the water, I might have answered, but it seemed as if someone had just thrown a pot of boiling water on me.

"I need to get out." I backed away from the spray, feeling my skin prickle. The water now felt as if it were boiling. Steam rose and covered every inch of the shower until I could hardly see him. Suddenly, his hand appeared through the steam, oblivious to the hot temperature, and he pulled me back under the spray.

"Keenan! It's too hot."

"That's because in two minutes the water will reach a scalding temperature causing first-degree burns to cover your skin. In four, you will suffer second-degree burns. Tell me who he is." He spoke with a flat tone. So unfeeling and cold. His expression was completely impassive as he watched me suffer under the spray of the water.

I sunk down to the floor of the shower. My body jerked uncontrollably as instinct kicked in, begging for self-preservation. "Please let me out," I choked out. "I can't breathe. It hurts so badly."

"Thirty seconds."

He continued to appear unaffected, and it was then I finally realized that he would destroy me if I let him.

"Keenan..." I found the strength to lift my head one last time and peered into eyes devoid of a soul, mercy, or love. "Go to hell."

The water had reached an unbearable temperature, and I could no longer stop the scream that ripped from my throat.

*****

SEVEN YEARS AGO

"Hey, beautiful."

I looked around in confusion until my eyes landed on an extremely hot guy leaning against the lockers. His dark hair was spiked, and the lopsided grin he wore spelled trouble by invitation. I recognized him as one the popular kids. The girls were always talking about him and his kissing skills... among other things.

"Are you talking to me?" He appeared to be waiting for someone, but it couldn't possibly have been me. Boys didn't talk to me. It was a rule set forth by my twin brother, who was older by a few minutes.

"I don't see anyone else who could possibly make me fall in love at first sight, do you?" Despite knowing it was a line, I found myself shaking my head slowly. "Come here."

"Oh, I, um... have to get to class."

He rolled his eyes as if annoyed. "Are you a nerd?"

"No way," I answered quickly and a little too defensively.

"So come to me... now," he ordered. The rough tone of his voice belied the easygoing smile on his face. I felt my feet move me closer to him even though my brain screamed to run the other way.

"Good girl."

"Uh, hi," I said needlessly when my mind drew a blank. I didn't know how to talk to boys because my dad and brother didn't allow me to date.

"You're Dash's sister, right?"

"Yes. We're twins," I offered lamely.

"I don't see how. Dash is ugly as hell."

I burst out laughing and felt the tension leave my shoulders and my nervousness ease.

"You have a beautiful laugh, Shelly."

"My name is not Shelly." I pouted in disappointment. Maybe he thought I was someone else despite knowing my brother.

"It's Sheldon, right?"

"Yeah," I piped up when he confirmed he did know my name,

"Well, I want to call you Shelly for short."

"Why?"

"Because no one else does." He leaned in close and whispered in my ear. "I'm going to be your first and your only everything."

"What makes you so sure?" I was surprised at my saucy tone but hid it well. I wasn't one who flirted, but I found with him it came naturally.

"Because I planned it that way." Before I could ask him to explain, he kissed my cheek and smoothly said, "I'll see you around, Shelly baby."

*****

I didn't know how long it would take for the burning sensation to fade, but when I woke some time later, I felt as if my skin were being pricked by thousands of tiny needles. I cried silently into the pillow, willing the pain away. The soft covers beneath me rubbed against my chafing skin. I didn't want to open my eyes because I knew what waited for me—it would mean this was real instead of a nightmare.

I couldn't see him, but I knew he was here.

When I finally opened my eyes, my gaze first landed on an old poster of Megan Fox posing in a superwoman costume. I remember the day we hung it up after fighting over who would get to keep her. He assumed at first that she was an inspiration for how I wanted to look. I revealed that I had an even bigger crush on her that I couldn't and wouldn't explain. It was also the first time he told me that he loved me.

At first, I laughed it off until I witnessed what had to be the first sincere moment we shared in the brief months we dated.

It just so happened shortly after the bliss of falling in love was followed by two years of heartbreak because of his cheating.

Before that summer day in his bedroom, he had been someone I could trust, but something shattered that. It wasn't until it was too late when I realized we had been doomed from the start.

"I thought about tearing it down."

Keenan's deep voice pulled me from the past. It was a constant battle not to live in the past, but it was an all-out war not to be afraid of the present.

"So why haven't you?" The raspy sound of my voice was a testament to the pain I had endured however long since I'd been passed out. I could still hear my screams from when the nearly scalding water poured onto my skin.

"Because there is no such thing as destroying a memory. It's impossible."

"It's not impossible. I managed to forget about you all these years."

"And yet here I am... Besides, we both know that's a lie." The bite in his tone was barely audible, but the resentment was there.

"What can I say? You're easily forgotten... or haven't you learned that from your parents?"

I was sure I had done it and that maybe he would kill me.

"How do you feel?"

Like I just took a round trip to hell and back. "Why do you care? So you can hurt me more?"

"Perhaps, but it isn't a reason not to answer the question. If I want to hurt you, Shelly, I will. Haven't I proven that?"

I sat up then, and my gaze instantly fell on Keenan sitting against the dresser with his knees drawn up and his arms resting against them. I wondered how he could tell I had woken up from his position. Even now, he watched me. His gaze never wavered.

I took a deep breath and matched his stare. Even if I felt none of the bravado I displayed, I had to make him believe it. "The only thing you proved is that you are unstable."

"I learned a lot about myself while I was away. I can promise you my mind is functioning better than ever."

"So, is that what you ran away to do? To find yourself?"

"No." He rose to his feet and left the room with silent steps. Despite my disgust, I couldn't help but admire him. Everything about him was different now. He moved and talked in the manner of a predator. It was as if he were hunting for something.

It was as if he wanted a victim.

I used the opportunity to check over my sore body that was covered in red patches. None of the injuries appeared too serious. The only scars I would carry were too far beneath the surface.

"Are you ignoring me?" My head snapped up and towards the bedroom door where Keenan stood watching me.

"What?"

He moved from the door to stand at the foot of the bed. When he leaned down to plant his hands on either side of my legs, I fought the urge to back away. "I've been calling your name."

"I obviously didn't hear you."

"Would you like more of before?" His expression hadn't changed, but his eyes were nearly black with ire.

"Please don't."

He said nothing as he stood upright and held out his hand. I stared down at his hand dumbfounded. "I can take you or I can make you," he said softly when I hesitated a little too long.

My hand slid slowly into his, and I could have sworn he rubbed my knuckles with this thumb before he pulled me to my feet.

"Slowly," I pleaded. My body was sore and my movements stiff.

He didn't reply, but his steps were slow as he led me from the room. When we entered the bathroom shortly after, I lost all the breath in my body and control over my limbs.

I fell to the floor, but his hand kept a tight grip on mine. "Keenan, no."

The entire time I pleaded, my eyes remained locked on the tub full of water. Sinister thoughts ran rampant in my mind. I didn't realize I was crawling backward until my back hit the wall.

"What are you doing?" His tone lacked patience as he took heavy steps toward me.

"Please don't make me go back in there. The water is too hot."

"It's not hot anymore. I changed it back."

"Changed?" Confusion replaced panic as I stared at him through the dim light of the hallway. What did he mean by changing it back? As soon as the question formed in my mind, the answer followed.

Not only had Keenan sought to punish me, but he had purposely made the water boiling hot to hurt me in yet another way that would cause irreparable damage. It must have been what he'd done when he messed with the handle.

"Yes, Shelly. I did it. Now come."

"No." I anchored myself against the wall as if it would really save me from him. Keenan was stronger and in control. How could I compete against that?

"The water isn't hot."

"Why should I trust you? What you did was sick." With a careless shrug, he forced me up from the floor.

"It was necessary."

"You have no right to be jealous of someone who doesn't exist," I snapped and prayed that he didn't hear the lie in my voice.

"Jealous? I'm merely taking back what's mine. How can I be jealous of that?"

He pushed me a little harder than necessary inside the bathroom. My attention was so fixated on the tub that I didn't notice his silence behind me until his next words made my blood turn cold.

"You had my name removed," he growled.

I whirled around to face him. Not only did the hatred in his voice make my spine feel as if it retreated to my body, but he was also blocking the exit.

The fire dancing within his dark irises should have made me back down, but Keenan would know the moment I did and then he would pounce.

The smile that graced my face couldn't be stopped even if I wanted. Never mind the fact that I stood before an angry Keenan in my birthday suit. No, it wasn't enough. I had to bait him. "Yeah. So?"

"Why?"

"I may be stuck in this hell hole with you, but that doesn't mean I answer to you anymore."

"Wrong, Shelly. You never stopped answering to me. That's why you could never seal the deal with your golden boy, isn't it?"

"You don't know what the hell you're talking about." He spoke as if he knew about Eric, but I knew there could be no way unless Lake told him, and I made her promise not to ever tell.

"Oh, I know plenty. I know when you're hot and ready to fuck and, baby, you were *always* ready to fuck. But when you look at him, I bet there was no passion and there was no lust. I bet he has never even tasted your pretty little pussy, has he?" His hand slid up my leg slowly and softly. So softly that had I not been so in tune with his touch even four years later, I might not have noticed. "I remember how much you liked that."

"I don't want you to touch me."

"Then why are your thighs quaking?"

I tried to still the trembling of my legs and fight the memory of how he would wrap them around his neck and spending what felt like hours tasting me… but all that was tarnished by the reminder of the cruel, sadistic person he had become.

"If you beg me, I'll do it for you, right here and now. But if you don't…"

He stopped speaking to lead me to the tub with a tight grip on my wrist.

"If I don't?" I hated that my voice sounded breathless and my body responded to the pure unadulterated promise of sex. Knowing he wouldn't go easy on me didn't make me want him less. Knowing what he could and would do made me want him more.

"I'll do it anyway. At least, if you beg, you will feel like you have a choice."

Because I was left without a choice, I lifted and lowered my foot into the water, which was shockingly cool and served as a balm to my skin. I was more grateful that the water would hide my true reaction to his promise.

"You can do what you want to me, but I won't be begging."

He lowered to his knee until he was eye level with me. The heat in his dark eyes was unmistakable. "Beg now or beg later, but you will beg." Without warning, he stole my lips but not to kiss. He clamped down on my upper lip until I cried out. When he retreated, I lifted a tentative hand to my lip just before I tasted a drop of blood.

"I think I like the taste of your blood just as much as your pussy," he chuckled before rising to his feet to tower over me.

At the same time, I shuddered with revulsion, my tongue unconsciously flicked over my lips, curious of the taste. When I recognized the familiar copper tang of blood, I glared up at him.

"What do you want from me?"

"Right now, I just want you to bathe and then I want you to sleep."

"I can sleep at home."

"Why? What's waiting for you there but an empty

apartment?"

"It's not empty." The temperature in the room seemed to drop a hundred degrees when he froze from picking up my clothes. "My daughter is everywhere in that apartment," I clarified. "It's where she took her first steps and learned to talk. Every smell and surface belonged to her. We have so many memories there, and I just want to be there with her."

I was begging, and I didn't even care. For her, I'd beg. For her, I'd give up anything. But it wasn't the Keenan who came back to me that I was pleading to—I pleaded to the Keenan who was still running away. I knew he could hear me. The evidence was in the emotion hidden behind the anger. It was right there in his eyes for the world to see. You just had to know what to look for.

His gaze was locked with mine for the longest time, and for a minute, I thought I'd gotten through. He made a quick turn on his heel and tossed over his shoulder, "You have ten minutes to be done."

*****

Keenan had taken off but not before cuffing my hands together and locking me in his bedroom, only saying that he would be back before retreating. It was more of a warning than the reassurance it should have been.

I wondered when he'd changed the locks on the door because he had never been able to lock the door with a key in the past.

He planned this.

I drifted off to sleep before I could figure out why he would go to the trouble of keeping me against my will.

I awoke sometime later to the feeling of his long

fingers circling my wrist. He unlocked one cuff and then the other before silently turning away. I ignored the dull ache in my wrists as I sat up and fought away the remains of sleep.

"Anything?"

His face remained impassive as he spoke. "We went back to the house in Camden, but there was no one there. I don't think anyone has lived there for years."

"How did you get in?" Instead of answering, he sent me a look that said I needed to use my head.

"You broke in."

"Yes."

I silently sat back and tried not to let the slump in my shoulders be visible. Our leads were dropping like dead flies, and each day, it seemed less possible that I would ever see Kennedy's face again or hear her voice.

"Are you ready to tell me who you've been seeing?"

"You are unbelievable. How could my dating life possibly help us find her?"

"Use your fucking head, Shelly. It could have been anyone. We need to explore every option."

"Isn't that what the FBI is for?"

"We haven't heard anything from them in days. They know less than we do. How long before this case goes cold for them?"

I didn't want to think about that. "There is no one. I told you that."

His eyes narrowed as his jaw hardened. "If I find out you are lying to me, I will make you pay, and you will never see her again."

"You can't keep my daughter from me."

His hand flashed out to grip my ponytail, pulling my head back until my neck felt as if it would snap. "I can if you're dead so think hard about who you really need to protect."

With that, he released my hair and stormed from the room.

There was no reason to put Eric in that kind of danger. The consequences of revealing his name were far too deadly. Eric had never even met Kennedy. I never talked about her to him. I'd always been careful. A part of me never wanted her to mistake anyone as her father and the biggest part was the maternal instinct to protect her. What kind of mother would I be if I brought someone in her life at such a tender age? I wasn't in love with Eric, and deep down, I knew I never would be.

I had no reason to feel guilty.

I wanted to find her more than I wanted to breathe, but finding her shouldn't mean the innocent life of another, should it?

I cried myself to sleep thinking about everything I had lost and everything I would still have to sacrifice.

Sometime during the night, my restless sleep turned into an erotic dream. It started with my lips followed by a light touch on my neck. My breasts were begging for attention by the time every inch of my neck was blessed with sensual kisses.

"I want you to open your legs." Dream me obeyed happily. My legs spread under the command. "Now open your eyes." The familiar voice floated into my dream, corrupting the bliss and turning it into something real.

Oh, fuck.

My dream wasn't a dream, and I was currently spread open like a wanton slut.

Keenan stood next to me, shirtless, like a sexy shadow in the darkness. The intention in his dark eyes was very clear even as my vision fought to adjust.

The moonlight highlighted his chest, and I held my breath as the full vision of his chest became clearer.

Were those nipple rings? Silver barbells protruded from each of his nipples giving his chest an exotic appeal. Intricate tattoos adorned almost every inch of skin.

It was disturbing how much my body responded to his. Even now, I could feel my sex clench and release with anticipation. I sat up in a panic and desperately pulled the covers up over my body. His t-shirt I turned into a sleep shirt was cut down the middle, revealing my naked body underneath. I choked down the sorrow from the ruined shirt that I could never again find comfort in.

"What are you doing?"

"Are you going to pretend you didn't know this was coming?"

"I would like to think I have a choice in the matter."

"You can decide how you want it." He lifted the covers from my hands and peeled them back, revealing my body once more. "But decide fast because fuck you or hurt you, I'm going to do it all, and when I do, you'll feel me. I can stretch and fill you over and over until you come, or I can make you scream another way."

"Keenan..." I could barely manage his name. It didn't matter anyway when he flipped me onto my stomach without warning and peeled the remains of his shirt from my body.

"Raise your hips."

Stupidly, I obeyed.

He ran tentative fingers down my already dripping sex although his intentions were less than such. Back and forth, he continued to rub, creating a delicious friction that I fought to hate yet craved. My hips tensed with their need to move against him. My pussy was weeping from the need of him, and all the while, I silently cried into the pillow. I was thankful for my position so he wouldn't see my tears. He would likely delight in having made me come undone.

I wanted him.

It was a fact as much as it was painful.

"We can't do this." It was wrong for so many reasons, and if I gave into him, what would that make me?

"Your pussy tells me you want this even if it is with me. I know your body better than you know yourself. You still belong to me, and I won't let you forget it again."

He was wrong. I never forgot it in the four years we've been apart, but every day I fought it.

"I haven't—" It was a good thing his tongue picked that moment to touch my sex or else I would have confessed to it all.

I was a moaning, gasping, writhing mess in no time at all.

"I take back what I said earlier. Your pussy is still the best thing I've ever had in my mouth."

CHAPTER THIRTEEN

KEENAN

IT WAS LIKE an explosion of everything wonderful assaulting my taste buds. Her cries drowned out the moans I released in her pussy.

She'd already come once, and I was fighting for a second. Her trembling body was putty in my hands and weak from my mouth.

"Keenan, please."

That's it, baby. Beg me. Just a little more.

"Please, please, please," she chanted. I knew the perfect way to push her over the edge, and it was right where I wanted her.

I strummed my tongue a little faster against her clit, and when her thighs shook uncontrollably, I smiled against her skin.

"Fuck me."

She whispered it so low, if I hadn't been listening for that very plea, I would have missed it. I continued to suck up every bit of come from her sex.

The pleasure of knowing she still craved my cock

inside her was almost better than payback. She turned around to face me on her knees, reaching for my belt buckle.

My hand on her wrist stopped her. "What's wrong?" she asked. Confusion and lust were written all over her features.

"I think we're done here." I made it out of the bedroom just as her angry scream ripped through the air.

Mission accomplished.

I headed for my father's liquor cabinet in the basement. I had all of my hope on finding Kennedy in that house tonight just to find another dead end.

A part of me wondered what I would do if I ever found her.

She belonged to me just as much as her mother did, and I knew I wouldn't be able to ignore my instincts to keep them. Staying away had destroyed me. Walking away wasn't something I couldn't do a second time.

I retrieved an unopened bottle with plans of finishing the entire thing by morning and turned back for the stairs. I stopped short at the sight of Sheldon creeping down the stairway.

"What are you doing down here?" I asked with impatience evident in every syllable.

"Where the hell do you get off?" She stopped halfway down the stairs and folded her arms across her breasts. Not ogling them was damn near impossible. She had always been generous in that department. The way they would bounce whenever she rode me was a permanent memory I willingly called on whenever I needed a release.

"I didn't, but you did. Twice."

"I ask you to fuck me after you threatened to do it anyway and you walk away?" Humiliation pinked her cheeks even as she stood before me with her head held high.

"You didn't ask, you begged, but fortunately for you, I got bored."

The truth was, I walked away because, though I wanted her body, I could see myself really hurting her. I craved it more than I wanted my next meal.

"Whether I asked or begged is irrelevant. Know that you won't ever touch me again. You did me a favor, really. I'd forgotten how mediocre your fucking can be." She took a step backward up the stairs, but there was no way in hell I was letting her get away after that.

Call it an ego trip, but it had just gotten her thoroughly fucked, but not in the way that she expected.

"Fine. You want to be fucked?" I dropped the bottle, letting it tumble and shatter down the stairs and grabbed her wrist to spin her around, slamming her against the wall of the stairway. Shock and fear tumbled out from her lips as a breathless gasp.

"Let me go."

"Shut up. If we're fucking, I want your ass first."

She must have been extremely pissed to come down completely naked, but it worked to my advantage. I kicked her feet apart and nestled my own between her legs.

"Are you still a virgin?"

Mutely, she nodded. When we were together, I half-heartedly attempted to convince Sheldon to let me take her there, but she had always turned me down. Up until now, I had respected her wishes.

Her breathing was thick and heavy as she braced herself against the wall with both hands seeming to accept what would happen.

We both needed this.

I gripped her jaw hard and applied pressure until she opened up. Slowly, I slipped two fingers inside and ordered her to suck them. Meanwhile, I unbuttoned my belt and jeans and lowered them enough for my cock to slip free. I was still hard and throbbing from eating her pussy. The sight of her naked body only served to harden me even more.

"Enough." My voice was gruff with lust making my command rougher than I had intended, but the slight tremble down her spine let me know she responded well to it. I slipped my fingers from her and lightly trailed them down her spine.

I sunk down to my knees and gripped her ass in my hands before spreading her so I could feast on the sight of her little pink rosebud.

"Fuck me," I growled before taking my first taste.

"Oh, God. Keenan, what are you—" Her breath cut short when I sunk two fingers inside her pussy, one at a time—slowly. Simultaneously, I fingered her pussy while eating her ass and enjoyed how she came apart under my attention.

"Come here," I ordered after rising to my feet. I gripped her hair and turned her around before pushing her to her knees. "Suck me."

She wasted no time, taking me in her mouth. I held her hair high like a leash while her head bobbed eagerly. I'd forgotten how good it felt to have her lips wrapped around me. My head fell back, and I released a grunt when I felt my orgasm building. The need to come was strong, but there was only one place I planned to release.

"Stand up."

She rose to her feet on shaky legs. "After I come in your ass, I'm putting my stamp back where it belongs." When she opened her mouth to protest, I twisted her nipple and growled, "Don't fuck with me on this."

I would reclaim what was mine.

All she could do was nod before I planted her hands against the wall again and spread her legs before bending her over. I took care to lube my cock as much as possible before settling the head against her still wet ass. I had to go slowly since I didn't have more than our combined saliva as a lubricant.

The heat from her ass, as I began to enter her, inflamed me. Although I couldn't see her face, I knew she was crying by the uneven hitch in her voice as she gasped each time I sunk deeper.

"Hurts," she whimpered, and fuck me if it didn't make my cock grow. I had only just breached her with my cock head.

"That's because you're fighting it. Let me in."

"How?" she cried.

"Stop thinking, that's how." I wrapped an arm around her waist and anchored her to me. The move caused her ass to suck me in deeper, and I almost came instantly.

Just a little more.

I slid the fingers of my other hand around until I was touching her pussy, which still dripped despite her protests.

She moaned shakily as I rubbed her there, teasing her and lifting her to a high she had never experienced before and never would unless I allowed it.

"Inside me."

"What?" I started moving slowly inside her ass. My hips thrust in a rhythm that had been unfamiliar to me for the last four years.

"I want your fingers inside me... please."

"Why?"

My pace increased infinitesimally. I would introduce her to hard fucking once again, but first, I needed to take my time. I didn't want this to end until she submitted to me.

"I just need," she mumbled incoherently,

"My cock?" She leaned her forehead against the wall and nodded, but I was having none of it. I gripped her throat and brought her back flush with my front. "Tell me it's my cock you need."

I increased my pace just a little more. Her ass was giving way to my ownership, and soon, she would, too. I just needed the words.

"Say it, baby. Tell me what you feel—" I thrust my fingers deeper inside her pussy and whispered in her ear, "Right here."

"Fuck... Keenan."

"Say it," I barked.

"You own me!" she screamed and convulsed against my fingers as she came.

"That's right, baby. Your sweet little ass belongs to me, and so do you."

My rhythm quickly transformed from a slow tease to a forceful pounding. I gave up everything to the fuck.

Her ass welcomed my unforgiving strokes while her screams spurred me. When she could no longer hold herself up, I took her down to her knees. She quickly planted her hands on the steps and braced for my relentless thrusts inside her body.

My fingers were no longer thrusting inside her. Instead, I gripped her hips to pull her deeper onto my cock.

"It's hurts so good. Oh, baby, I'm going to come," she pleaded.

"Fuck, yes. Come on my cock. I want to feel your ass suck me in."

Her legs shook and her breath came out in shorts gasps as she came hard forcing me to follow after and empty inside her.

The force of our orgasms seemed to suck the strength out of us both as we collapsed on the stairs.

We'd fallen asleep where we were on the staircase, and it was my phone ringing sometime later that woke me up.

"Yeah?" I grumbled lazily into the phone. I wasn't even sure I had answered until the caller spoke two words that made my heart stop.

"Lake's gone."

I jumped up immediately and pulled up my jeans. Sheldon started to come to when I yelled into the phone. "What the fuck do you mean she's gone?"

"I mean she slipped out sometime during the night," Dash gritted.

"Night? Wait... What time is it?"

"It's after six in the morning. What the fuck are you doing over there?"

"Nothing," I answered a little too quickly. "I was asleep."

"What's going on?" Sheldon mumbled sleepily.

"Is that my sister?" Dash yelled through the phone.

"Is that Dash?" I nodded quietly to her before ordering her upstairs. For once, she listened without argument.

"Have you called her?"

"Several times. She won't pick up, but I know she sees me calling because she keeps sending me to voicemail."

"Why would she leave?"

"Probably because Keiran rejected her visit again."

I clenched my eyes closed and swore. "He's going to kill us and then her."

"Yeah, and sooner than you think. We managed to convince the private investigator and the hospital to drop the charges."

"How?"

"Money. How else?"

"So when is he being released?"

"In three hours."

"Fuck!" I shouted. "So we have three hours to find her. Have you tried her aunt?"

"I'm on my way there now."

"I'm on my way." I hung up without saying more and ran full speed up the stairs to the first level, hooked a right, and ran up the second set of stairs.

"What's going on?" Sheldon asked as she pulled on her jeans from yesterday.

"What are you doing?" I stopped short and glared down at her. Sheldon was average height while I was tall, and I used it to my advantage each time I sought to intimidate her.

"I'm getting dressed. I can't exactly go home naked, can I?"

"You're not going anywhere, so naked shouldn't be a problem. Think of this as your home until we find Ken."

"Don't call her that. You don't get that privilege."

"As the man who fertilized your egg, I think I do."

"But that's all you were." Her voice rose with each word as she yanked on her clothes.

"Because the bitch who birthed her didn't try to inform me that she had my baby."

"Don't blame me because you're a coward. What was I supposed to do? Search all over the world? Turn over every rock you might have crawled under?"

"Yes," I answered simply. "It's what I would have done if you had run away—if you *do* run away."

She planted her hands on her hips and regarded me coolly. "Is that a threat?"

I walked up to her until my chest was flush with

hers. I gripped her chin gently and lifted her face so I could look into her eyes. "It's a threat, a promise, a commitment, and a vow. Take it seriously, baby, because if you ever leave, I will find you, but I can't promise you will survive it."

"I miss the old you," she whispered unexpectedly. The pain in her eyes was unmistakable.

"That's too bad because he's gone." A broken heart couldn't be mended.

"Forever?"

"Yeah, baby. Forever."

She slipped her chin from my fingers and took a step back. "Then there's nothing left to say. I'm leaving."

I nodded once, and she seemed to take that as acceptance, but when I picked her up and tossed her on the bed, she screamed and fought.

"Be still, or I'll fuck you right here, and this time I won't wait for permission."

"You wouldn't rape me." The fear evident in her eyes belied her challenge.

"Oh, yeah? Try me."

"I'll fight you."

"I'll like it."

She fell silent and still, so without another word, I ripped the jeans from her body and stood up. On the way out, I picked up the rest of her clothes and stormed out, slamming the door behind me for good measure.

Regret snuck up on me as I leaned against the door. If I could kick my own ass, I would. I sounded like a creep even to my own ears, but what was I supposed to do?

I couldn't let her leave, but a part of me wished I hadn't taken it that far.

Maybe I should let her go.

The longer I was around her, the more dangerous to her I became, but the selfish part of me that was most dominant just couldn't let go.

*****

I pulled into the driveway of Lake's childhood home. Dash's R8 was already parked on the street so I went to the door and rung the bell. I didn't expect Dash to be the one to answer the door, but as soon as I stepped inside, I knew why.

"Just tell me where you are, honey. We're worried about you... Yes, I know your boyfriend is an inconsiderate asshole, but remember why you love him... you don't mean that." I listened closely to the one-sided conversation, but when it appeared to be going nowhere, I silently indicated for the phone.

"Lake?" I spoke into the phone.

She huffed and asked, "Yes?"

"Keiran is being released in about two hours." I hung up the phone and handed it back to her aunt.

"Why did you do that? We may not get her to answer again."

"She'll come," Dash answered.

Carissa folded her arms and regarded us with skepticism. "Lake is perfectly capable of making her own decisions. While I like Keiran a lot, he does not and should not have that kind of power over her."

"Then clearly you've never been in love."

Less than an hour later, Lake slammed through the front door, rolled her eyes, and marched upstairs. Carissa followed her upstairs after recovering from the surprise of how fast her niece returned.

It was a wonder she was even surprised given the kind of man her husband is. Years ago, I got the impression that he wasn't someone to be fucked with. He happened to be one of the best private investigators in the world and one who could no doubt find Kennedy. Unfortunately, shortly before Kennedy was taken Jackson went off grid in some third world country on a case.

"Where's my sister?" Dash asked, breaking me from my thoughts.

"My uncle's place."

"So what did you guys do last night?" I cut my eyes to see him regarding me with narrowed eyes.

"Is that any of your business?"

"Someone had to make her their business since you haven't been concerned for the last four years."

"What the fuck do you want from me? An apology letter?"

"I want you to man the fuck up and realize we aren't kids anymore. My sister doesn't deserve to bear the brunt of your grudge, and if you even think of hurting her again, I will kill you, motherfucker."

"Well, then I suggest you kill me now because whether I leave or stay, she will get hurt. It was a mistake bringing me back here, so if you want to blame someone blame the person who started all of this."

"You're not making it any better. Why can't you see that?"

I laughed despite the seriousness of our conversation. "Because I don't want to make it better. I have no intentions of doing so. I came to collect. So, as I said before—kill me or stay out of my way."

CHAPTER FOURTEEN

FIFTEEN YEARS AGO
KEENAN

MY DAD HAD just come home with a strange boy who was around my age. At first, I was excited about having someone to play with, but as soon as my dad left us alone, the boy he called Keiran disappeared.

I searched all over the house until the only place left was the basement where I wasn't allowed to go. My mom had said it was dangerous, but she hadn't been home for a while, and I doubt my dad would notice. He never noticed me.

Slowly, I ventured down the dark stairs. When I made it all the way down, I realized the basement was cold and creepy.

I looked left and right but couldn't see anything for the lack of light. Since I'd never been allowed to come down here, I didn't know where the light switch was.

"Why are you following me?"

The voice seemed ghostly filtering through the dark. How did he know I was here?

"Where are you?" Slowly, I ventured deeper into the dark in the direction his voice came from.

"What do you want?"

"Don't be afraid," I said softly. To be honest, *he* made *me* afraid.

His laugh was unusual and not at all friendly. It was scary like he was, and I got the feeling that being down here alone with him was dangerous.

When he finally finished laughing, he said, "You shouldn't be here."

"Neither should you," I countered. "We aren't allowed down here."

"Says who?"

"My dad. We'll get in trouble."

"Will he kill me?"

"What? No! Why do you think that?"

"Because I'll kill him if he tries to hurt me."

"He won't. Please don't kill him." I wanted to run away, but I stayed because I wanted to know more. The sound of his voice became louder as I got closer.

"Why do you care?"

"Because he's my dad. Don't you have a dad?" I frowned because he acted weird. Kids weren't supposed to talk about killing.

"Yes, but he isn't nice. Is your dad nice?"

"He can be, but he's busy a lot, so I don't ever really see him. I never have anyone to talk to or play with either, so I was wondering..."

"I don't know how to play."

"But you're a kid. Kids always know how to play."

"I'm not a kid. I'm a slave."

"What's a slave?" I felt foolish talking to the dark, but it was better than not having anyone to talk to at all.

"I don't really know, but I always have to do what I'm told or they'll kill me."

"Who?"

"The trainers."

"They sound like bad people."

"They are."

"Are you bad?"

"Yes. You should stay away from me."

"Maybe all you need is a friend."

Suddenly, he was right in front of me. The frown on his face was scary, and before I could run away, he pushed me down.

"Don't you get it? I'm bad. Bad people don't play."

*****

Dash and I drove separate cars to the local jail. John and Mr. Chambers were already there waiting. Shortly after arriving, Keiran walked through the doors and practically ran down the steps. After so many times being locked away, I had become familiar with what happens next. Keiran would be in more of a pissy mood than normal after being locked away like an animal.

"Come here," he said to Lake as soon as his foot touched the pavement. He completely ignored the rest of us and marched over to where she stood. Even after four years of being together, his obsession with her was as strong as when he hated her. Maybe even stronger.

She resisted his attention for only as long as it took him to become pissed. In no time at all, he had her locked in his possessive embrace as he devoured her face.

"All right, you two. Get a room. We still have my granddaughter to find," Mr. Chambers chastised. The reminder that Kennedy was still missing seemed to snap Keiran out of it.

"No more bullshitting around," Keiran barked. "We

find her tonight, and no one fucking eats or sleeps until we do."

Ten minutes later, we were all gathered in the living room of my childhood home, minus John who said he had somewhere to be (a.k.a. Mitch). I had found Sheldon some old shorts and a shirt to wear from my preteen days. Everyone lifted a brow at her attire, but wisely, no one said a word.

After about another hour of Keiran's grilling, we had all grown impatient. "The ransom note didn't give us much to go on, and we've searched everywhere. Do you know something we don't?"

"If we searched everywhere, Kennedy would have been found. What's the deal with the house in Camden?"

"It was a dead end, but we've been keeping surveillance on it. Nothing's popped up on the radar."

"Q, when do you have to go back?"

"I'm good for another week."

"Jesse, how safe are we hacking these satellites?"

"As long as I continue to jump between satellites, I can be in and out before anyone can pick up I was ever there."

Keiran had begun to pace back and forth, and when the silence stretched too long, I interrupted. "What are you thinking?"

"There's one place we haven't looked."

"Where?" we all collectively shouted.

"Four years ago, John told me the story of how he met our mother. Mitch kept her prisoner in a house no one knew about until John found them. I don't know how he found them, and he also never told me where it was... Where did he say he was going again?" Keiran asked as he pulled out his phone.

"He didn't," Q answered before cutting his eyes toward me.

Fuck. There was no way Q could know where he had gone, but I knew he suspected something. The look he gave me confirmed it.

I had promised John I wouldn't tell Keiran where Mitch was but was a secret built from the need for revenge really worth my daughter's life? I had just made my decision when Keiran started to speak into the phone.

Keiran hung up a short time later with a tense expression.

"What did he say?" Sheldon asked. Her hands shook and her chest heaved up and down. I took in her body and once again noticed how thin she had become in such a short time. It was something I noticed last night, but my head was too clouded with lust to look into it further. Thinking back, I hadn't seen her eat or drink so much as a bottle of water since waking up in the hospital a week ago.

"He said he was on his way."

That explained the frustration he wore on his face. I pulled my vibrating phone from my jeans and read the message that lit up the screen: Don't say anything.

It was a text from John. I considered ignoring it, but what would it mean for Kennedy if I did? Would John keep the information secret if I spilled his? What would it mean for Kennedy if I didn't tell?

"How long until he's here?" I hadn't realized I was staring hard down at my phone until Sheldon's voice snapped me back to the present.

"He said a few hours."

I jumped to my feet and looked around the room at all the tired faces. It was evident that each person in this room had hardly slept since Kennedy was taken. The love that clearly surrounded her was something I had not seen at her age. For as long as I could remember, I had only been given isolation.

"Well, I'm going to go help your mother with the volunteers," Mr. Chambers announced. "Dash, are you coming?"

"No, I think I'm going to stick around in case something comes up."

The way he looked at me told me the real reason he chose to stick around. He didn't trust me, and I gave him every reason not to. In some way, I also think he was hoping I'd change my mind. That was Dash. He was always the positive one.

"Be careful, Dash. Just remember what's at stake. Empires don't run themselves."

"Dad, my niece—your granddaughter is what's at stake. I'll do whatever it takes," he responded coldly.

Given the conversation between Sheldon and her mother at the hospital, I wasn't surprised at his reaction. However, Keiran was completely oblivious and currently looked on the verge of murdering him where he stood. Mr. Chambers wisely stormed out without a response.

"What the fuck was that?" Keiran asked as soon as the door closed.

"Leave it alone," Dash gritted.

They seemed to have some sort of staring contest and neither was willing to give in.

"Baby," Lake called. She stood to lay a hand on his chest and started to rub in a soothing motion that defined how adept she'd become at abating his anger. "I'm really tired, and I know you must be, too. What do you say we get something to eat and relax while we wait for John?"

Her attention seemed to work when Keiran and Dash backed off each other. I couldn't help but be a little disappointed. The dynamic duo had never been at odds with each other until now. Ruining Keiran's friendship with the only person who had been brave enough to stick by him all these years would have been the cherry on the top.

Lake led Keiran upstairs by the hand, and Dash left shortly after receiving a phone call. The tense look on his face only deepened so I knew the phone call couldn't have been a good one.

"What do you say we get something to eat?" I asked Sheldon once we were left alone.

"I'm not hungry."

"I can see your bones, so hungry or not, you're eating." I retrieved her clothes and ordered her to shower and dress.

*****

I took Sheldon to a restaurant just outside the city that was known for their pancakes. I hadn't realized all the little things I gave up when I left.

"I don't see why we had to come out to eat," Sheldon griped as we took our seats. We were seated immediately due to the late hour for breakfast. "I'm sure there is plenty of food in your kitchen."

"I wanted to make sure you ate since you can't take care of yourself, and it's not my kitchen."

"I can take care of myself. Anyway, why should I eat when I don't even know if my daughter has eaten in a week?"

"So, starving yourself is going to bring her back? You can't punish yourself."

"No, I can't, but only because you've been doing a good enough job of it for me."

"Did you honestly think I would make this easy on

you?"

"No. I've learned not to expect anything good when it comes to you. You wrecked me, Keenan. In more ways than one."

The waiter came for our orders before I could respond. To Sheldon's annoyance, not only did I order for her, but I also ordered an entire platter of breakfast all of which I knew she would never be able to consume.

"I can speak for myself, and I can't eat all that."

"Too bad because you aren't getting up from this table until you do." I smiled wide for good measure, which only served to piss her off more.

"You're feeling incredibly sure of your power today."

"Last night, I had my cock buried deep in your ass while you screamed for more... why wouldn't I be?"

"Because it was a mistake that won't be happening again."

"It will happen again as often as I want it. It can happen now, right over this table if you don't eat your food. My daughter is going to need her mother in good shape when she comes home. She doesn't deserve to see you like this."

That seemed to shut her up, forcing us into an uncomfortable silence. The waiter came with our food and we ate silently. I happened to look up from my food in time to catch her wipe a tear away.

"Does it bother you this much?"

My question seemed to break down the floodgates. "I need her back. I feel helpless because I don't know where to look, and I don't even know why she was taken from me, but what I do know is that she is with strangers who don't know how to take care of her. What if she has a seizure?"

"She'll make it through this."

"How do you know that? You don't even know her."

"Because I know her mother. She's grown into an incredibly strong woman who can fight." I lifted her chin and forced her gaze on me. "And she'll continue to fight because she knows that's all she can do."

"Why are you being so nice to me? Don't you hate me?"

"I owe it to the daughter I've never met to keep her mother in one piece," I said dismissively. I didn't like the hopeful way she watched me. We weren't living a fairytale anymore, and it was time she remembered that.

"You should fix yourself up. Crying made you look like shit."

I managed to shock her into a stunned silence before a scowl transformed her features. She angrily pushed back her chair and stormed off to the back of the restaurant.

When she was out of sight, I took some of the food from her plate and rearranged it to make it look full. I didn't know where my need to look out for her came from, but I had to be careful.

Sheldon was easy to fall for.

And if I didn't tread carefully, she could very well own me all over again. After breakfast, she managed to convince me to take her to her apartment for a change of clothes. I had just taken a seat when the sound of glass shattering broke the silence.

I ran the short distance to her bedroom where I assumed she had disappeared.

There she stood in the center, holding a note. The paper I instantly recognized as similar to the ransom note we'd found rattled unsteadily in her bleeding hand. Glass shards from the broken mirror littered the floor around her feet.

Wordlessly, I plucked the note from her hand and guided her to sit on the bed. Her gaze was locked straight ahead as she sat frozen.

Mentally, I braced myself for what had sparked such a violent reaction. After unfolding the paper, I silently read the next clue to my daughter's disappearance.

ARE YOU WILLING TO KILL?

* * * * *

Thirty minutes later, I had Keiran, Lake, Dash, and Q seated around her small living room. I handed the note to Keiran who silently read it before handing it to Dash.

"This doesn't make any sense. Who could want my sister to kill and why? She's not a killer."

"No. But Keiran is." Everyone turned to Q who now held the note.

"What?"

He held up the paper. "It's addressed to him."

I took the paper from his hand and sure enough, written in bold letters on the back was his name. "The first ransom wasn't addressed."

"Keiran?" Sheldon had emerged from her bedroom. She still looked as if she'd seen a ghost but appeared steadier on her feet. "Why would they take my daughter if this is about you?"

"Whoever wrote this note knows about my past. It has to be someone I know."

"So what are we supposed to do now? Wait around for another ransom note?"

"May I see it?" Lake held out her hand for the note, and when I handed it to her, she read it over. She flipped it at least ten times and each time she read it, her skin paled.

"Do you see something else?"

"No. But I—I don't think the note is meant for Keiran."

"What do you mean? His name is written on the back."

Her hand clapped over her mouth, and she quickly ran from the room before she could explain. Keiran followed after her while the rest of us stood around dumbstruck.

"Because he's not the addressee," Q finished. "He's the answer."

Someone wanted my brother dead in exchange for Kennedy?

At that moment, Keiran walked back into the living room alone wearing a hard expression. "We need to find Mitch."

Shit.

"Keenan!"

At the sound of Sheldon's voice, I looked around, but she was nowhere in sight. I hadn't even noticed when she left the room, which was a first.

I followed the sound of her crying and found her in what must have been Kennedy's bedroom. I hadn't realized the rest had followed me until a chorus of swearing sounded behind me.

Written on the wall in red ink was a message:

SHE DIES IN 24 HOURS.

CHAPTER FIFTEEN

SHELDON

NONE OF US knew where to begin after finding the message in Kennedy's bedroom. We were short on time and leads, and we hadn't heard from John.

"When was the last time you were here?" Keiran questioned.

"Last night," Keenan thankfully answered. My throat was still clogged, and I was afraid I would choke on my own tears if I spoke too soon.

My daughter would be dead in just a few hours.

Was I willing to kill?

More importantly, was I willing to kill a friend for my daughter?

There had to be another way. I had to believe it because any other possibility was too painful.

"We need that address," Keiran growled. "Where the fuck is John?"

"Maybe Keenan knows," Q offered. The glare he sent Keenan's way was challenging, but Keenan managed to keep his composure despite being backed into a corner.

This secret John *guilted* Keenan into keeping was getting out of hand. I silently pleaded with him with my eyes, but Keenan ignored it and pushed away from the wall he currently leaned against.

Three hard knocks on the door interrupted whatever Keenan had been about to say. He made a detour for the door and opened it to reveal not only John but also Jesse standing on the other side.

"Where have you been?" I grilled.

"I came as soon as I could. Can you let us in?" John quipped.

Begrudgingly, I stepped aside to let them in. Jesse made his way to the small dining table Sheldon had positioned in the corner and began to set up.

"I went home first, but when I only found him," John indicated to Jesse, "I came here next."

"We received another ransom note. We needed you here hours ago."

John's expression darkened as he looked around the room. "Son of a bitch. What did the note say?"

"If Sheldon doesn't kill Keiran in twenty-four hours, Kennedy will die. Does that sound urgent enough for you?"

"We need that address now," Keiran ordered. The angry vein in his forehead was beginning to pulse.

"We need to talk, son."

Kennedy could die soon, and he wanted to talk? "Please, John. Just give us the address." He turned to me with sad eyes full of regret but no answer.

"What could we possibly have to talk about right this second?"

"Mitch."

"Yes. I am preparing to blow his head off and bring my niece home. What is there to discuss?"

"Mitch wasn't the one who took Kennedy."

"You don't know that for sure," I directed to John.

Keiran looked from me to John before pinching the bridge of his nose. "Someone want to tell me what the fuck is going on?"

"Mitch is dying. He has been for the last three years."

"And you know this how?"

"Because I've been keeping him in a cancer facility a few hours away."

The room chilled noticeably following John's revelation.

"Come again?"

"Your father came to me three years ago after being diagnosed with a cancerous tumor. By the time he came to me, he was far too weak to take care of himself so I took him to an after treatment facility."

Keiran was nearly rabid by the time John had finished explaining. "Where?"

"He's under my protection, Keiran but know this is to protect you, too."

"Yeah?" Keiran asked. "And who will protect you?"

"Look, the only reason I told you was because I didn't want to waste the little time we have on a dead end."

"Bullshit," Keenan countered. It was the first time he'd spoken since the confrontation began. "If it's a dead end then give me the address and let me make that decision. You have nothing to lose except your life if you don't."

I had never seen Keenan this way before. Threatening people was Keiran's thing, which made me wonder once again just who it was that returned from California, and could I trust him with my daughter?

Right now, he was part of the hope I held of bringing Kennedy home, and once she was home safe, I would do whatever it took to protect us from him once and for all.

As if sensing my thoughts, he turned to face me, his eyes darkening with each second that passed. He seemed to be sending a silent message, one that I wasn't too sure I wanted to decipher.

I looked away but not before catching the slow, sinister smile that made him look almost evil.

I could no longer see the person he was.

I look at him and all I see is a fallen angel because, in many ways, he is.

"One way or another, we are getting my daughter back tonight," Keenan announced. "So here is the plan."

*****

"I don't feel good about this," Lake said for the thousandth time as she paced back and forth. The guys minus Dash and Jesse had taken off for a town about three hours away where John had first found Sophia and Keiran.

If I weren't so afraid, I would have laughed at how life could come full circle when you least expect it, but nothing about this night was laughable.

Keenan and Keiran had chosen to go with their gut with only just a few hours left. If they were right, Kennedy would be back in my arms tonight. If they were wrong...

"I feel like I should be doing something."

"There's one little detail your boyfriends seemed to have forgotten about," Jesse quipped without taking his eyes from the computer. He had been silently working on pulling up a satellite feed of the house.

"What's that?"

"The FBI," he spelled out slowly. "Has anyone bothered to fill them in?"

"Believe me, they didn't forget," Dash stated. "If Kennedy is in that house, then no one involved will be walking out alive. Besides, the FBI hasn't been too helpful and neither have the private investigators my father hired."

"I think the only thing left to do was to deny their services after Keiran bludgeoned one of them, don't you think?" This came from Lake, who had now taken to jamming her fingers through her hair.

"It's going to be okay, Lake."

"But what if it isn't and Keiran goes away forever? God, he was finally shedding the slave and becoming his own person, but then suddenly someone comes back to finish the job." She sunk down the wall until she reached the floor. "Even if he doesn't die or isn't sent away forever, what if this resets him? We all saw what happened in the hospital."

"What I saw was someone who would do anything to protect his loved ones. That's who he is today. He's able to love and you have to believe that it's the only thing motivating him. If you can believe in anything, believe in love."

She seemed to be thinking it over before she locked her gaze with mine. "Will you be able to do the same?"

CHAPTER SIXTEEN

KEENAN

"WHAT DO YOU see?"

We made the three-hour trip in half the time and had been staking out the house for the last thirty minutes. The house was average in style and size and wasn't a place anyone would expect an abducted child to be held making it the perfect spot.

"Nothing. This is the place," Keiran stated, echoing my inner thoughts.

"What are we going to do about the Feds?" Q asked from the backseat.

"Once we confirm Kennedy is here, we'll report it, but not a minute before. I want the motherfuckers who took my little girl to suffer."

"How do you want to do this?" Keiran asked.

"Hot and fast. There's no way of telling where Kennedy is in that house. I don't want to give them a chance to have the advantage. We make quick work of it. Sheldon said there were two men who took her. There could be more, but we leave one alive for questioning before we kill him. John, do you remember how you got in before?" According to John, the locks were designed to keep anyone who didn't have a key from getting in or out.

"I've got it covered, son."

"Good. Once you get us in, Keiran and I will take the lead. You and Quentin will pull up the rear. There are four rooms plus the common areas. Kennedy is likely being held in one of the rooms."

There was a fifty percent chance we'd fail and lose everything including our lives, but I owed it the child I created to try. It was more than my parents had ever given me.

"John," I called back for my father's attention.

"Yes, son?"

"I want you to know that if my daughter is in there, I will kill you myself." From the corner of my eye, I saw Keiran turn his attention from the house and on me. I boldly met his gaze, daring him to protest, but when he simply nodded, I relaxed.

John wisely chose not to respond. Father or not, he had screwed with my daughter's life to protect a man that didn't deserve to live. I could care less what his intentions were.

We approached the house quickly, taking care to stay hidden in the shadows. I listened for voices, and when I heard the low but unmistakable sound of voices, I was ready to burst through the door. The reminder from my conscience that it could very well be a family having dinner was the only thing to keep me from ruining the entire mission.

John made quick work of the door, and in no time, we were through. The entryway was dark but empty, and as we moved deeper inside, I could hear deep voices drifting down from upstairs. We followed the sound to a door on a top floor.

"Do you think she'll do it, Vick?"

Vick? I wondered how good of a chance it could be that this Vick was the same investigator the Chambers hired to find Kennedy.

"If the bitch knows what's good for the little brat, she will. She's only got a couple hours."

"How are we supposed to know if she killed him?"

"We wait until we get the call."

"But how will he know?"

"It's not our problem. Once we get the call—"

His head was blown off before he could finish speaking. As soon as his body dropped, I trained my gun on the freckle-faced guy with carrot-colored hair. He didn't appear old enough to even be out of high school.

"If you don't stop screaming, you'll join your buddy."

He frantically looked around the room for an ally before he settled on Q as his best bet. "Don't look at me, bitch."

"Take anything you want, just don't kill me."

"Do you know what I'm here for?"

"N—no." He shook his head hard for emphasis.

"Do you know who this is?" I asked pointing to Keiran. He blinked a few times, focusing his gaze on my brother and shook his head again.

"This is Keiran Masters." Recognition had shone in his eyes before terror took over.

"If you're Keiran," stammered, "then who are you?" he asked.

"I'm the father of the little girl you took." And that's when the begging began. I had to hit him with the gun a few times to get him to shut up long enough. "I'm trying to have a polite conversation with you, but you keep interrupting me."

"I'm sorry, sir." His sniffling was starting to bug me, so I decided against torturing him.

"I'm only going to ask this once so pay attention. Where is my daughter?"

"She's in the guest room down the hall on the right."

Wow. That was easy.

I hoped the surprise I felt didn't show on my face, but judging by the terror still evident in his eyes, I knew I still looked like a man bent on killing.

"Please, just let me go. I didn't even want to do it." He screamed hysterically.

"But you did, my friend." I was surprised by the calm in my own voice even though every nerve, vein, and blood vessel inside me raged.

As soon as I walked out, leaving Keiran and Q behind with him, the screaming began again. John followed me, claiming he didn't have the stomach for torture.

I followed the simple directions to a door just down the hall. I put my ear to the door and listened for voices just in case it was a trap. I heard the small sound of crying on the other side and threw caution to the wind.

I tried the knob, but the door was locked so I threw my shoulder against it. Eventually, the door gave way and I burst through. Wood chips fell around me and temporarily blocked my vision of the small bundle huddled on the bed.

"Kennedy?" her crying had become little whimpers. She tried to make herself appear small out of fear. I suddenly realized I didn't make the greatest entrance into her life.

"Keenan?" I turned towards John, who had a hand held out as if to block me. When he noticed the look in my eyes, he said, "Do you really want her first memory of you to be like this? She doesn't know you, and she is already scared."

"Papa?" The angelic yet timid sound of her voice nearly made me come undone. She recognized John and tried to sit up, but I noticed that her movements appeared sluggish.

Had she just woken up?

"Papa, I'm scared and wanna go home now."

"Oh, sweetheart, we're going to take you home right now. Your mother has missed you so much."

"The bad man hurt mama." She looked at me when she said it, and I couldn't help the guilty flush that heated my skin. She looked just as her mother described. The perfect mix of her mother and me.

"She's just fine, angel. She has been worried sick so let's not waste any more time." He picked her up, and I hated the way she clung to him. Jealously ripped through me fast and hard. I wanted to take her from him but knew it wouldn't be a smart move. I was essentially a stranger to her.

"Who's he?" She looked at me once again and ducked her head to hide against John's neck. John looked to me for an answer, but I shook my head.

Seeing her in the flesh, I realized I wasn't ready.

Would I ever be?

"They've been drugging her," John stated as soon as we had Kennedy settled in the car. She fell asleep against the back seat almost immediately.

"How do you know?"

"Her pupils are severely dilated. Her movements are sluggish and her words slurred. She's very developed for her age and can talk like a child twice her age. Sheldon has done very well with her."

"Are you defending her?"

"I know what you are thinking of doing. Sheldon is a good mother and you were gone. Do you really think she would have kept her from you if she knew where you were?"

"Yes," I answered without hesitation. "She would have though she likes to think she wouldn't have, and if I'm wrong, she will now."

"With reason, I'm sure."

"Would you like for me to carry out my promise now so my daughter can have nightmares of your death for the rest of her life?"

"Do what you want to me, son, if it will make up for all the years I—" He stopped and stared off into the distance for a few heartbeats. "If I had known what my absence then and later had been doing to you, I wouldn't have—"

"I don't believe it and neither do you. You would have because you were in pain, but most of all, you were selfish and weak."

Footsteps approaching cut short our conversation, and when I looked back, Keiran and Q had emerged from the house. The blood that lightly splattered their shirts became more evident the closer they came.

"Don't let Kennedy see your shirts."

"Damn... a daddy for three minutes and you're already bossy," Q joked. Keiran wordlessly removed his shirt, followed by Q.

"What did you find out?"

"He claimed he didn't know who his employer was. He kept talking about some rich guy who promised them a lot of money to kidnap Kennedy. He said they were promised double if they had to kill her."

"Did you take care of it?"

"What do you think?" Keiran countered darkly.

"I don't know what he thinks, but I think we need

to call the Feds and get rugrat home soon," Q interjected.

*****

Up until the wee hours of the morning, I had gone through the interrogation process that usually followed a murder.

No, I didn't act with malicious intent.

Yes, it was self-defense.

No, I was not given information on the whereabouts of Kennedy before acting.

They were all lies that I managed to tell well. I had no idea how Keiran fared given he'd just been released from jail on assault charges and not twenty-four hours later had been located in a house of dead bodies.

By noon, we were all standing on the sidewalk appearing none the worse for wear. Dash was there minus the girls as instructed.

"How is she?" I asked as soon as I was in talking distance.

"She's fine. Sheldon wanted to take her back to her apartment, but we managed to convince her to stay at least one more night. It was an emotional night for them both. You should have seen them together."

"Take me to them."

An hour later, after showering and changing, I walked inside the Chambers Mansion just in time to see Sheldon serving Kennedy breakfast. Her gaze collided with mine as soon as I walked through the entryway. Even from across the room, I could see how her hands fluttered and her pulse quickened.

So many emotions passed between us in a short span of time.

"Mama, it's him!" I looked down to see Kennedy

pointing and staring up at me in awe. Her expressive round eyes still held the innocence of youth despite her abduction.

"She hasn't stopped talking about you."

"It's fitting really because I haven't stopped thinking about her." I closed the distance between us and added, "Or you."

I brushed her cheek with my fingers, but rather than responding, she flinched away from my touch. Instinct screamed at me to grab her, but I now had to remember the ever-watchful eyes of my daughter.

"Have you told her?" She shook her head and continued to watch me with a wary look in her eye.

"You?"

"No. Last night didn't seem like the best time." Her shoulders visibly relaxed.

"Good. I wanted to talk to you about that."

The finality in her tone set me on edge and immediately put me on the defensive. Rather than going off on her in front of Ken, I pulled her out of the kitchen and into the large pantry.

"Whatever it is you think you should say to me, I want you to think about it again."

"I don't have to think about it. I don't think you being in her life is a good idea. It's too late—"

In that moment, I could really see myself killing her, so I shut her up the only way I knew how. The kiss wasn't meant to arouse. It was hard and punishing. She fought to get away, so I crushed her against me. When she finally accepted the loss of control, I turned the kiss into a sensual embrace.

There was nothing I wanted more at this moment than to take her right here against the shelves full of canned vegetables and tomato sauces. The way she pushed her breasts against my chest and moaned into my mouth pushed me dangerously close to testing out the sturdiness of the shelving.

When she opened her mouth for my tongue to explore deeper, I threw caution to the wind and found myself saying, "If I stripped your clothes away and bent you over for my cock, could you take me quietly?"

When she nodded slowly, I hid my surprise and wasted no time slipping down her tiny sleep shorts. I was lucky and elated to find that she was naked underneath. I didn't want to risk her changing her mind because I wasn't sure I could stop if she did. I turned her around and lifted her right knee to rest on a middle shelf.

"Keenan, hurry."

I curled my hand around her neck and brought her ear close to my lips. "How bad do you want it?"

"I'm desperate enough to ignore common sense."

I chuckled and witnessed the way the sound made her skin vibrate. My jeans came undone and my hard cock pushed through the opening seeking entrance to her pussy.

"Condom," she gasped when I began to enter her. It was amazing how wet and ready she already was.

"No."

"What?"

Her right hand held onto the shelf so I rested mine on top of hers and slammed into her hard. "I said no."

"Oh, fuck." After fucking into her a few times, her gasps slowly ascended to low screams.

"And fuck I will, now quiet down. Our daughter is in the next room." I moved inside her, each invasion harder and deeper than the last. The cans rattled with the force of my thrusts as I picked up speed. I could feel her hand grip the shelf tighter under my hand. Eventually, I was forced to cover her moans with my hand and sunk my teeth into her shoulder to mask my grunts.

"Now that I have your attention let me explain something to you. I'm not going anywhere. You are mine and Kennedy is mine."

The whimper against my hand was likely a protest, but I kept going. Her hips met mine as she fucked herself on and off my cock, searching desperately for a release I was only glad to give her.

CHAPTER SEVENTEEN

SHELDON

THERE WEREN'T ENOUGH adequate words to describe the plethora of feelings that currently assaulted me.

My daughter had finally been returned home last night after being abducted for over a week, and here I was screwing her father in the pantry of the home I grew up in the very next morning.

Having sex with him was unprecedented. I had no warning or profound reason suitable to explain why, once again, in a forty-eight hour period, I had managed to be coerced out of my panties with little effort.

Maybe it was overwhelming lust.

Or maybe it was the fact that I hadn't had sex in four years.

I moaned and mewled against his hand like a wanton slut, which was exactly how I felt. In the past, he had always been able to make me feel like a slut and a lady whenever we made love.

But we weren't making love now.

No, this was fucking at its finest. I quickened my hips to match pounding thrusts. My orgasm built first from my soul before ripping through my heart and releasing from my mouth as a muted scream.

It was a good thing his hand was there. I didn't relish the thought of explaining the throes of passion to Ken at such a young age. Something told me that her father wouldn't appreciate the burden either.

When the fog started to clear, I became aware of the cans littering my feet and how my nails dug into the wooden shelves. A warm sensation traveled down my thigh, and I knew it could only be one thing.

I could feel his chest move against my back and the sweet smell of his breath fan across my skin. The jingle of his belt buckle as he fixed his pants echoed around me.

I was already answering to the consequences of my decision. It was in the possessive way he handled me as he pulled up my shorts and wrapped his strong arm around my waist to guide me from the pantry.

When we entered the kitchen, I was lucky to find no one waiting other than Ken, who appeared none the wiser. She'd made a complete mess of her pancakes as usual, and in my absence, had managed to pour nearly the entire bottle of syrup on her food.

"Ken, what did I tell you about pouring your own syrup?"

"I was hungry."

It was official. I'm the worst mother in the world. I wanted to cry and assure her that she could pour all the syrup in the world, but I knew it wouldn't reverse the last week or the last ten minutes.

I wet a towel and proceeded to clean up her face and hands. She usually fussed when I cleaned her up, and I realized that her attention was completely fixed on Keenan. They stared, completely enraptured by one another.

"Hi," she greeted softly.

"Hello, Kennedy." Keenan shook his head as if to clear it and said, "It's nice to finally meet you."

"What's your name?"

"I'm... I'm..."

For the first time since arriving, or facing a girl ever, he seemed to be at a loss for words. She looked at him expectantly, and what happened next shocked me to my core.

Keenan fell to his knees.

Right there on the kitchen floor he collapsed.

Kennedy left her seat and walked to him. Slowly, I freaked out inside because what was happening before me only a monster could tear apart. How could I protect her from him if she accepted him without ever knowing who he was to her?

"Are you scared?" He nodded numbly, and so she rested a hand on his cheek. "Auntie Lake said no one can hurt you if you don't allow it." It came out a jumbled, three-year-old mess, but I'd been there when Lake told her, and so I recognized what she meant.

"She's right," Keenan spoke. Although his voice shook, he still sounded strong. Kennedy nodded once as if accepting his acceptance. "My name is Keenan."

"Keenan," she repeated, but it came out more like Keena. "Are you mommy's friend?"

"Yes, I'm mommy's friend, but I'm your friend, too."

"You saved me from bad men."

"Did they hurt you?" I held my breath even though I had asked her the very same thing last night along with the doctors who checked her over. When she shook her head, I exhaled quietly. Keenan took his eyes off

Kennedy long enough to nod in my direction. "I'm sorry I wasn't here for you sooner."

The hard edge in his voice told me that he meant more than just last night. There was no way I could let this happen now if ever.

"Kennedy, why don't you go upstairs and get ready so I can take you to the beach."

Her excited shriek ripped through the air and just like that, the spell was broken. "Can Keenan come?"

I ignored the flinch from Keenan at hearing her call him by his name. "I don't think Keenan wants to come with us."

"Keenan does and Keenan will," he said, but it came out as a threat. Fortunately, Kennedy seemed completely oblivious to the drastic change in his mood and atmosphere. She screamed her excitement before taking off to retrieve her bathing suit.

"Do you think a trip to the beach is a good idea so soon?"

I felt a flash of anger at the idea of him questioning my parenting skills so soon after just meeting her.

"I think it's exactly what she needs. I don't want this to be something that traumatizes her."

"You don't think it already does? She may not understand, but trust me when I say she'll never forget. If you don't think I'm right, try talking to Keiran."

"It's not the same thing."

"But it could have been which is exactly why I'm sticking around. You can't protect her on your own. You almost died because you can't even protect yourself."

"Are you blaming me? This is your fucked up family's fault." We were now shouting, but I couldn't bring myself to care.

"Guys." Dash's voice intruded on our heated moment, and when I turned around, I saw why. Holding

Dash's hand was Kennedy, who looked on the verge of tears. Before I could think of something comforting to say, Keiran, Lake, and Q filed past them, which meant they must have all heard, too.

They each took a seat and pretended nothing was wrong, all except Keiran, who watched me with a cold look in his eyes. Lake cast worried glances between Keenan and me while Q silently observed.

Dash thankfully broke the silence again. "Kennedy, why don't you go play with your toys while your mother and I have a talk?"

"Will you play with me?" she directed to Keenan.

"I need to talk with your mother too, but I'll play as soon as I'm done."

"I'll come play, sweetie," Lake offered. She patted Keiran's shoulder on the way out, and just that simple touch from her seemed to calm him.

"Why are you guys here?" I asked as soon as Lake led Kennedy from the room.

Keiran and Keenan quickly ran down the events of last night leading up to Kennedy's rescue. "One of the men who took Kennedy was one of the investigators your father hired to find her."

"How is that possible?"

"That's something we'd like to ask your father," Keiran replied with ice dripping from every syllable.

"Are you seriously suggesting my father had something to do with his own *grandchild* being abducted?"

"What I'm suggesting is that we ask him. He at least has to know some information about the men he hired that could lead us to why he hired them in the first place.

"Which man was it?"

"The one Keiran didn't try to kill," Q answered matter of factly.

"And if my father doesn't know anything?"

"Then we start looking at him as a suspect."

"Yeah, but there is just one little detail you're missing. Why would my father want you dead? This whole nightmare started because of you. Someone is after you, not me, and not Kennedy."

"As long as she's a Masters—"

"She's not. She's a Chambers."

Keenan and Keiran each narrowed their eyes in a similar fashion, and if I weren't so pissed, I would have been amazed by how alike they truly were. It had been impossible to see in high school because while Keiran wore his crown proudly, Keenan had been the devil in sheep's clothing.

"A fact your parents seem to hold against you."

"Enough," Dash barked. "It doesn't fucking matter what her last name is. We protect her regardless. Now, my father is no saint, but having Kennedy abducted is not something he would do despite how he feels about paternity."

"So what are you saying?" Keenan asked, but it sounded more like a challenge.

"I'm saying we ask him for the information on the investigators he hired, but we consider other angles. Keiran, you're going to need to think harder about your past, and be sure there is no one left who would want to hurt you."

The doorbell rang so I used the opportunity to escape the overwhelming tension currently circulating the room.

"Good morning, Ms. Chambers." The federal agents assigned to Kennedy's case stood on the front porch.

"Good morning. I promise I was going to come in. I just—"

"No need for apologies. The important thing is that

Kennedy is home safe. We've covered most of the questioning with her father, but as her legal guardian, we wanted to ask some additional questions. They are routine if you have a few moments."

"Yes, of course." I moved aside to let them in.

"Is there somewhere we can speak in private?" I led them past the kitchen to the small library down the hall.

"Can I offer you something to drink?"

"No, that won't be necessary. This will only take a few minutes."

"So, how can I help you?"

"The men who found your daughter last night found themselves in a sticky predicament. Two men were killed rather gruesomely, particularly one whose throat was cut and then stabbed nine times in the heart. How much do you know about the events that took place?"

Bile rose up in my throat at the mental picture he unnecessarily painted. "Not much. I wasn't there."

"Were you aware of what they were planning to do before it happened?

"By aware, do you mean if I knew if they planned to kill those men?"

"We're concerned, given the history of the men involved, particularly Keiran Masters. Throughout this entire investigation, we've been given little information and are curious as to how a house a few hours from here was suddenly happened upon."

I didn't know if it was paranoia, but I suddenly had the feeling that I was being tricked into a corner, only I wasn't the prey.

"I'm sorry... you said there were routine questions you needed to ask?"

"Yes, we just wanted to check in to make sure little Kennedy is settled in okay. You take care now."

The agents were gone as quickly as they came leaving me confused and nervous. I rushed out of the library to warn the guys but found that no warning was necessary. Keenan, Keiran, Dash, and Q had the agents surrounded and though they appeared casual, I knew it wasn't anything other than a threat.

"Did you forget something or did you just miss us?" Keenan taunted. I was rooted to the spot because, for a minute, I saw the old him.

"We were checking up on Ms. Chambers and Kennedy now if you'll excuse us." They squeezed through the small opening of the circle and disappeared out the front door.

"Have you all lost your minds?" Lake shrieked. I hadn't seen her standing on the stairs. Thankfully, Kennedy was nowhere in sight. "Those are *federal* agents."

"Baby..."

She held up her hand. "Don't, Keiran." She turned and headed back upstairs.

"You're in trouble," Q sing-songed. Keiran shoved him into the table and stalked off toward the back of the house. "What did I say?"

*****

Somehow, our weekend trip for two turned into eight. We piled into three cars and made our way to the California coast. Kennedy had managed to bounce around in excitement for all of thirty minutes before falling fast asleep.

"She has a lot of energy," Keenan remarked shortly after her eyes drifted shut. It was the first that Keenan had spoken since we left. We were in Keiran's car alone together with Kennedy while Keiran and Lake rode with Dash, and Q and Jesse rode together.

"Kids tend to do that," I replied dryly. Among the other things about him that angered me, I was still more than a little annoyed that he had insisted on not only inserting himself into our trip but also our lives. I told myself I wouldn't dwell on it. This weekend was for Kennedy. I wanted to fit as much good and happiness into her life, needing to erase the terrifying week she'd endured.

"What I'm trying to say is she seems like a happy kid. John was adamant that you've done a great job with her."

"Remind me to thank him for the compliment."

"I do not like your attitude, Shelly." His voice deepened from lighthearted to dangerous, but I refused to let him intimidate me.

"Bite me."

Real mature, Sheldon.

I'd no sooner spoke the words than Keenan hazardously turned the car onto the side of the road. I thanked my lucky stars that traffic was light while keeping the panic at bay. We stopped with a screech of tires as rocks and dirt flew around us.

"Have you lost your mind?"

He ignored me as he pulled out his phone. His keystrokes were quick and angry. Whatever message he sent must have been short because he had already pocketed it again.

Shortly after Dash and Q's cars pulled up beside us. Keenan hopped out and opened the backseat, unbuckling Kennedy's seatbelt, who by some small favor was still asleep. "What the hell do you think you're doing?"

I quickly unbuckled my seatbelt, but by the time I made it around the car, Keenan already had Kennedy strapped in Dash's car.

"What's going on?" I heard Dash question.

"Sheldon and I need to have a private conversation. Take Kennedy and we'll follow you."

"Dash, don't!"

I expected that if anyone helped, it would be Dash, but when he shook his head, I felt my confidence waver and panic rear its ugly head. "I can't help you anymore if you're going to keep giving in. You need to work it out," he said before driving off.

"How could you just take my daughter?" My rant was cut short when Keenan tossed me over his shoulder. "Stop!" He walked the short distance back to the car, but when he bypassed the passenger and rear door, confusion took the place of my anger.

He quickly popped the trunk, and the next second, I landed inside. The hard impact jarred me and before I could recover, the door slammed shut.

*****

After an hour of riding in the trunk, I suffered from motion sickness. If I didn't know any better, I would think he purposely weaved in and out of traffic to taunt me. Another hour passed, and I had just begun to drift to sleep when the car came to a hard stop. Before I could brace, I rolled and hit the wall of the trunk, and with a grunt of pain, I settled back into place just in time for the trunk to open.

It took a moment for my eyes to adjust. Keenan's face was a blank mask of indifference that was far more chilling than anger. At least, when he was angry, I could tell what he was thinking and even predict his next move.

"Are you waiting for an invitation?"

I allowed for my contempt for him to show and then slowly climbed from the trunk. My muscles screamed in protest so I took a moment to stretch and breathe in the fresh air.

"Feeling better?"

"Why did you do that to me?"

"Because you needed it."

"I needed it? You think I needed to be locked in your trunk like a bag of groceries?"

"I meant you needed time alone to think. You were acting like a child so I treated you like one. Think of it as a timeout."

"You son of a—"

"Finish that sentence, and I promise you'll make the rest of the trip feeling worse than a bag of groceries."

"I hate you." Surprisingly, saying it out loud didn't make it feel real—as I would have hoped.

"You don't hate me yet, but you will. I'll make sure of it."

I stared at him incredulously. "Why would you want me to hate you?" *And why did I care?*

"Because it will make being with me that much harder on you, and then you'll feel what it was like to be without you."

"After four years, you still don't get it, do you?"

"What am I supposed to get, Shelly?"

A part of me couldn't believe that I would do this on the side of a barren highway, but I couldn't hold it in any longer.

"I didn't leave you because I didn't want you. I left you because I realized how much better and stronger I was without you. You, who were cocky, arrogant, spoiled, and unfaithful, you actually believed you deserved—no, you believed you were *entitled* to me. You weren't, and you never will be. It doesn't matter how much pain you cause me or how much control you have.

I'll never truly be yours again."

A whirlwind of rage clouded his dark eyes making them appear almost black. I could no longer make out the irises until what was left of them resembled a soulless window. "You don't have to be mine, but you'll never belong to anyone else."

Chapter Eighteen

KEENAN

AFTER THE CONFRONTATION with Shelly, the beach was the last place I wanted to be. If I followed my instincts to be a bastard, I would have taken her somewhere private where I could enact just how she would stay mine. But Kennedy called to me. After only just meeting her, I couldn't stay away.

How could someone so innocent possess that kind of control with little effort?

"What took you guys so long?" Lake questioned with suspicion in her tone. She glanced over at Sheldon before turning narrowed eyes toward me.

Sheldon chose to remain silent so I spoke up. "We got confused about the direction we were going, but we straightened it out." It was a hidden meaning that only Sheldon seemed to catch judging by the look she sent me.

"Mommy!" Kennedy ran full speed through the lobby of the resort while the rest followed. For the first time since unlocking Sheldon from the trunk, a smile graced her lips as she stooped just in time to catch Kennedy. "We go to the beach now?"

"Mommy just needs to put on her bathing suit, and then we can go, okay?"

Kennedy got a disgruntled look on her face and then peered down at her empty wrist as if checking the time. Her little head popped up and a flash of mischief appeared just before she said, "Mama come naked like the shower!"

Now there's an idea.

I couldn't stop the laughter that bubbled up inside, spilling out until it filled the lobby. Everyone, including Sheldon followed while Kennedy looked on in confusion before joining. Once I was back in control, I scooped down next to Sheldon.

"I think that's a great idea, Kennedy, but your mother may not be allowed on the beach if she isn't dressed properly. What do you say your aunt and uncles take you, and we come find you when we're done?"

"Can Uncle Keke come, too?"

"Who?" I looked to Sheldon for help.

"Keiran. She can't say his name well, so Lake got her to call him that. I think he is still making her pay for it."

"Of course he can. In fact, he's going to hold your hand all the way there. Sound good?"

She nodded enthusiastically, but somehow, I knew she wasn't satisfied when she didn't immediately take off. Keiran came forth and picked her up, but before he could walk away, she asked, "Are you coming, too?"

The worried look on her face as if she were afraid to lose me gave me pause. At that moment, I wanted to promise her the entire world with none of the bad if she wished for it.

"I wouldn't miss it," I promised.

Once everyone cleared the lobby, I placed my hand at Sheldon's back and led her to the front desk. "I have a reservation for three."

After giving the clerk my information, he handed me a set of keys. I clamped a hand around Sheldon's arm and steered her toward the elevators.

"Please tell me those are keys for two rooms."

"Why would you think that?"

"Because Kennedy and I need our own room."

"You both are staying with me." The elevator doors opened, and thankfully, no one was around to enter with us. I could feel my temper spiking.

"I'm not putting my daughter in a room to sleep with a stranger."

I'd lost the fight. My hand was around her throat, and I'd forced her back until she was trapped in the corner. I could only hope there weren't cameras.

"I'm not a stranger to her anymore. I'm her father. A fact she will be told tonight." The pressure I applied prevented her from responding, which was the safest route.

Only when the doors opened, did I release her. I struggled internally with myself. The old me may have lived a forged lie, but I never would have touched her that way, and even now, I felt sick with myself.

Once again, I placed my hand on the small of her back with an ease that belied the brute force a few moments ago.

"The only way to survive is to hurt those against you before they can hurt you, and if they succeed, you welcome the pain and make them pay."

Back then, Keiran's advice had only made me afraid, but now it gave me purpose. I hardened my resolve by reminding myself that this wasn't a fairytale. This was just the beginning of her imprisonment to me.

* * * * *

Sheldon had not breathed a word and still looked a little shell-shocked since the incident in the elevator, but I was determined not to feel guilt.

When we made it to the beach, Keiran and Lake were nowhere to be found. Dash was laid out in the sun reading a book while every girl on the beach watched on with sultry fascination. I looked around for Kennedy and found her splashing in the water with Q and Jesse. Q was attempting to teach her to surf, in shallow water no less, while Jesse watched. Amusement poured through my senses erasing all the tension from the past few hours.

"Three-year-olds don't surf, dude." Jesse deadpanned.

"This isn't just any three-year-old. Isn't that right, rugrat?" A spark of jealousy flowed through me at the realization that everyone seemed to have a relationship with Kennedy except for me.

"Mama... Keenan, look!" Kennedy struggled to stand even with Q's hands holding her, but when she finally succeeded, the brightest smile appeared. Sheldon wasted no time running into the water, creating a splash while I ogled her lush frame in the two-piece. Motherhood had done her body well.

For a few hours of beach fun and the happiness of my daughter, I let go of the past and my plans for the future. I taught Kennedy the basics of swimming and used it as an opportunity to bond. I was amazed at her passion for the water at such a young age.

Keiran and Lake materialized after we had exhausted ourselves in the water. The guilty blush that heated her cheeks and his smug smirk provided a detailed description of what they had been doing for the past few hours.

"Nice of you two to join us finally, but I'm hungry," Dash announced.

"Why didn't you get one of the women who can't stop staring at your crotch to get you some food?"

"Because then they would expect me to put out, and my mother taught me that what's inside my cookie jar is precious."

"That was me, idiot." Sheldon rolled her eyes as she toweled off Kennedy.

"Since Keenan abandoned us to live out here, why doesn't he pick a place?"

I sent Dash a look to fuck off and packed up the bag that Sheldon had packed for Kennedy. "I don't live around here so I wouldn't know."

I turned to Sheldon just in time to see the play of emotions on her face before she covered it up with a blank expression. Could it have been the reminder that I left or that I'd created another life? When we began our trek back up to the resort, I shrugged it off. Whatever we were before now no longer mattered.

Back at the resort, we agreed to meet in an hour for dinner before going our separate ways. "Are the three of you in the same room together?" Lake asked after the rest had left. Her expression turned down into disapproval.

"Yes, we are."

"But you haven't told Kennedy," she continued while looking between the two of us. "Won't that confuse her?"

"Believe me, I've tried to tell him," Sheldon griped.

Kennedy was already half asleep on my shoulder and wasn't likely to notice anything, but I saw Lake's point even though the last thing I wanted was to agree with her. I struggled to gain leverage and looked toward Keiran for help, silently communicating with him.

"We'll take Kennedy since we're already showered." He lifted her from my arms and took a hold of Lake's elbow, steering her down the hall.

Sheldon watched them walk the short distance to their room before angrily jamming the keycard into the lock. After about three unsuccessful attempts, I brushed her aside and opened the door.

"I'll shower first so I can get Kennedy ready," was all she said before disappearing into the large bathroom and slamming the door. The walls vibrated from the force of her anger causing the gold framed artwork to rattle on the walls.

I waited until I heard the shower run before I stripped away my swimming trunks and followed after her. It had been torture watching her glisten as she played in the sun and water and not be able to touch her. I figured since she was mine, I may as well indulge.

When I stepped inside the bathroom, steam was already beginning to form, but I could still make out her silhouette in the large shower stall made for two. I took a moment to admire her naked frame through the glass door before opening it.

She jumped and let out a low gasp before her amber eyes turned dark with anger. "Get out."

"No."

It was all I could muster before I gave in to the lust pounding through my veins straight down to my dick. I sealed any further protests by sticking my tongue as far down her throat as I could get, and surprisingly, she took me.

I soon learned, however, that the pleasure of her surrender didn't come without a little pain. She raked her nails down my chest. I flinched at the same moment my cock surged to life, becoming harder than before.

When I finally let my lips drift down to her neck, she whispered, "I can't seem to deny you and more terrifying is that I don't want to, even though this is all we'll ever have. I hope it's enough for you."

"Shelly, I'll never get enough." I lifted my head to meet her eyes. "So I guess I'll have to keep fucking you." I lifted her leg and hooked it around my hip so I could enter her slowly. I couldn't stop until I was seated inside her fully, and I loved the flash of pain in her eyes just before she surrendered to the pleasure.

"Keenan, you fill me so full," she moaned just before her eyes fluttered closed.

"And you still own me, baby. Fuck you." My hips slammed into her until it became frenzied fucking. Her gasps and moans were so guttural that I could feel them travel up my own spine until it eventually came out through my throat with a grunt. "It's never been like this," I growled against her neck before biting down onto it. I wanted to hurt her more than I wanted to breathe, so I bit down harder until she cried out for mercy.

It was too bad I had none to give.

Blood rushed through my body heightening my need. I found myself yanking her up higher around my waist, but when that wasn't enough, I anchored her against the shower for my cock to have its tortured way with her.

Her pussy sucked me even deeper even when her little whimpers begged me to slow down.

"Keenan!"

Her scream made my cock twitch inside her. I fucking loved my name on her lips, and I'd give anything to keep it there.

"Don't ask me to stop, baby. I can't." I tightened my

arms around her and gave her the friction she needed to propel her over the edge and straight into orgasmic bliss. Just as she started to come down, I pushed deeper inside her body for my release.

"You can't come... inside me... again," she panted. I released her and turned away.

"Aren't you on birth control?"

"No, I'm not."

I took the time to grab soap and lather before responding. "We'll schedule an appointment when we get back."

"That's all you have to say?" she snapped and snatched the soap from my hand. "What if I get pregnant again?"

"Then I'll be here for you." Even to my own ears, it sounded more like a threat than a supportive gesture.

"That won't happen. You ruined my life once. I won't let you do it again."

"Are you saying my daughter ruined your life?"

"Yes—no. I'm saying *you* ruined my life. Kennedy is the best thing that ever happened to me. I just wish you weren't a part of her."

The ferocity at which her statement hit me caused my self-control to explode. I ripped open the shower door and dragged her out behind me—soapy skin and all. She didn't attempt to get away, and so I was able to easily sit her on the marble vanity.

"Spread your legs."

I don't know if it was the tone of my voice, the scowl on my face, or the possibility of another mind-blowing orgasm, but she spread her legs without argument, and I quickly gave her every inch of me inside her pussy while swallowing her cries.

"I'm going to make you regret that."

* * * * *

An hour had passed a long time ago I realized when I checked my phone and saw a message from Keiran stating that they took Kennedy out to eat along with an address to the restaurant.

"Are we done fighting for the day?" she asked. Her voice was hoarse and weak from hard sex and sleep. I didn't notice when she began to trace my chest with her fingers. Over four years, I collected tattoos on my chest as a way to forget the night my entire life became a lie, and I started living in the nightmare instead. Each tattoo, all of them meaningless except for one, covered the six bullet wounds I carried from that night. I would always hear how I was lucky to be alive though I felt far from lucky.

"They're gone," I stated harsher than I meant, but I constantly found myself in a state of frustration when it came to her.

"No. It's here..." She kissed the spot near my lungs before moving on and making her way up my chest. "And here..." She pressed another lingering kiss over the spot where my heart lay. I felt a drop of moisture and looked down to see another tear escape. "They will never be gone. Tattoos won't fix the pain. It's so much deeper than your skin."

She looked up and met my gaze once more, but this time she held it. "Why do you keep looking at me like that?"

"Like what?"

"Like you're searching for something."

"Because I am."

"And what are you searching for?"

"Him."

"Him?"

"The boy I fell in love with."

"Why would you do that?"

"Because I've wanted to tell him for a long time now that I still love him."

My ears rang with the force of my heart pounding in my chest. I searched for sincerity or for a sign that it could still be a lie.

She still loved me?

No... Not me.

Him.

"What?"

"I want him to come back. If not for me, then for Kennedy."

"He was cocky, arrogant, spoiled, and unfaithful, remember?" Her opinion of me would forever remain in my memory. I didn't have the right to feel hurt over it. I'd more than earned it.

"Yes, but he also followed his conscience and loved with his heart on his sleeve. He would have given his life for me rather than threaten to take mine in more ways than one. He *left* because deep down he couldn't let me go any other way, so he did what he could to set me free."

She trailed her finger to a specific spot on my chest just below my heart. Caged in between the broken vines were the words—*A broken love can still last forever so long as you carry the pieces close to your heart.*

"I forgave him years ago, and I carried the pieces too, waiting for him to come back, but he never did. I had to learn to live without him."

She looked up at me with so much hope and love that I had no choice but to let her go and leave the bed. In truth, I was at a loss for words. I quickly gathered my clothes to dress and headed for the bathroom. The door closed, but not in time for me to miss the sound of her cry.

*****

When we arrived, the restaurant was alive with locals and tourists. The bar was already crowded and every table seemed to be filled. I quickly spotted our party seated at a table in the back and led Sheldon by the hand, much to her chagrin.

"Nice of you to join us," Dash greeted sarcastically.

"You really need to find a girl so you can stop acting like such a cock block," Keiran remarked.

"Keiran!" Shelly scolded as she took her seat on Kennedy's right. I took the seat on Kennedy's left and reached for the waiting glass of water.

"I'm not cock-blocking. I'm hungry."

"Uncle Keke, what's that?"

"Shit."

"Oooh, mama. Uncle said a bad word."

"Congratulations, douchebag. You have officially corrupted our niece."

"What's a doo?"

"You're both dumbasses." Q laughed.

"Dumb ass!" Kennedy repeated and then laughed outrageously.

"For fuck sake, everyone stop talking before you all corrupt my daughter." Everyone at the table grew quiet at my outburst including Kennedy. Sheldon's gasp was audible, but I had eyes only for Kennedy and her for me though hers were rounded with wonder. I wondered if she could understand what had just happened. I chewed on my bottom lip wondering what I should do next.

"What's fuck?"

Everyone burst out laughing.

"Kennedy, that is a bad word that little girls should not say and neither should grown-ups when in the presence of a sweet little girl like you. I am so sorry."

She nodded and turned her attention back to eating her chicken tenders as if nothing had happened. When she dipped a chicken tender, I noticed she had ketchup and honey mustard mixed together just as I do.

"We ordered for her so she wouldn't have to wait for you to finish bumping uglies like the rest of us," Dash griped once again.

"You are suffering from serious blue balls, my man."

We ordered and conversation flowed easily for the rest of dinner. I learned a lot of what had taken place in my absence.

Sheldon was scheduled to graduate with a pre-medical degree next Saturday. She wanted to study to be a pediatrician. This was news to me given that she'd always wanted to be a fashion model. I had a feeling that Kennedy had something to do with that.

Keiran was studying for a degree in computer science. That gave me the longest pause. He had received an athletic scholarship to play basketball for Arizona so I knew obtaining a degree was a part of that deal, but I hadn't expected him to choose something that didn't involve sports.

Lake was studying for a degree in education. Her plan was to become an elementary school teacher specializing in learning disabilities.

Dash studied business while playing ball at Arizona much to the displeasure of his father who preferred his heir and only son to attend an ivy league or more specifically his alma mater. He was already beginning to take over business operations from his father.

Quentin had joined the army straight out of high

school when he claimed college life wasn't for him and a little structure and violence never hurt anyone. Jesse surprisingly hadn't although he was raised in a military family. Everyone expected him to simply follow in his father's footsteps but instead chose to work with them instead.

It seemed that everyone had taken great steps and moved forward while I still felt as if I were standing still.

"So where's Willow? Was anyone ever going to bring her up?"

"On that note, I think I have to use the gentlemen's room," Jesse coughed.

"Willow is, um... well, she..."

"She went to Nebraska and we haven't seen or heard from her since."

I made a point to glance over at Dash, who sat glowering at the tabletop. "So she is literally the one that got away, huh? I guess charm and money doesn't work on everyone."

"What's your problem?" Dash said finally looking up.

"You are. You're stupid."

"And that makes you?"

"Cocky, arrogant, spoiled, and unfaithful. Did I get it right, Shelly?"

"Yes, but I believe I forgot one. You're also a coward." She pushed away from the table and stood up from her chair. "Lake, can you look after Kennedy?" She didn't wait for an answer before walking away. I tracked her movements until she disappeared inside the ladies room.

"If you want her back, you're going about it the wrong way," Keiran stated.

"Are you supposed to be an expert?"

Instead of answering he turned to Lake. "Baby, do you love me?"

"Yes. Do you love me?"

"Forever," he whispered softly. His hard gaze shot to me. "See? It's that simple."

"Is it?"

"It is. You just have to be smart enough to realize it before it's too late."

"How about we take Kennedy with us and put her to bed so you and Sheldon can have some alone time?" Lake offered.

I wasn't going to argue with that possibility.

"Kennedy?"

"Yes, Keenan?" I had to swallow the urge to tell her that I was her father for the umpteenth time before speaking.

"Your aunt and uncles are going to take you back so you can get some sleep. Your mother and I will be right behind you to tuck you in."

"Come on, you little juvenile delinquent. Let's see how much trouble we can get in before bedtime." Keiran scooped her up and tossed her over his shoulder much to her delight. Her squeals of excitement echoed through the restaurant as he led the rest of them out.

It took me another moment to realize that they'd all left me to pay the bill. As I was fishing out my credit card, Sheldon emerged from the restroom. Even from here, I could see how red and puffy her eyes were.

"Shelly?"

My ears began ringing from the sound of some prick calling my girl by the nickname I gave her when we were in love. Sheldon had been on her way back from the restroom, with me clocking her every step when this blond, frat-looking guy approached her. When his fingers slid around her waist and pulled her close for a kiss, I was out of my seat and closing in fast. Her back was to me so she didn't see me approach them.

"Eric? How—what are you doing here?"

"I'm having lunch with my parents. I told you I'm from this area. Are you okay? I've been calling and looking for you everywhere."

"I'm fine. I've just been going through a really tough time with the stress of finals and medical school admissions."

"You're still coming to the graduation, right?"

"I'm not sure, and I'll tell you all about it later, but I have to get back."

"There's no need to rush off, *Shelly*. Everyone left. So who's your friend?"

Her complexion noticeably paled at the sound of my voice invading their intimate moment. I schooled my face into a complacent expression, but judging by the way she was shaking, she already knew it was an act.

I warned her of what would happen if I found out she had lied. I knew she had been lying to me. She'd forgotten just how well I knew her. I also knew one day I'd come face to face with the guy she thought she could use to forget about me.

"I'm her boyfriend. Are you a friend of the family?"

"No, I'm the father of her child, and the man she'll be fucking for the rest of her life... however long that might be." I made sure to make eye contact with her when I said the last. "So now that we are all clear about the role in her life, I'm going to have to ask you to remove your fingers from her body before I break each one of them."

"Shelly, who is this guy?"

I snapped and I wasn't even sorry for it. Screams

rent the air after I knocked the frat boy on his ass and made quick work of bashing his face in.

"Keenan, please!" Sheldon screamed, but I heeded to none of it. Visions of the two of them together assaulted me and each blow to his face and body was my way of beating them away.

"You're killing him. Please stop." She tugged on my shoulders, and with each desperate attempt to stop me, her strength grew until I could no longer ignore the scene I had created.

The black fog slowly lifted, and when I stood to my feet, I grabbed her hand and walked her back to our table as if nothing had happened. I switched from card to cash to pay the bill and led her out of the restaurant, blatantly ignoring the bloody mess that was left by her boyfriend and the man who might have gotten her killed by the end of the night.

Chapter Nineteen

SHELDON

A RIVER OF sweat had formed over every inch of my body. We had been driving for almost an hour now, and I had no idea where we were going. He never said a word other than to order me inside of Keiran's car after nearly beating Eric to death.

Keiran had always warned me what would happen when he found out, but I hadn't believed him just as I never truly believed Keenan would come back. I had been searching for a way to tell him about Eric despite our not being together. I knew he would be upset, but the level of brutality he unleashed in that restaurant went far beyond everything I thought I knew about him.

After another hour, I couldn't stand the silence and fear of the unknown, so I curled as far against the door as I could and let sleep take me.

The rough slam of a car door jolted me awake some time later. "Where are we?" I asked as soon as the door was opened.

"You're home. Now get inside."

Home?

Did he say home?

The city lights that filtered through the windows of the parking garage were a far cry from the peaceful dark nights of Six Forks.

The eerie look in his eyes set my heart racing. There was nowhere to run so I sat back in the seat. I could tell by the hard set in his jaw that he took the move as defiance rather than fear. When he leaned down, the sweet smell of his skin and cologne invaded my senses, temporarily causing me to forget that I was with him against my will.

The click of the seatbelt unlocking cleared the fog of lust.

“You have tried my patience for the last time, Sheldon. Get in the fucking building or you will spend the rest of the night regretting that you disobeyed me.”

I took his threat for what it was worth and stepped from the car. The elevator ride to the very top of the building seemed longer than it should. Maybe because it felt like I was on my way to my impending doom? Maybe it was because I held my breath?

The elevators doors finally opened up to a large, spacious apartment. It’s sterile, trendy look with hard lines and glossy surfaces didn’t give the feeling of home.

Keenan had to place his hand on the small of my back and force me into the apartment. I looked around for a place to hide if need be but quickly figured it would be useless since it was his place.

Regardless of the size of the apartment, there wouldn’t be many places to hide, and he’d likely know where to look. I turned to face him finally, seemingly accepting my fate. I just prayed that maybe he’d calmed down during the drive.

“Did you fuck him?” His voice was calm, giving the

appearance of a casual question, but the quiet, deadly storm brewing in his eyes was anything but calm. I took a slow step back hoping he wouldn't notice my desperate attempt to retreat. His gaze slid down and slowly back up, letting me know that he had noticed.

"Where will you go, Shelly?"

"Keenan, you're scaring me."

"Am I?" I could only nod due to the tremble of my lips increasing beyond control.

"Sheldon... I asked you a question. One you have yet to answer. Please don't make me force the answer from you."

I barely noticed the skilled way he stalked me. He moved so silently, and before I knew it, I was backed through the open doors of the balcony with nowhere to run.

Being cornered surprisingly gave me the opposite effect than I had anticipated. Instead of cowering in fear, my own rage pounded through my veins.

"You have no right to be upset. So what if I fucked him? I belong to him, Keenan. I don't belong to you. I haven't for four years... maybe I never did."

I choked on my last words when his hands closed around my throat. My feet fought for the ground when he lifted me high.

We were moving, but I couldn't see where. It wasn't until my ankle banged against the railing that I realized I was dangling over the edge with only his strength and mercy to keep me from falling twenty stories.

"Answer me," he demanded. "Or I'll make our daughter a motherless child." Coldly, he made a show of releasing a hand from my neck. I was only held up by one.

I told myself not to struggle, but I couldn't help but to do just that.

My vision blurred.

My face heated while the rest of me had gone cold, and suddenly, I couldn't fight anymore.

I made the effort to take one last look, hoping to find the boy I fell in love with a lifetime ago.

I froze.

When my eyes finally locked with his, it wasn't rage I found in his expressive depths.

Tears streamed down his face, and all I could see was hurt, panic, and lost love just before it all faded away.

*****

SEVEN YEARS AGO

"Are you cold?"

"A little."

Keenan shrugged off the hoodie I often saw him wear and wrapped it around my shoulders.

"How's that?"

"Better." To be honest, I was still a little cold but I appreciated the effort. We were having a late night, forbidden picnic in the park. I wanted to look my best for our first date so I foolishly chose the thinnest and shortest dress I could find in my wardrobe. I had only just turned fifteen, so I didn't have many that my mom deemed appropriate for a girl my age.

"Liar."

He grinned just as his arms came around. I didn't expect it or for him to settle me on his lap and wrap them tighter around me. My body instantly warmed from the feeling of his. It was equal parts flustering and body heat.

"How about this?" he whispered against my neck.

"I definitely feel warm now."

"Good. I wouldn't want my girl getting sick."

"Your—your girl?" I stammered.

"I told you I'd make you mine."

Keenan hadn't wasted any time asking me out. It had only been two days since he first spoke to me in the hall. He said he had a few hoops to jump through first, a.k.a. my brother. Yesterday they'd gotten into a pretty bad fistfight. Dash wouldn't agree to let him take me out and apparently, the confrontation escalated. What I didn't understand was how they could possibly still be friends.

Keenan currently sported a black eye and several bruises that disappeared inside his shirt. Dash hadn't fared any better from the fight.

In the end, Keenan made the decision that he would take me out on a date, and Dash couldn't stop him.

"I won't be yours for long if I don't get back home soon. My parents will kill me if they find out I snuck out."

We'd actually gone on our date earlier to the movies but a few hours after returning me home, I'd heard the first tap on my window. When I asked what he was doing at my window so late, he had charmingly declared that he couldn't wait to see me again. I had melted right there against the windowsill and didn't care who might see.

"If my queen wishes... but first things first..."

"What's that?"

I could literally feel my heart race with excitement at the look in his eyes. It was a look I was quickly becoming accustomed to seeing. Sometimes, he would just stare at me as if unwilling to let me go so he kept me captive with his eyes.

"Have you ever kissed anyone?"

Should I lie or tell the truth? Would he think I was a loser if I told him the truth? Would he think I was a slut if I didn't?"

"If you're thinking about lying to me, I would love it if you didn't. Whatever your answer is, I will still want you."

For the second time tonight, I melted. I realized that with Keenan, it was a constant state of being. "No, I haven't ever."

The wide, boyish smile that graced his lips put me at ease. His hand boldly slid up my front. My dress bunched slightly.

All the while, I anticipated the moment he would touch my... ribs?

His hand stopped there to pull me closer before skipping over my breasts entirely and gripping my neck. "Can I be your first?"

I barely finished nodding before his lips brushed mine in the softest caress. It was a feeling I would never forget and one I'd hope to never lose.

* * * * *

PRESENT

They say true love's kiss is the most powerful sign of love in the world. It's the moment when you find the person to who you are meant to trust the rest of your life.

Nothing was ever said of life ending on a balcony because of true love.

While I had lived, true love died.

"You tried to kill me," I shuddered. I'd come to on

his bed. He sat on the edge, watching me.

"You lied to me even when the lie meant our daughter. I should have killed you."

"Eric doesn't know about Ken. He's never even met her."

"How noble of you, but that doesn't change things. While I couldn't kill you, I promised you'd be sorry for lying to me. It was a promise I was prepared to fulfill because I know you, Shelly. That means I know when you're lying."

"What are you going to do?"

"What I should have done four years ago when you told me no. I'm taking you prisoner. Take a look around, my love. This is your cage." He magically produced a set of handcuffs. "Are you going to make me use these? You could consider them your wedding ring. "

"Keenan, this—"

"Beg."

"What?"

"If you want to be set free, the only thing I care to hear from your lips is the sound of you begging. I'm not interested in anything else."

"Please."

"That's more like it," he smugly replied.

"I wasn't finished." I'd snapped, but I couldn't care about the consequences. "I meant please spare me your jealous rage. You don't seem to be much of a forward thinker. They will look for me."

"You haven't been paying attention, have you?"

"What am I supposed to be paying attention to?"

"They're hoping we have a chance of falling in love again and think we need some alone time."

He stood from the bed, pocketed the cuffs, and made his way for the door.

I sat up and ran after him, but he managed to shut

and lock the door. I pulled and tugged and beat on the door, hoping it would give. When my throat had finally grown hoarse from screaming, I rested against the door, too weak to move away.

I had to get out.

CHAPTER TWENTY

KEENAN

"NO WAY! I am not playing babysitter. Your bitch of a girlfriend hates me, remember?" The next morning, I had called Di over and had been trying to convince her to play guard.

"Don't call her a bitch and you won't need to speak to her. I just need you to bring her food three times a day. The master bath is accessible to her. I may only be gone a few hours, but this is just a precaution."

"Oh, God. We've just gravitated from stalking to kidnapping."

"Don't grow a conscience on me now, and I've never stalked anyone.

"No? What do you call sending me back to spy on a town full of people you abandoned four years ago?"

"I paid you so why does it matter?"

"I didn't need your money, which you have been well aware of since the moment we almost fucked on it."

"But you took it anyway. Look, I'm asking you this as a favor. You won't be mixed up in anything."

"So what are you going to tell your big, bad brother when he finds out she's missing?"

"I'm going to tell him the truth."

"Do you think that's a good idea? Scratch that. Clearly, you aren't concerned about making smart decisions. What if he tries to stop you?"

"He won't. He knows better than that."

"I kind of got the impression that Keiran isn't afraid of much, least of all you."

I couldn't tell if she meant it as a warning or insult. Knowing Di, it was the latter. "He's not invincible."

"Wow." Di shook her head and for a moment, she looked worried. "You're really going to do it, aren't you?"

"Do what?"

"You're going to try and build a wall against everyone who cares about you. As a friend, I have to be honest and tell you that you're going to lose."

"Thanks for your vote of confidence."

"Just keeping it real."

"Before this gets any more real, I need another favor."

*****

Keith met me in the building's garage, and I tossed him the keys to Keiran's ride. I hopped in the car I had purchased a couple of years ago but never really used. An hour later, we were pulling up to the resort. Beach goers already littered the beach even at the early hour.

"Wait here," I instructed Keith.

He absently nodded as he inspected the beach likely looking for his next groupie. The man was a bigger whore than I ever was.

I had knocked on Keiran's door for ten minutes before he answered the door appearing very much awake, dressed in loose sweatpants and dripping with sweat.

"You had me standing out here for ten minutes so you could finish fucking?"

"What do you want?" he asked.

"My kid."

The tension between us was palpable only when we were alone. I had the feeling Lake had something to do with that. For someone who mercilessly tormented, taunted, and belittled, he did any and everything he could to keep her happy. If she so much as broke a nail, he would be ready to murder an entire city.

"She's down at the beach with Q and Jesse."

"Are they her nursemaids? Where is Dash?"

"She knows them—better than you even. Dash had to go back. His father demanded his presence for some business dealings."

"Jeez, he doesn't let him breathe much, does he? He's going to pay for not going to Yale or Harvard for the rest of his life."

"Dash is a big boy. He can handle his father."

"By being at his constant beck and call?"

"Hi, Keenan," Lake interrupted. She ducked under Keiran's arm with only his t-shirt to cover her. He scowled down at her head and then at me when he caught me purposely ogling her legs. "Where's Sheldon?"

"She's tied up at the moment." I meant it as a secret joke, but judging by the frowns on their faces and suspicious looks, it didn't go over their head as I had hoped.

"Is she okay?" she asked slowly.

"She's fine. Don't you trust me?"

"No," they said simultaneously.

"Oh, look at you two. You're practically finishing each other's sentences."

Keiran pulled Lake inside by her waist to her annoyance and growled, "Fuck off, Keenan."

"I plan to, but first I wanted to return your car keys."

"How are you getting back?"

"I have my own ride, a fact I made very clear when you kidnapped me a week and a half ago."

"Then who the fuck is driving my car?"

"A friend." Keiran fully stepped from the room and shut the door behind him. I could tell by the angry vein that he was pissed. "You do know that you just locked yourself out, right? Lake probably won't let you back in since you won't let her out to play."

"What friend?" he asked, ignoring my taunts.

"A simple one."

"Di?"

"Why would you think it's Di?"

"Do you think I'm stupid? How do you think I found you?"

"That's bullshit." My mind was racing even after denying it. *Had Di betrayed me?*

"She wasn't too careful the last couple of times she came to Six Forks. On her last trip as your spy, I spotted her. She gave me your address only if I promised not to kill you."

That explained the hysteria when I disappeared. She wasn't worried. She felt guilty.

"What does it take for a little loyalty," I mumbled.

"You tell me."

We glared at each other for long moments, neither one of us willing to fold. It was the elevator opening and the sound of Kennedy's excited chatter that forced us to end the silent duel.

"Keenan!" She freed herself from Jesse and ran to me as fast as her short legs would let her.

I stooped down to eagerly accept her hug. "Good morning, princess. How are you?"

"Fine. Thank you. Where's mama?"

"She's waiting for you right now to come and play. Will you come with me so I can take you to her?"

She nodded and looked up at Keiran. "Uncle, can I go?"

Behind her, I glared at him feeling jealous rage. My fists clenched at the smug look on his face before he answered. "Sure, kiddo. Be sure to tell your mother to call me."

He sent me a warning glance, which I chose to ignore. After gathering our bags from the room we never used, I put the resort in my taillights.

My plan worked without so much as a hiccup and the only remorse I felt was for having to lie to Kennedy. I had no intentions of letting her mother near her anytime soon.

Not until after I punish her thoroughly.

* * * * *

I let Di know picking up Kennedy was successful, and after dropping off Keith, we met at a mini mansion across the city from my apartment. I was still surprised at how easy it was despite Keiran's subtle threat. I knew they would eventually search out Sheldon, so I implemented the second part of my plan.

"And who is this little darling," Di cooed.

"Hi," Kennedy greeted shyly. She then wrapped her arms around my leg and ducked her head. I was humbled by the knowledge that she trusted me to keep her safe.

"Are you going to be okay here?"

"Why wouldn't I? I'm a big girl," Di replied flippantly.

"Because I know what this place did to you." I convinced her to let me use her father's house where she lived for most of her life and where her father had pimped her out to his various business partners. It was also where we had found the safe full of money that had totaled up to about eight million. We split the money and never returned. "Can I trust you?"

"Do you have a choice?" she joked. The smile on her lips died at my unmoving expression.

"I'll be back tonight and when I do, we need to talk."

For a few heartbeats, she stared at me with confusion and then awareness. "He told you." I didn't reply and didn't give her a chance to explain because I walked away.

CHAPTER TWENTY-ONE

SHELDON

THE SOUND OF the lock and the door opening alerted me to Keenan's presence. I had given up on trying to escape and had begrudgingly thrown myself on his bed where I stayed until he returned.

I was mourning the loss of Kennedy. I had only just gotten her back only to be taken from her in return.

"I need to get back to her," I said after the silence had stretched for too long.

"She's in good hands."

"She'll be better in mine."

"You'll get her back when I think you deserve her."

"Excuse me?" I was out of his bed and in his face faster than I could breathe my next breath. "I am her mother. She needs me."

"A fact you forgot when you chose to protect your boyfriend over our child."

"Eric had nothing to do with her abduction."

A cloud of hatred wafted around us. His eyes changed from impassive to furious as quickly as if someone had pushed a button. His hands were in my hair, tugging me down until I knelt at his feet, but I refused to cower before him. I glared up at him with equal hate.

I didn't see the knife, but I felt it at my throat. "If you say his name in my fucking presence again, I will end you."

"Then do it," I challenged. "I will never give you what you want. I will never be yours." Silence was all we had between us as I waited for the press of the knife, but it never came.

"Maybe not here," he whispered as he trailed the knife from the throat to my chest where my heart beat underneath. "But you will in everything else."

He lifted me into his arms and carried me out of the bedroom. I looked around as much as I could. Nervous anticipation built until I was shaking with it. He carried me into the kitchen and set me down gently on the tabletop. The coldness in his eyes remained so I scooted away, but his hand on my thigh stopped me. "Don't move."

My clothes were shed under his hands, and while I wanted to fight him, the warning in his eyes made me hesitate.

When I was completely naked, he nodded to the chair, and I quickly sat in it. I pushed forward and used the tabletop to shield as much of my body as I could. His smirk told me that he noticed.

He turned his back and quickly set about making breakfast. I watched him from the corner of my eye, but he never turned to acknowledge me. When he was done, he set a plate in front of me with the order to eat and then turned back to clean the dishes.

"Who said I was hungry?"

"It doesn't matter if you are or not. You do what I

say and that means eating when I say."

"Or what?"

"Or I'll punish you."

"This isn't punishment?"

"You aren't suffering... yet. So don't try my patience."

The dangerous edge in his voice made the threat seem all the more real, so I silently picked up my fork and ate. I was surprised at how good it tasted.

When did he learn to cook?

Like me, he had barely been able to defrost a chicken without screwing it up somehow. An ugly thought formed, and I was disturbed by jealousy.

"This is good. Did your girlfriend teach you how to cook?"

His bark of laughter surprised me. "I don't have a girlfriend. I haven't for four years."

"Fine. Your slut buckets. I'm sure you have tons."

He turned to face me, gripping a plate in his hand. "I don't have tons... only one." He took a seat and regarded me with lust in his eyes. "Come here," he ordered. He pushed his untouched food away and patted the space on the table in front of him. Ever aware of my naked state, I climbed on the table to the spot he indicated. "Spread your legs for me. Let me see what's mine."

My trembling legs seemed to fall apart under his heated gaze, warming my sex in return. His hands ran the length of my thighs, but he kept this touch light.

"I've always loved the feel of your skin. So soft and supple. Touch yourself. Feel what I feel."

My fingers hesitantly pushed through the warm lips of my sex.

My body quivered in answer, and I could almost feel everything he was thinking of doing to me. Everything he *would* do to me.

"I won't need to ask if you're ready for me. I can see the evidence dripping from your fingers." I wanted to beg for him to touch me, but that would be surrender and I couldn't do that. "I know what you want, but you won't ask for it, will you?"

I continued the light touch of my fingers and even went as far as to insert one. If he could tease then so could I. His indrawn breath was barely audible, but my senses were too in tune with his not to hear.

"You're going to fucking kill me," he groaned. His mouth descended, and the moment his lips met mine, I came apart and filled the kitchen with my cries.

I could feel my willpower weakening along with my body. I didn't even realize that I was falling. In more ways than one. My back now rested on the tabletop, and my legs opened wider for greater access.

"Take it all," I whispered just before the force of my release sucked the air from my lungs along with my will.

"I plan to," he whispered back. Regret that he'd heard me was quickly replaced by the sudden and merciless invasion of his cock. The table rocked and the chairs collapsed under the force of his hips. I swallowed back my cries until they were nothing but whimpers. I wouldn't give him that. "No, baby, don't you hold yourself back." He slid his hand between our bodies and tortured my clit. "Scream for me."

*****

Keenan had spent the morning taking me, and not once did I resist.

He had done things to me that still made me blush. There wasn't a part of my body that he left untouched.

"What are we doing here?" I asked much later as I

looked around the empty tattoo shop with irritation.

"Righting a wrong." He started setting up as if getting ready for a client.

"Is this your shop?" I tried not to sound impressed when I asked but failed.

I had always wondered what Keenan had gone on to do and if he had found someone else. He left before he could graduate due to his long stay in the hospital, and given his quiet yet desperate need for attention and affection, it was impossible to picture him without someone.

"It's mine." He patted the leather chair. "Hop up and lay on your stomach."

"But I don't want a tattoo."

"I wasn't asking, Shelly," he threatened without looking up.

"You're being ridiculous."

"You can do it willingly, or I can strap you to the chair and do what I want anyway."

I struggled with my choices and realized I lacked an advantage or the words to convince him that what he was doing crossed too many lines.

The foolish teenage girl in me still hoped...

I quickly did as he ordered before he could see my tears. I rested my head against the soft leather in defeat and willed my body to keep still.

I drowned it all out.

The hum of the machine.

The feel of his hand.

The needle's piercing vibration against my skin.

I let it all go for the past.

* * * * *

SIX YEARS AGO

"Are you afraid?"

It took me a moment to gather myself after he'd just gotten through kissing me senseless. We were in his bedroom with romantic music playing softly in the background. I had to admit that he was pulling out all the stops.

A twinge of sadness and anger flowed through me as I remembered our recent but short breakup and why. I'd forgiven him, but the urge to beat the brakes off Jessica Stanton was still strong. She had been a friend, and the two of them had done the unthinkable when they made out at a party.

"A little. I've never done this before." The cutest grin spread to his lips and eased some of my nervousness.

"You don't know how happy that makes me."

"Why? Because you're damaged goods?"

"Ouch. That hurt." He clutched his chest as if seriously wounded.

"Maybe this will help," I whispered and quickly shed my dress before I lost the courage.

I was surprised at how brazen I was even though it was all an act. His eyes boldly traveled every inch of my body, and I shivered from that contact alone.

"Are you sure you want to do this now? We can wait if you want."

I nodded my head even as I crossed my arms over my breasts. I had turned sixteen the month before, and I felt I was as ready as I would ever be. "What better day than Valentine's day?" I joked.

"Your wedding day," he answered. His face turned

down with guilt, and he backed away, but my hand shot out to stop him.

"I know. I was only kidding, but I want you now. I choose you. I choose this moment."

"I don't deserve you."

"Well, I am pretty amazing."

"I'm sorry, okay? It will never happen again. I don't want to hurt you like that again."

As much as I didn't want to risk this night, I couldn't hold back my feelings. "Why did you do it?"

His head fell forward and his shoulders shook as he gripped the sheets. I watched the veins in his hands bulge and stretch. "I wish I knew."

*****

PRESENT

He'd lied. After the first time, he hurt me much worse each time after. The pain yesterday didn't heal with time. It only festered.

"Where did you go?" I felt myself being lifted until I was now sitting upright. I felt the soreness on my ass and looked down to see what he had done but found it wrapped.

"What?"

"Where did you go just now? You were as stiff as a board."

"In my memories, Keenan. It's my only comfort. What did you do to me?"

"I told... I needed to right a wrong."

Realization hit, and I was left shaking with anger. "You tattooed your name again?"

"Not quite."

"What. Did. You. Do?"

"I left a reminder of who you belonged to. It's more

for me really."

"Your arrogance is unattractive." I may have sounded petty, but it was all I had at the moment—short of killing him.

"Are you saying you don't want me?"

"More or less."

"Let's test that theory out." In one fluid motion, he flipped me over and had my shorts around my ankles.

"Is this how it's going to be? I'm not your toy, Keenan."

"No, baby. You're not. You fuck too well to be a toy." I could feel him peeling the wrap away from my ass. "Mine," he growled and palmed me.

"You keep saying that."

"I mean that's what the tattoo is. It says 'Mine.'"

"Please tell me you didn't." I attempted to stand up, but his hand on my back kept me in place.

"I did and I enjoyed." He peeled down my panties with his thumb and kissed down my back.

Somehow, I found the strength I didn't know I possessed.

"Keenan, let me go." I turned my head to look into his eyes and let him see how serious I was. "I don't want this."

He stared at me frozen for so long that, for a moment, I didn't think he would let me go. He shoved away from me and kicked away his chair until it banged into the wall violently.

The next second, his fist flew into the glass frame nearby, and I watched in horror as it shattered and fell to the floor.

Without a word, he stalked toward the back of the shop and disappeared behind a door.

I spent the next few hours confined to a corner of his shop while he saw countless clients.

All of them were female.

I watched them flirt and touch and shamelessly throw themselves at him.

A few even had the gall to grab onto his cock and he just smiled.

Always smiling and welcoming.

I hated him.

He promised I would and he succeeded.

"So, Keenan, I was wondering if you would finally take me up on that date," a platinum blonde with a body full of tattoos asked. Seriously, where could she possibly have room to fit another tattoo?

"I don't know, Missy. I'm kind of busy. Maybe next time," he winked, and I almost threw up in my mouth at the way she gushed.

"How am I going to ever steal your heart if you won't let me take you out?"

"That's because my heart has already been stolen."

The platinum turned her nose up at me and snarled, "Her?"

He laughed. "Don't be silly." My heart plummeted at his blatant disregard for me. "I'm talking about my daughter."

"Oh, I bet you make pretty babies." She brazenly sat in his lap and ran a finger down his chest. "I bet we could make some pretty babies. So how old is she?"

"She's three and as sweet and cute as a button, unlike her mother who is a viperous bitch."

"Is that her?" She looked at me in disgust, and I couldn't help but flip her off.

"No, she's nothing to me."

"Then why is she here just sitting there?"

Keenan's jaw tightened, but the bitch was too busy sneering at me to notice.

"Missy, if you don't mind, I have another client in

five minutes, but how about I take you up on that offer this weekend?"

"That would be great."

"Cool. I'll call you," he said without looking at her. I rolled my eyes at the vision of her flouncing from the shop.

"You're a pig. It's a wonder you haven't contracted something."

"I'm always careful, Sheldon."

"I can't tell. You never use a condom when I ask you to."

"That's because you're different."

"A minute ago, I was nothing."

"What can I say? I have to keep my clients happy."

"In what way? With your dick? I don't care what they say. A slut is a slut whether it's a man or woman."

"You don't know what you're talking about," he gritted.

"I know you haven't changed. When does it ever become enough for you?"

"Shut the fuck up, Shelly."

"Tell me... how many women have you slept with since we've been apart? One a night? Two? Six?"

"Zero."

Maybe it was the pounding of my brain or the hammering of my heart that caused me to misunderstand. I managed to bounce back from the shock of his answer and say, "Not only are you an unfaithful whore, but you're a liar, too."

"When have I ever lied to you? I may have kept my shit from you, but when you found out, I never lied so why would I lie now? I'm not looking for a future with you. I haven't touched a single fucking woman in four years."

So many emotions assaulted me at once.

I swallowed the weight of it down, but it just kept coming back up until I puked my guts all over the floor. My dry sobs caused me to lose focus, and because of my spotty vision, I never saw him move, but I felt his hands lifting me.

"For fuck sake, Shelly. Breathe!"

CHAPTER TWENTY-TWO

KEENAN

I DON'T THINK I remember ever being this frightened. Not even when I met Keiran for the first time, or when I felt the first bullet enter my body and threaten to end my life. Not even when I was confined to a hospital to die.

"Shelly, please breathe, baby. Don't do this to me."

"Not... dying," she coughed.

"Then what the hell are you doing to me?" I hadn't realized I was shouting until her body flinched in my arms.

"Please, stop shouting." She groaned and leaned against my chest. I briefly wondered how tight I could hold her without crushing her.

I'm losing it.

She possessed the power to drive me insane without doing much at all.

"Were you serious?" she asked after some time had passed. I continued to rub her back, hoping to keep her calm.

"What?"

"I'm your first?"

"Well, not my first. Remember there was—"

"Keenan."

"Yes, you were my first and my last."

"Why?"

I blew out heavily and thought about the last four years. "I got the urges, but I couldn't do the deed. I don't know why."

"So you could be faithful to me when we're not committed, but not when we were together?"

"What do you want me to say? Give me the right words and I'll say them."

"It doesn't matter, and it's none of my business. I shouldn't have asked. Now, if you don't mind, the smell of my puke makes me want to puke all over again."

She slid from my arms, and I let her because I didn't know what else to do.

"Where is the bathroom?"

I pointed to my office, and while she was gone, I gathered some cleaning supplies and cleaned up the mess. Once the floor was spotless again, I went to check on her.

I found her standing frozen at the entrance of the bathroom. Her hand was held tight over her mouth as tears streamed down her face. I stood confused and followed the direction of her gaze until my own landed on the sketch of her that took up most of the right wall. It was in clear sight of the bathroom and would have been the first thing she saw when she came out.

My eyes closed with regret over my screw up. She was never supposed to see that.

I cleared my throat, but that proved to be another mistake. The lost look in her eyes fucking broke me.

"Keenan... what is this?"

Didn't she remember? She'd seen the sketch before. I woke her up to show her that night. It was when I found out how much of a grumpy sleeper she was.

"You know what it is."

"It's much bigger and it's here. Why?"

"Why not? I drew it. It's a good picture."

"Don't do this, Keenan. Tell me why."

"My goal was to hate you and never remember why I ever loved you. Looking at the sketch helped. It reminded me how you took away the one person who ever wanted me and the first love I ever felt was real."

"Keenan, please try to understand... you hurt me so much. Every time you were with them, I ached."

"Well, then you should feel satisfied. You paid me back in full."

*****

The dim club lights and pounding music from all sides were exactly what I needed to hide in plain sight. Drinks came and went from shameless female suitors. Many I had no clue where they came from, but I didn't want to care. I wanted to lose myself to the feeling of being wrong. The club was part dance and part sex with everything in between.

Everything goes.

Even murder.

I had my arm around the nearest brunette. I avoided blondes and anything that reminded me of the traitorous bitch who plagued my every thought.

After taking Sheldon back to my apartment and locking her in my bedroom again, I avoided her and as soon as night fell, I fled.

"Baby, you're so tense," the brunette cooed. Her hand trailed up my thigh and stopped just below my dick. "How about a blowjob?"

Four years ago, I would have found that type of slutty behavior appealing and dived right in. Now I only wondered why the fuck I ever looked her way.

Her long nails played with my zipper, and when I gave her a nod of approval, she lowered it and stuck her hand inside. When her fingers wrapped around my cock, I felt my skin crawl. I ignored her and sipped from my drink as she worked to make my dick hard.

Maybe I had whiskey dick.

Or maybe I wanted Sheldon.

Fuck it. I can't have her anyway.

She made it pretty clear.

A part of me nagged to just let her go again, but knew it would be impossible to let her go and stay away this time. How could I, knowing she had my kid?

Shit. Kennedy.

I looked down at the woman who was still working to get me hard. "Enough."

I checked the time and high tailed it out of the club, hoping I could catch her before bedtime.

The city was alive with people looking to have a good time to close out the weekend. Thirty minutes later, I was walking through the front door. I found Di and Kennedy camped out in the living room watching Jaws and eating ice cream.

"Seriously, Di?" She nearly jumped out her skin at the sound of my voice.

"Keenan!" Kennedy ran to me with her face covered in chocolate syrup. I caught her just in time and lifted her in my arms. "How are you, princess?"

"Fine. Where's mama?"

Guilt over my lie returned full force, and I felt like an even bigger ass. Keeping them apart had officially topped the list of worst things I'd ever done. I may have been angry over missing three years of Kennedy's life, but I knew Sheldon hadn't purposely kept me away. I made that mistake alone by leaving.

"She's waiting to tuck you in so I came to get you."

"Really?" Di asked, earning my glare. "Look who grew a conscience."

"Stay out of it."

"I can't. There's no one else to tell you when you're being a dick... and by the way, if that wasn't clear, you're being a dick."

"What's that?" Kennedy asked.

"Princess, go sit in the living room while I talk to Di." She ran off, and as soon as she was out of sight, Di started to back toward the front door. "Don't even think about it. You and I need to talk."

"Really?" she squealed and feigned ignorance. "About that?"

"First, why is my kid watching Jaws and eating ice cream this late at night. Speaking of late, why isn't she in bed?"

"Whoa, super dad. Calm down. I think the better question is why doesn't she know she's your kid?"

"It's complicated. Now answer the question."

"You had me help you basically kidnap them by setting up all these locks so you could 'stake your claim' and now you're chickening out?"

"It isn't kidnapping, and it didn't go as planned, but it doesn't matter because they are here now."

"It didn't go as planned because it shouldn't have ever happened. I'm just glad you came to your senses... sort of."

"Why did you rat me out to my brother?"

"Because you were homesick, and I knew he wouldn't hurt you no matter how many times he may have fantasized about it over the years."

"That isn't a reason."

"Would I knowing about Kennedy be a reason?"

"Come again?"

She took a deep breath and released it slowly. "He told me when he cornered me. At first, I thought it was a trick to get me to tell him what he wanted to know, but then I realized it was Keiran. He would have just tortured me."

"So how did he convince you that she was real?"

"He showed me a picture of her. She looks just like you, which is kind of a shame. I always wanted to know if those Maury shows were created with real material or staged."

"Di."

"Yes?"

"Thank you."

"What are friends for?" she grinned smugly.

"You fucking annoy me."

"And you're a slut."

CHAPTER TWENTY-THREE

SHELDON

I'D BROKEN FREE. Back at the shop, I snagged a couple of bobby pins and didn't allow myself to wonder how they'd gotten there. Thanks to boredom and YouTube, I figured out a long time ago how to pick a lock. Once I was free, I tiptoed out of the room and listened for any sign of Keenan. When I realized he wasn't in the apartment, I made a mad dash for the phone I spotted downstairs.

I tore the receiver from the counter and dialed Dash. When he didn't answer, I tried Lake, who answered almost immediately. "Sheldon! I'm so glad you called. I was getting ready to form a search party for you and a lynch mob for Keenan's head."

"So why didn't you?" I asked bitterly. It was all I could do not to scream into the receiver. I had been locked away in some undisclosed location for the past twenty-four or so hours, and Lake, one of my best friends, pretended as if I had just come back from some vacation.

"Well, I didn't want to disturb your romantic alone time."

"Come again?"

"Don't be so stingy with the details, girl. Spill."

"Lake… what the hell are you talking about?" I was yelling into the phone, clutching it with a grip more suffocating than death. "Scratch that. Where is Kennedy?"

"I thought Kennedy was with you guys. Are you okay?"

"No. I'm not okay. Keenan—"

"Mommy?"

I whirled around and almost tripped over my feet at the sound of my sweet little angel's voice. "Kennedy?" I could hear Lake calling for me in the background, but I absently hung up and ran the short distance to where Kennedy waited by the door.

"Ken! Oh, my God." I kissed her all over her face and completely ignored the fact that I could be scaring her. "Are you okay? Let me look at you."

"Mommy, I had fun." She began to fire off everything she'd done, and though I could barely keep up with her babble, I listened because I wanted to know exactly where she'd been. "Di show me sharks."

Di? Did she say Di?

"Di? You had my daughter around that slut?"

"Watch your mouth around my kid."

"I think I know how to raise my own daughter. I'm her mother."

"Then act like it. She needs a bath and it's late. Do it before I change my mind."

As much as I wanted to argue, he was right. It was almost midnight, and I was surprised she was still up and wide-awake. I could also smell the beach on her. He walked past me and shed his linen jacket that matched the pants he wore. I tried not to salivate over how suave he looked. It was a far cry from the jeans and tees he normally wore. He looked every bit of the man he'd grown to be and even older than his twenty-two years.

I ran a bath for Kennedy. Before long, her eyes were drifting close so I dressed her for bed. By the time, I had her nightie on her Keenan had entered and took a seat on the edge of the tub while I brushed Kennedy's hair. Her head rested against my chest, but when Keenan entered, she began to fight sleep.

Could she already be attached to him? If she was, then I knew it was too late. How could I rip them apart now?

"Why did Lake think we were spending alone time together?"

"Because that's what I told them."

"And they just believed you?" I felt as if I was sold to the highest bidder.

"I told you... they want us back together... even if we don't."

"They are being ridiculous."

His eyes narrowed and his hands clenched at my statement. Kennedy seemed to sense the change in her father because she lifted her head to stare at him. He noticed and snapped out of it immediately, and I couldn't help but smirk.

"I'm going to put our daughter to bed. I want you to wait for me in the bedroom."

"Keenan, I don't think this is a good idea. Maybe I should sleep with Kennedy."

He drew me close with a light hand around my neck and growled against my lips. "Go. Now."

I met my daughter's eyes, which were nearly shut from fatigue but still very much aware. Fighting with Keenan in front of her when he was still very new to her would only scare her.

I cleaned up the bathroom and made for the bedroom where I took a shower in the master bath. By the time I finished, Keenan was waiting for me on the bed. He'd shed his shirt and shoes and the sight of him shirtless and barefoot stirred unwanted lust. The tattoos covering his upper body contrasted greatly with the dress pants.

"You can stop drooling now."

I snapped my mouth shut and swallowed the moisture that had formed from the sight of him. "I wasn't drooling."

"If you say so." He smirked. "Here. I want you to wear this." He extended a slip of sheer fabric, and reluctantly, I took it and held it up for inspection.

"I think I will be a little over prepared to sleep, don't you think?"

"You can sleep naked if you want."

"Why can't I wear the pajamas I brought with me?"

Instead of answering, he wrapped an arm around my waist and pulled me between his legs and then plucked the lingerie from my hands. The towel was peeled from my body, dropping carelessly to the floor, and just as quickly, I was wearing the gown.

"Will you always need to have your way?"

"I'm afraid so." He stood to his feet, towering over me. "I'm going to shower, but I'll be back for you."

"Is that a threat?"

"It's a promise." He startled me by kissing my nose softly and then disappeared into the bathroom.

What the fuck?

I all but ran out the room feeling confused and on edge. Why had he changed his mind about Kennedy? Why was he being gentle and almost likable? A part of me hoped it was real while the other feared it was just another mind game.

I entered the bedroom where Kennedy was fast asleep and watched her chest rise and fall for the longest time. With each breath she took, my heart felt lighter. She was safe. She was home. We had each other.

"We have to tell her soon." My head turned toward the door where Keenan stood, his hair and body both dripping wet with a towel wrapped around his waist. "You're drooling again."

"Your dick is practically making a tent in that towel."

"There is nothing practical about my dick, baby."

"Why are you sweet talking me?"

"Would you rather I threaten and yell at you?"

"At least it would be real."

"Then let me show you what real feels like," he gritted as his eyes darkened to pitch black. I suddenly regretted what I'd said. It scared me how quickly he could change. "Let's go."

He turned away, assuming I would follow.

I did.

And I cursed myself the entire way to his bedroom.

He took a seat on the edge of the large bed and crooked his finger.

Stupid me followed.

"Face the wall."

I did as I was told though my brain sent my body the command to run.

You can do this.

No matter how much he hated me, I had to remember that somewhere deep inside he was still Keenan. My Keenan. The Keenan who always had a ready joke and a loving touch.

Only... at this moment, here, together, he wasn't my Keenan. He was my ruination.

I heard him move but somehow knew that turning

around would be a mistake. The room filled with the slow and sexy croon of a man who sung about a lost love replaced with hate and sex.

"Dance for me."

At his command, my hips began to sway. The sheer fabric he ordered me to wear did nothing to hide the curves I earned from my pregnancy. His eyes just before I turned as they scanned my exposed body told me he appreciated.

"Your ass is even more beautiful than I remember. And your tits..." His groan was low but perfectly audible. "You're a woman now." His warm breath whispered over my skin, heating me up, but at the same time, raising chill bumps. I never even heard him move. "Did my child do this to you?"

"What do you think?"

"I think you're sexier than ever. Perfect even."

His hand came between my thighs and slid up until his fingertips rested just underneath the flimsy nightgown.

"Perfect?" I could barely manage to speak the word when his fingers briefly strummed my sex before moving away as if it never happened.

"Perfect," he repeated. "It's too bad really." A kiss on my shoulder left me needing more than just a promising threat.

"Why is that?"

"Because you won't be when I'm through with you. I'm going to be the devil you made of me."

"Maybe you were always this person, and the guy I fell in love with was the façade."

He turned me around to face him with his hands on my hips. "Congratulations, Shelly. You're finally thinking with your head."

He pushed me back onto the bed and crawled on

top of me. "It's too bad your head isn't needed for what I'm about to do to you."

"I never said I wanted to fuck you."

"You didn't have to. Your body tells me everything I need to know." He trailed his hand up my thigh and rested it just where my thigh met my sex. "Your pussy doesn't lie either. I can feel all this heat between us right... here." He trailed a finger down my sex and my traitorous body quivered.

"Because you don't play fair." I pushed the towel from his hips and he yanked the gown over my head. My hand immediately gripped his cock and guided him inside me.

"I never claimed to," he groaned when he was seated fully.

"Then what do we do now?"

"We fuck." His lips met mine at the same time he began to move inside me. My legs wrapped tighter around his waist, and I pulled him into me. His dark gaze pinned me to the bed just before his hands did. "Only I control this fuck, baby, so let go and let me."

I had to grab onto his hips to handle the harsh but slow possession of his body. It was the same song and dance every time I gave into him. It was me fighting not to let him see how much I craved the surrender.

*****

He rolled onto his back, taking me with him, and stared up at the ceiling. My limbs felt like rubber and my entire body ached from overuse including the forbidden parts.

Keenan had explored me thoroughly throughout the night. My mouth and ass had taken the brunt of his lust.

"Why did you change your mind?" I whispered into the dark.

"About?"

"Taking Kennedy away from me."

"I never took her away from you, and even if I had, nothing's changed, Shelly. I'm still the bad guy."

"Protecting yourself doesn't have to mean hurting others. You don't have to be that cruel."

"You want to know about cruelty? There is nothing worse than being in love with someone you want to hate."

"What are you saying?"

"I think you know."

I did, but some things were better left in the dark. I definitely didn't want to believe it.

We each gave in to our private thoughts. The rise and fall of his chest was starting to lure me to sleep until my mind began screaming for me to ask the question that still stood between the two of us.

"Why did you fuck her?"

He was silent for so long I thought he might have fallen asleep until his heavy sigh told me he wasn't. "Because I would have lost you either way. At least the way I chose I knew I could have a chance at keeping you and you would be okay."

"What do you mean you would have lost me? Where would I have gone?"

"Let it go, Shelly."

"I can't do that."

"You don't have a choice." I sat up and searched his face, maybe hoping he would give in, but his steely gaze met mine unwaveringly. "Drop. It."

"One of these days, I'm going to finally accept that you will never stop being a coward." I moved to my side and faced away from him while fighting back tears.

For the longest time, the only sound that could be heard was the sound of my incessant sniffling until he spoke so quietly I almost didn't hear him. "You read those text messages but did you understand them?"

What?

"I read enough." There weren't many between them, and after four years, I could probably only guess that there were no more than a handful spanning two weeks.

"No, Shelly. You didn't."

*****

FOUR YEARS AGO

"Are your parents' home tonight?" Keenan nuzzled against my neck and groped my ass to lift me into him. We had just finished making out in the driveway

"I don't know, but Dash could be back any moment." I giggled.

"No, he won't. He's busy chasing Willow's ass. I don't blame him either." I hit him on the chest and considered kneeing him.

"Don't joke about my friends," I warned.

"Baby, I was only kidding. You're the sour apple of my eye."

"You're really asking for it tonight, aren't you?" I meant it as a threat, but the lust in his eyes increased tenfold.

"I'm damn near begging for it, Shelly. Are you going to give it to me?"

"That depends..."

"On?"

"How well you beg."

"I can beg very well, baby. If you take me inside

right now, I can show you just how well I beg with my mouth on your pussy."

We were upstairs and locked away in my room in sixty seconds flat. We continued to kiss with an intensity I still had not become entirely used to.

"Your lips taste like I'd died and gone to heaven, but your pussy will make me want to die for that little slice of heaven. Turn around, baby, and bend over the bed."

I did as he instructed without hesitation.

"Lift your skirt and slide your panties to your ankles." I felt awkward completing his instructions in my current position, but I managed it without embarrassment. "Good girl," he praised. His voice sounded far away, so I turned my head to find him standing near the far wall, watching me with his ankles and arms crossed.

"Why are you playing with me?"

"I'm admiring. Playing starts now." He shed his hoodie and shirt and knelt behind me. "Fucking beautiful," he groaned before his tongue swept my sex.

From that moment, he kept me in a constant state of weeping and shaking as he ate me hungrily. When he finally decided I had enough, he positioned himself on top of my powder blue coverlet and ordered me to ride him.

After three rounds, we finally caught our breath.

As I was drifting to sleep, I felt him kiss my nose. I opened my eyes in time to see him slip from the room. As soon as he closed the door, his phone vibrated with a message.

I groaned and rolled over, ready for sleep to take me. Five minutes later, his phone continued to vibrate obnoxiously. Thinking it might have been an emergency I grabbed his jeans and fished his phone from his pocket:

Unknown: Why are you ignoring me?

It appeared to be the first messaged that had come through from an unknown number. There were at least five more, each worse and more incriminating than the last: Unknown: Is your little girlfriend around?

Unknown: She can't love you like I do.

Unknown: I want more Keenan.

Unknown: How many other boys can say they fucked their chemistry teacher?

Unknown: We have something special. I haven't stopped thinking about your cock.

The last one was the most confusing of all.

Unknown: I told you... if you want to keep her, you need to see things my way.

I quickly scrolled to the top and read through the messages. Keenan had only responded twice in the two weeks the messages spanned. He had told her their deal was done and the second message read that what had happened was a mistake. The phone slipped from my hands to the floor, and I followed after it when my knees gave out. What deal could involve sex with Ms. Felders? *He fucked Ms. Felders.*

This wasn't the first time he had cheated on me, but I never thought we would go this far. I hadn't realized I was crying until I felt his arms around me, pulling me up from the floor.

His voice was barely heard over the sound of my heart shattering to bloody broken pieces. If I looked close enough, I might have been able to see it lying at my feet.

He lifted my naked body and gently laid me down on the bed and then quickly looked over me. When he didn't see physical signs for my current state he asked again, "Why are you crying, Shelly?"

"You said it wouldn't happen again." The last of my

tears had shed and in their place was anger.

"I'm not following." Confusion flooded his features as his eyes searched mine.

"Then maybe your phone can bring you up to speed." I jumped from my bed, retrieved his phone from the floor, and threw it at his bare chest. "You and the chemistry teacher seem awfully familiar with each other. Is it because you fucked her? The chemistry *fucking* teacher."

"Fuck." He stood from the bed and reached for me, but I backed away. The thought of his hands on me now made my skin crawl. "Sheldon, it was—"

"A mistake? I know. You told her as much after her many messages sent to you just *begging* for more of your dick."

"It was only once. I turned her down after that."

"What should that mean to me? It should have never happened."

"But it's not what you think."

"Is it ever? It wasn't with Jessica Stanton or Casey Whitmore or Brittany Anderson. How strong do you think I am, Keenan? Or do you just think me that much of a fool? No, don't answer that. I am a fool, but more than that, I'm done."

"Don't do this, Shelly." He begged and pleaded, but I heard none of it. "Don't walk away again."

"Keenan, I'm not walking away. I'm shutting the door. Now please get out."

"I'm not leaving, Shelly, and neither are you."

"I can't be with you anymore, Keenan. I can't compete with your demons. They consume you. I hate you so much that if you died right now, I wouldn't even care."

CHAPTER TWENTY-FOUR

KEENAN

A WEIGHT ON my back had woken me and when I opened my eyes and turned my head, I was met with my own reflection staring back at me.

"Keenan. Up."

"Princess? Why are you out of bed?"

"I draw."

"Oh, no," I heard Sheldon grumble from under my arm. Sometime during the night, I had curled her under with her back resting against my front. We were both completely naked underneath the covers so getting out of bed with Kennedy there was not an option. Especially not with my morning wood that currently rested between Sheldon's thighs.

"What's with this?" I asked Sheldon, indicating toward Ken.

"Every morning, she gets out of bed and finds a way to make my morning a long one. Your daughter is a criminal mastermind."

"I see..." I turned back to Kennedy, who was currently occupied playing with my hair. "Kennedy can you wait for us outside the bedroom, please?"

"Keenan, come now and see my draw." She pouted.

I don't know how she did it, but just like that, I caved. I couldn't let my little girl be unhappy, could I? I would kill anyone who tried so I had to live by it.

I worked the sheet around my waist, careful to hide my hard-on and took her by her hand. I could feel Sheldon's eyes on me and heard her laughing just before I shut the bedroom door.

"Lead the way."

I followed after her and into the living room. At first, I didn't see it, but the faint red coloring on the wall from one of the markers I used to sketch caught my eye. She ran to the spot and pointed, excitement lighting up her face. It was just a bunch of lines and shapes, but to me, it was the greatest creation in the world. Never mind the deposit that I wouldn't be getting back.

"Pretty?" she asked.

"It's beautiful." I thought about it long and hard before asking, "What is it?"

"Mama... me... you."

A sudden indrawn breath shifted my attention from Kennedy and her wall of art to her horrified mother standing behind me and covered in my dress shirt. She looked ready to collapse. I crossed the short distance between us and pulled her into my chest by the back of her neck.

"Does that scare you?" I whispered against her neck. She nodded against my chest but remained silent. Kennedy tugged on the sheet wrapped around my waist.

"Mama sad?"

I scooped her up and made room for her between us. She rubbed her mother's head and then frowned when she didn't lift her head.

When her lips started to tremble, I felt my temper rise.

"No, baby. She's not sad. Isn't that right, mommy?"

The warning in my tone finally convinced her to lift her head from where she was crying softly against my chest. She smiled brightly at Kennedy, and though it was forced, it seemed to appease her.

"Are you hungry?" Sheldon turned her teary gaze on me and only after a second too long did she reluctantly nod. "What about you, mini me?"

"Keenan," Sheldon scolded. My reference to Kennedy being mine went over her head, so I ignored Sheldon's warning and set Kennedy on her feet once more.

"I want cereal."

"Cereal, huh? What kind do you like?" She rattled off an entire list of cereals long enough to include every cereal in the world, but somehow, never listed a single flavor I had. "How about pancakes?"

"Yes, please and cereal, too?"

I looked to Sheldon for help, but she only shrugged and said, "It's one of her favorites."

I went back to the bedroom and quickly dressed in sweatpants before leading them into the kitchen. Kennedy babbled a mile a minute about everything under the sun while I cooked. I never knew until now how kids questioned everything they saw. When I was finished, I spooned the food onto the plates and carried them to the table where Sheldon blew raspberries in Kennedy's neck. While she was preoccupied, I took the opportunity to do the same to Sheldon's whose neck was exposed. She jumped in surprise and Kennedy laughed outrageously.

"Daddy, silly."

I stiffened at the sound of the word, and I could tell without looking that Sheldon had the same reaction. I finally mustered some motion and turned to face Kennedy's bright grin shining toward me. She squealed and clamped her hand over her mouth as if she'd just told some big secret.

"Did you tell her?" Sheldon's accusation only served to piss me off before I could revel in the idea that my kid knew who I was.

"No, I didn't but does it matter? I am her father unless there is something you'd like to tell me." I knew it was bullshit as soon as I uttered the words, but I wanted to strike back. Kennedy was mine. Every single inch of her was me.

"She can't know."

"It looks like she does," I smugly replied.

"She's three, Keenan. It means nothing." Her eyes flashed deviously when she sat back in her seat and crossed her arms. "She thought Keiran was her father once too, you know. Right around the time she began to talk..."

The smile that appeared on her lips hurt worse than the bullets that almost took my life.

I counted the seconds it took me to realize that what I thought I heard her say was real.

I wanted the anger. I wanted to rage. I wanted *blood.* But all I could feel was devastation. Kennedy had known someone else as her father. So where did that leave me?

"Get out."

She flinched at my command, and if my daughter had not sat watching, I would have thrown her out on her ass.

"I'm not leaving without my daughter."

"Fine. Then get out of my sight before I lose what little control I have left and snap your neck."

"Don't talk like that around my daughter."

"GET THE FUCK OUT, SHELDON!"

I gripped the counter until my nails dug into the granite because, while I may have lost my temper, I still held a feeble leash on my control.

Kennedy was now crying and watching me as if I were going to hurt her next, and I never wanted that. I watched Sheldon with pure hatred flowing through my veins as she reluctantly left the kitchen.

"Mama." Kennedy held out her hands for her. Sheldon turned back for her, but my look stopped her. I let go of all the warmth from mere moments ago. She deserved the hard, cold exterior, not the person on the inside clawing to get out and save her from me.

When she was finally gone, I turned to Kennedy, who now watched me with sad eyes. My own reflected back and I could feel the slump in my shoulders. "I'm sorry you had to see that, kid."

I'd lost my appetite so I contented myself with watching her eat her pancakes once she calmed down. She wasn't her usual talkative self, which made the atmosphere awkward, so when my phone rang, I welcomed the distraction.

"Keenan, you need to get here now." Keiran's gruff voice filtered through the phone before I could speak, but he sounded off.

He sounded scared.

"What's going on?"

"It's your father."

"My father?" *John... or Mitch?*

"John," he clarified as if he could read my mind.

"What does he want?"

"He was shot, man, and it's not looking good. Get here."

CHAPTER TWENTY-FIVE

SHELDON

KEENAN HAD ALL but thrown us into the car without a word of where we were going and why. More than once, I had to ask him to slow the car and remind him that Kennedy was in the backseat, but he never responded. He would just grip the steering wheel tighter and let off the gas until whatever plagued his mind returned and then he would gun it again.

We made the eight-hour trip in just less than seven and went straight to the hospital. I still had no clue what was going on, but I knew someone close must have been in trouble judging by the look of terror and pain etched all over his features.

I grabbed Kennedy and chased after Keenan, who had parked in the emergency lane and ran into the building. He was at the reception desk, rattling the poor nurse who scrambled to find what I assumed was a room number.

"Keenan, you have to calm down before they kick us out." He pinned me with a look that would have killed me on the spot if such a thing were possible.

"Yes, John Masters is in room 345. You take a right—" Keenan had already taken off before the lady could finish her directions. I followed at a much slower pace feeling far too numb to move any faster.

Something had happened to John, and I could only guess that it was serious given the severity of Keenan's mood.

I spotted Lake as soon as I entered the hallway where John's room was and rushed toward her. She appeared lost in her thoughts. Her gaze was fixed on the wall. I set a sleeping Kennedy on a nearby couch before speaking. "Lake, what's going on? What happened to John?"

She snapped to at the sound of my voice, and when she looked from me to Kennedy, she broke down and rushed out the events leading up to this moment. "He was shot at a stoplight on the way home from town. The few witnesses say it all happened too quickly."

"So what are the doctors saying? Is he going to be okay?"

"No, Sheldon. He's not. He's bleeding slowly around the heart and the doctors aren't able to stop the bleeding."

"Then wh—" No matter how many times I tried, I couldn't complete it. I couldn't bring my fear to life. Keenan was going to lose his father?

"He's going to die and he doesn't have long. They said it would be in the next couple of hours or so."

This can't be happening.

Why is this happening?

"Who did this?"

"I don't know. Keiran has been in there for hours and hasn't come out. I've never seen him like this. I don't know what to do."

"Have you gone in?"

She shook her head and said, "He told me to wait out here."

"I can't do that." There was no way I could stand here and do nothing. I pushed through the door of the hospital room and found Keenan, Keiran, Dash, and Q surrounding the bed with grave expressions. None of them noticed me enter so I stood frozen against the door.

"Tell me who did this," Keenan demanded.

"I can't do that, son. I would rather leave this world knowing you two were finally at peace. I don't deserve to have my death avenged. It's time I pay my dues." John's voice, once strong and deep, was now weak and sickly sounding. The hard, strong man suddenly looked frail.

"What are you talking about?" Keiran barked. "If you deserved to die, I would have done the deed a long time ago."

I should have been appalled by his behavior, but after so many years of friendship, I knew being hard was his way of showing his pain.

"Boys—"

"No, John—dad—fuck!" Keenan visibly struggled with words and the emotions he desperately tried to keep in check. He was fighting a losing battle.

"I am your father, son. I don't care about the biology."

It was then that I remembered a paternity test had never been taken even when the question arose. Could John really be his father? With his death, Keenan would never know.

"Just tell us who did this to you."

"Here is your chance to make it up to us. Tell us who did this," Keiran pressed.

"Whether he's guilty or not, I would be encouraging the murder of a man and sacrificing your futures. It doesn't matter what I allowed in the past. All that matters now is what I do in the present." He took a deep breath and continued speaking.

"I've lived my life with one regret after another, but the regrets I'll carry with me wherever I go from here is not protecting the two of you and giving you the best of me. I regret not being there. I know I have no right to ask, but I want you two to make me a promise."

I risked venturing further into the room because his voice was weakening with each word and his eyes grew heavy. The guys didn't verbally acknowledge his request, but their attention never wavered.

"Promise me that you both will be a better man than I ever was."

Time stood still and then stretched impossibly long as each person in the room waited to see what Keenan and Keiran would decide.

At once, they finally nodded, offering some small mercy and comfort to the dying man who was the only father either of them had ever known.

I expected more.

Redemption.

Acceptance.

Love.

In the end, John died and neither of them ever shed a tear.

*****

No one knew what to say so no one said a thing. It was devastating how unexpected and pointless death could be. The doctor announcing the time of death still echoed in my head.

What do you say to someone whose father just died? Are you okay? Sorry for your loss? It's going to be okay?

The real tragedy was in the lack of emotion that followed his death. Keenan and Keiran had both walked away without looking back. The only one who couldn't seem to get a hold of their emotions was Lake.

Dash had agreed to take Kennedy to our parents' home for the night, leaving me his car while he hitched a ride with Q. I paced the hall while Keenan and Keiran talked to the doctors searching for something to say.

When someone dies, you grieve. I didn't know John all that well due to his absence, but he had become someone I could count on for Kennedy in the last four years.

I was so deep in my thoughts that I hadn't noticed when Keenan approached and stood in front of me, watching.

"Are you okay?" The raspy sound of his voice drew my attention.

"I'm supposed to be asking you that." He only shrugged, and I watched his emotionless eyes stare back at me blankly. "Keenan... what's going on in your head?"

"My father just died. I don't know what you want me to say."

"Talk to me. You have to feel something. I know you do."

"I couldn't even tell my own father that I loved him before he died and you know why? Because I didn't. I couldn't fucking love him. Our history is too ugly. How the hell will I ever be able to love my own kid?"

"Keenan, sometimes it's not that simple. You're not your father and Kennedy isn't you."

"Yeah? Well, I don't think that's a chance I'm willing to take any more."

And just like that, for the second time in my life, he walked away from me. Only this time, I followed. Right through the hospital doors and into the night.

During a less emotional time in the future, I may wonder why I chased after him. He sped from the hospital grounds, and I struggled to keep Keenan in my sights as I raced behind him. The roads were slippery from rain and traffic seemed to pour from every direction. He was leaving. How could he leave?

Why was I trying to stop him?

His father had just died, and without missing a beat, his only thought had been to get away. Maybe it was just for a few hours, but the look in his eyes had sent warning signals to my gut not to let him get away.

The course of this night would lead into forever, and it was up to me to choose the path. Right or wrong. I had to choose. So I did.

"Come on, Keenan. Please slow down. Slow down. Slow..."

He shot through an intersection just as the light turned red and I had no choice but to floor it so as not to lose him.

It was a mistake that became apparent by the blinding lights of an oncoming car, hindering my ability to see even more but it was too late anyway.

I had never heard a worse sound than metal crunching and grinding, and there was no greater fear than the fear of falling.

Actually, that was untrue. The feeling like you were going to die was greater. The fear of all you would leave behind by dying was the greatest of them all.

CHAPTER TWENTY-SIX

KEENAN

I NEEDED TO turn around. Something was telling me to turn around, but which would I be listening to if I did—my head or my heart? Rain poured by the boatload making it hard to see. I sped through the streets heading for the exit out of Six Forks.

My father was dead, and I couldn't feel a damn thing. Tonight proved how empty I was, and I couldn't get out of my head how Sheldon looked at me.

Like I was evil, unworthy, and cold. At least that's how I felt. I couldn't place the blame on her.

The stoplight up ahead turned yellow and I had to make the choice to stop or speed through. I chose the latter because stopping meant having the chance to look back.

I made it through just as the light turned red and thought I was home free until a series of horns blasted around me. At first, I chalked it up to disgruntled drivers until I looked in the rearview in time to see a car stupidly follow behind me. The car was quickly t-boned and spun out of control until a pole stopped it. Painfully, I watched the car wrap violently around the pole.

There was no way the driver could have survived.

In the space of seconds, the world seemed to stop when I recognized the car. It belonged to Dash, but he had left earlier with Kennedy and caught a ride with Q.

Fuck. Sheldon.

I jerked the car to the side and hit the ground running. A crowd formed around the wreck, and I had to muscle through to get to her. The car had flipped over and was completely totaled.

Desperation and shame flooded my senses. Sheldon had been chasing after me.

I did this.

"Young man, you shouldn't get too close. The car is leaking gas."

A quick inspection of the ground confirmed the older woman's warning. Already, I could hear sirens in the background, but I couldn't wait for them. I called out to Sheldon, but when she didn't answer or move, I realized she was unconscious. Blood leaked from her head and given her recent head injury, it made the situation all the more detrimental.

I yanked on the door handle, but it wouldn't budge. The glass was completely shattered so I reached inside cutting my arm and hand in the process. No matter how hard I shoved and yanked and pounded, the door wouldn't budge. I ran around and tried all four until the rear passenger door gave way.

"Oh, dear," the older lady from before gasped. "Son, you better get away and wait for help to come. That pole is beginning to spark."

It didn't take an explanation to know what would happen if a single spark reached the ground and gas that traveled closer to the pole by the second. I refused to lose my father and her in the same night.

"Son, get away from there. You're going to get yourself killed," a faceless voice yelled from the crowd. There was no way I was leaving her or standing by for help. If it came to it, I would die with her.

Without her, I was dead anyway.

I crawled inside just as she began to come to, and I said a quick, silent prayer that she was still alive and reached out for her.

Screams ripped through the air, and when I looked back, I saw a single spark falling. I watched it fall for all of two seconds and then moved with renewed determination. I reached out again, but just as I did, hands grabbed onto me, pulling me away.

"No!" I screamed and clawed at the hands grabbing me, but there were too many pulling me further away. The spark had now reached the ground and raced toward the car. I threw an elbow and my head back, not caring who was on the receiving end and managed to break free.

Adrenaline surged through my veins.

On my hands and knees, I scrambled for the car once again and dove in without hesitation. I ripped the seatbelt away and caught her just as the car caught the first fire. Instantly, I could feel the flames heating my skin. Smoke filled the car making it hard to see, and the way I came in was already engulfed leaving my only way out through the driver's door.

With little room, I kicked at the door, aware at any moment the car would explode. Even now, I could feel myself tiring from the smoke that filled my lungs. It was becoming impossible to breathe and even the force of my kicks decreased.

I began to see my life as it had been and then my life as it could be.

"Keenan," Sheldon groaned before she went still.

Just the sound of my name from her gave me the strength I needed, and with one last kick, the door finally gave way.

*****

ONE MONTH LATER

"I still can't believe you closed the shop. However will you service all the women of Los Angeles?"

"Would you stop with the slut jokes? I haven't slept with a single woman in California."

"Oh, I know, but it's so much fun to see your panties in a twist."

"Get lost, Di." I pretended not to care but quickly gave up the fight. "How did you know?"

"Because you were so much more happy go lucky when you were getting laid on a regular basis. Since you left, you've become a grumpy asshole. I would say even worse than brother dearest."

"Are you here to help me unpack or reflect on my character?"

"I can't believe you really left."

"You can always stay. Keenan and Di—on the road again."

"Umm... live in Six Forks? I don't think so. I need the glam life in the city."

"Or maybe you're scared," I teased.

"There is nothing in Six Forks that scares me." The frown she wore was troubled. I cocked an eyebrow at her but didn't respond. Unlike her, I didn't push.

I looked around my father's house that he left to Keiran and me along with every single thing he owned. Keiran had immediately rejected everything while I chose to donate everything minus the house and his business. We had our differences as fucked up as they were, but I couldn't bring myself to give away everything he built.

I had the attorneys divide everything that belonged to John, and everything that was inherited, and had them donate the inherited funds to various organizations with the larger portions going to foundations dedicated to battered women and children.

"So what's next?"

"What do you mean?" I asked absently as I cut through the tape on another box. Michelangelo stared back at me in the form of a backpack. The little green monster was smirking while he stood ready in a pose for combat.

"Are you going to fight for her this time?"

"Who?"

"Does it matter? They're a pair now, you know. Two for the price of one," she joked.

"What's that?"

"Oy... pay attention, will you? The woman you've been in love with, the mother of your child, and the woman you pulled out of a burning car is out there falling in love with someone else and you're here decorating."

"She wants nothing to do with me, Di. She made that clear."

"Well, you had just almost gotten her killed because she was worried about you when you couldn't be bothered to care for yourself."

I took a deep breath and closed the box full of my daughter's things that were left behind that morning a month ago. "Who have you been talking to?"

"Lake. She and Keiran are doing great in Hawaii, by the way."

Keiran and Lake had temporarily relocated for the

summer until Lake starts graduate school at Stanford in the fall. Keiran's brush with his past after four years was hard on Lake who hadn't been able to relax since.

Keiran had taken his inheritance and funneled a large portion of it into Jesse's company, becoming a partner. It was hard to believe Keiran fought past his jealousy and now actually worked with the man. No one knows what he did with the rest of his inheritance. He only claimed it was no longer his.

Apparently, he made this decision long before the NBA offers poured in. All of which he'd turned down.

Even though our relationship was still rocky, I couldn't help but respect his decision. Something told me Lake had something to do with it. Indirectly, of course. Anyone with eyes could see that Keiran sought her approval. He wanted to be worthy of her.

It also explained the degree in computer science.

I didn't think I would ever get over that one.

"That's great. When are they coming back?"

"In about two months, but don't try to change the subject. What are you doing?"

"I'm trying to be a decent human being for once."

"By denying your feelings and a child her father?"

"Kennedy doesn't know I'm her father. It's better this way. I won't have to spend the next fifteen years afraid that I will become my father and her suffering for it."

"So fulfill the promise you made a dying man during his final moments and do the right thing."

Chapter Twenty-Seven

SHELDON

I READ THE words of the letter for what seemed like the hundredth time.

I did it.

After four years of wanting to pull my eyeballs through my skull by my hair, I'd accomplished what I set out to do. Medical school was calling my name.

Worry tried to worm its way through, but I wouldn't let the stress of the past few weeks or my future obstacles as a med student and single mother ruin this moment.

I needed to call someone.

Eric surprisingly popped in my head, but after Keenan had beaten him to a pulp in front of a restaurant full of people, including his parents, he made it clear I wasn't to contact him, especially after I told him about Kennedy.

Apparently, his parents had a certain image preset for him that my baggage and I would tarnish. And so ended a one-year relationship that would have never developed past the limit I had set of my own.

I was even more grateful that I never slept with him.

I never even had the urge.

It was time to for me to make Kennedy's lunch so I checked on her first. It was a full-time job keeping her out of mischief. For the first time, she took the initiative to actually draw on paper instead of the walls or furniture. Her head was bent and her face serious with concentration as she doodled. I was beginning to believe that drawing was something she loved to do like her father.

Don't think about him, Sheldon.

Don't think about how he hadn't called nor had he stayed.

Nope. He went back to California to his tattoo shop and high-rise apartment and... Di.

I wondered if they ever had sex or if their friendship had been completely platonic.

There was something about her that didn't meet the eye. I didn't know if it was good or bad, but I knew she was more than she showed the world. Maybe it was why I didn't trust her.

Or maybe I was just jealous.

After all, she had been in his life for the last four years when I hadn't.

Did he realize he loved her and that was why he never came back?

More often than not, I wondered if he ever thought about us.

It was hard for me not to think of him or what he had done for me. He had risked his life for me in the craziest of ways. Not only had I heard about it, but also some punk kid had the gall to videotape it and upload it to YouTube.

Now every vagina around the world and woman with girlish dreams wanted him. And all I wanted to do was to stake my claim and forget how I turned him away after surviving the crash.

I half expected and half hoped he would threaten and stake his own claim, but instead, he walked away from us quietly.

Was it unreasonable for me to hate him for it?

"Kennedy, it's time for lunch," I shouted over the thunder that had suddenly broken through the sky. A quick peek through the windows showed torrential rains pouring onto the street below.

"Mama, it's raining now. Can I go play?" I smiled and like always, shook my head. I think Kennedy was the only child ever who didn't understand that rain-storms were not for playing in. My little daredevil bare-ly noticed a sunny day.

"We talked about this, Ken." I set her plate full of square-cut peanut butter and jelly sandwiches in front of her just as a hard knock sounded on the door.

I debated answering because I wasn't expecting an-yone. After Kennedy had been kidnapped with no leads to who was responsible, I was being extra cautious.

When I picked up the large kitchen knife on the way to the door, I realized that paranoid might have been a better term.

Keenan and Keiran had suspected my father, but after damn near interrogating him, they laid it to rest. My father's only crime had been his carelessness and putting business before his grandchild.

Greg and Vick had approached my father with false credentials as private investigators after 'hearing about her kidnapping' on the news. It had been a long shot, but one they lucked out on after his men had already been placed on another assignment concerning a business deal in Germany that my father had been cultivating for a very long time.

The only question now was who hired them to impersonate private investigators. We already knew why. Someone out there wanted Keiran dead bad enough to kidnap an innocent child, and without a name, he was still in danger along with Kennedy.

"Just a second," I called when the knocking continued, becoming louder with each knock. I opened the door and stared at the person on the other side in surprise.

I wasn't expecting him.

"Can I help you?"

"Yes, I'm here to install your new cable and internet service." A middle-aged man in faded jeans and even more faded t-shirt with the cable company's logo stood with a smile. I quickly slid the knife down my sleep shorts and pasted a smile.

"I didn't schedule for a cable installation."

The man frowned and then looked down at the tablet he carried. "Are you Sandy Chaplin? Apartment 203?"

"No, I'm sorry. That apartment is around the corner and two doors down."

"My apologies. Have a great day." He ambled off and I closed the door feeling silly. I had just made it back to the kitchen when the knocking returned. This time I left the knife.

I assumed the technician might have gotten lost again so my smile was ready when I opened the door. The person standing on the other side of the door this time swept my smile away.

My brain screamed at me to close the door and pretend it never happened, but I stood transfixed.

Keenan stood on the other side with his head down,

drenched in rainwater. His white t-shirt was plastered to his muscular chest making his tattoos visible while his jeans hung off his hips in the way that I liked so much.

"Are you going to let me in or continue to eye fuck me," he smirked. Instead of waiting for an answer, he took my hand and stepped inside, closing the door behind us. All the while, I stood with my mouth agape.

He's really here.

"What—um... what are you doing here?" I had to clear my throat multiple times to speak intelligibly. I glanced toward the kitchen nervously and debated kicking him out. I didn't want Kennedy to see him if he wasn't here to stay...

What was I thinking? Did I want him to stay?

Kennedy had been depressed over Keenan's disappearance and had only just stopped asking for him. For the longest time, she'd cry herself to sleep, and I didn't understand even though I wanted to cry with her. She had only known him for a weekend.

Love didn't kindle that fast, did it?

I felt like a hypocrite for even thinking it. Keenan and I had fallen fast and hard for each other. Why couldn't the same be for father and daughter?

"A good friend of mine reminded me that I wasn't fulfilling my promises. I realized that every promise I made, since I walked away from you four years ago, involved you. Even the promise I had made to my father before he died."

"What are you talking about?"

"I'm talking about you and Kennedy and the very permanent fact that the two of you still *own me.*"

My head swam with the possibilities of what he could mean. "I don't speak in riddles, Keenan. Why are you here?"

He ran his hands through his already spiky hair and blew out a breath. "I'm here because I want to beg... if you'll let me."

He seemed at a loss for words so I asked, "What do you want to beg for?"

"For you and my kid."

I took a step back, letting my hand slide from his tight grip. Surprisingly, he let me go although he flinched from the loss of contact. "Are you actually asking for another chance?"

"No."

"Oh..."

"I'm asking for you to save my life because with every breath in my body, I love you. I'll love you until my last. Without you, I am no longer someone with a reason to live."

"I'd like to believe that, but I can't. You have a problem that I can't overlook anymore. I can't spend the rest of my life worrying that one day you'll find the woman who is not only worth betraying me for, but is also worth breaking my heart forever."

His eyes became desperate and frustration lined his features.

"I was filling a void created by my parents. I was invisible before you. I was unwanted and unloved. I lived that way until I found a way to fill it, even if they were only temporary fixes. I was an addict but not in the way that you think. I craved the attention and the intimacy I never had and was too stupid to realize the gift you gave me was far more precious. I wasn't worthy of you, but you filled the void. And then, somehow, this image of my mother walking away from me forever became you. I was scared, Shelly. I was terrified that you would one day realize I was unworthy and leave so I found a way to fight the insecurity while holding on to you. It made me feel like I was in control, and that no matter what, someone would want me."

"So I was replaceable."

"No!" he shouted and I glanced nervously toward the kitchen. He lowered his voice and said, "Not replaceable. You were unobtainable."

"But you had me."

"I had my mother once too, and then I lost her."

"So what makes you think it will be better now?"

"Because I realize my mother and father made their choices, but their choices didn't have to reflect mine. I'm not afraid to love you anymore."

"You didn't even love me enough to fight for me. Instead, you ran away the first time I hurt you when I forgave you each time you broke my heart. I risked everything to be with you—my self-respect, my sanity, and my heart—and now you're asking me to risk it all again?"

"If the risk means my surrender, then this..." He kneeled and my heart ricocheted around my chest. "This, Shelly, is me surrendering to you."

"I, uh... what?"

"Princess," he shouted. "Could you come here, please?"

Tiny footsteps sounded, but I was still frozen to the spot to react. "Keenan!" Kennedy ran into sight and launched herself into Keenan's arms.

"I missed you," he whispered to her.

She clung to his neck until he sat her on his knee. "Baby girl, I have a confession to make that you may not understand, but I need to do it anyway. Are you listening?"

She nodded and he cleared his throat.

"Four years ago, I hurt your mother really bad in more ways than one." Kennedy seemed to understand because her face fell, but she continued to listen.

"I thought I could protect her from a really bad lady by doing something that I knew would break her heart. I took the chance to keep her father from taking her away from me because the bad lady knew we were naughty kids."

He grinned at the last, and I cleared my throat.

"Anyway, the bad lady video recorded us with her phone when we did a naughty thing at school and threatened to show her father along with the whole world if I didn't do what she wanted. She also threatened to fail her if I said no and failing meant your mother would have to go somewhere far away from me to finish school. I made a deal with the devil, and although I saved your mother from the bad lady, I lost her, too. I was selfish, Princess, and I took your mother for granted, but if you can forgive me, I promise to spend the rest of my life never taking her for granted again."

He looked up from Kennedy to meet my gaze. "Can you forgive me, baby?"

I don't know how long we gazed into each other's eyes before Kennedy stood up from her father's lap to stand in front of me. "Keenan sorry, mama."

"You little traitor," I whispered to her before a smile broke free. I felt my tears but ignored them because there was something I needed to say. "I'll forgive you on one condition." He looked wary but told me to name it without hesitation. "You tell Kennedy that you're her father, and you better have a ring somewhere on you because we aren't accepting anything less than your full commitment."

His boyish smile that I recognized from so long ago broke free as he stuck his hand in his pocket and produced not one but two rings. "Princess, come here." She turned to him and he took her left hand. "Kennedy Sophia Chambers, will you accept me as your father?"

Kennedy nodded with her gaze transfixed on the ring that looked like a real diamond although tiny to fit her finger. I suppressed the urge to scold him for buying a three-year-old a ring that no doubt cost a lot of money. He slid the ring on her tiny finger, and to my surprise, it fit. He grumbled something about changing her last name before turning to me.

That was the moment I began to feel my heart beating against my chest a little too hard. "Sheldon Chambers, will you do me the honor of accepting my surrender to you and being my wife?"

* * * * *

TWO MONTHS LATER

"Let me see the ring! Let me see the ring!" Lake pushed aside everyone in her way to get to me. Seriously, someone would have to speak about what we started to call her *Keiran Tendencies.* We were currently having a barbecue in our backyard to celebrate their return from Hawaii.

She gushed and cooed over my engagement ring before she started crying. "I knew he was likely to stop being a coward."

Everyone in the vicinity laughed except for Keenan, who pouted. He could still be such a baby. There were days when Ken was more of an adult.

"So when is the wedding?"

"November 24th. Two days before Thanksgiving."

"I'm so happy for you, I could just cry."

"I think you already are...?" Keiran remarked, earning an elbow to the gut. He rolled his eyes and began to nibble on her neck, and just like that, I was forgotten. I had to clear my throat to get their attention again.

"Do you guys ever use a bedroom?" More than once, I had walked in on them during their spring break. It was right after Kennedy was born, and the first time I had walked in on them going at it on the kitchen counter. Granted, it was his home but still...

"Keenan, get your fiancée out of my sex life," Keiran replied. "Someone might think you can't please your woman."

Laughter surrounded us, and though I was the brunt of the joke, I was elated to see them trying once more. They still tiptoed around each other, but some of the tension had dissipated. Their bond started to reconnect at John's funeral shortly after his death. I had attended despite my decision to stay away from Keenan because I couldn't bring myself to not be there. There were days when Keenan would come across something of John's and a dark cloud had taken residence while I waited him out, and like always, he'd come back to me.

"Shelly, can I talk to you in private?" Without waiting for a response, he took my elbow and steered me into his childhood home that was now ours.

"If you are dragging me off for sex, I told you there is a waiting period. We just did it on the washer an hour before the barbecue started."

"I found the letter," he said once he shut the door to our bedroom.

"Huh?"

"The college acceptance letter to Stanford. I found it hidden in your panty drawer."

"What were you doing in my panty drawer?"

"That's not the point. Why didn't you tell me about this?"

"Because I've decided not to go."

"Say what?"

"I decided not to go. Stanford is in California."

"I'm well aware of where it is. What I don't get is why you threw away this opportunity?"

"Because our life is here in Six Forks."

"No, Shelly, our life is where ever we are as long as we are together." He shook his head, and I felt like a scolded child. "I'm disappointed in you."

Now I was the one to pout. "What do you want me to say, Keenan? It's too late."

"That's where you're wrong. Early admission is coming. I've already collected everything you need. Tonight, before you even think about having me between your thighs, I want you to start on it and make whatever preparations you need to."

"Don't I get a say in this?"

"You already had your say, now it's my turn."

"But I like it here."

In truth, I didn't know why I was objecting. Medical school was what I wanted ever since Kennedy had her first episode. To some people, it may not have been a reason to decide the path I would take, but I never wanted to feel that helpless again, and not only could I help Kennedy but other sick children. I could make a greater difference than being a fashion model.

"We can return in a few years when you're done, and Kennedy will have access to a beach anytime she wants."

Kennedy was insatiable when it came to the beach. Anytime she saw water, she was asking to go to the beach. Bath time was a real treat.

"What are we going to do about the house?"

"It's paid for and it's ours. It's not going anywhere."

"Are you really willing to do this for me?"

"Ask me that again and I'll spank your ass."

"I just—"

"Sheldon."

"Sheldon? Since when do you call me Sheldon?"

"Since you started asking to be bent over my knee."

My body answered to his statement long before I could. "Instead of your knee, maybe you could tie me to the bed again." I lifted my dress over my head, revealing my naked body underneath. "Remember how we conceived Ken?"

"Fuck yeah, I remember." His voice had turned husky and his eyes darkened with the need to fuck. "Get the belt."

CHAPTER TWENTY-EIGHT

KEENAN

I watched Shelly do as I ordered with a teasing smile on her lips and thought about how, for the rest of my life, I would get to see that smile every day.

I'd never felt so fucking needed than I did when I was with her and Ken.

All my life I had been searching for feeble attention when all this time I had been granted a love that was just for me.

And though our love may have been broken, it was still ours.

Chapter Twenty-Nine

IT'S NOT OVER...

"So who is the poor soul who suffered this unfortunate fate, and more importantly, who did he piss off?"

"Mitch Masters. Age forty-eight. No wife or kids to speak of. The family is an unclear subject. His brother, John Masters, admitted him to the facility, but was also murdered a few months ago and no leads have been found for that either." The detective circled the crime scene carefully, but when his gaze landed on all the blood on the wall, he looked away and studied the body instead. "So his eyes were open?"

"Yeah. The poor bastard saw his death coming."

The bloody mess on the walls was hard to stomach, but this time, the detective didn't look away immediately.

Written in crimson red, were the words, 'For John.'

"I think we just found our lead."

The End

But What About…

- Who was behind Kennedy's kidnapping?
- Who killed Mitch?
- Who was Keenan's father?
- Where is Willow?

…and more.

The series continues so stay tuned for an important announcement.

Interview With Keenan

If you could have a phone conversation with Keenan, what would you say?

Nualla DaSilva: What were you really feeling when Sheldon didn't come see you?

Keenan: The one thing I had left to live for walked away. I felt like death.

Lauren Stryker: You need to make up with your brother!!

Keenan: If it's meant to be, it will be.

Rachel Campbell: How dare you be pissed at Sheldon not being there for you after you humiliated her over and over by screwing around.

Keenan: I'm a man, baby. What can I say?

Maria Williams: Why do you always cheat on Sheldon? What has she ever done to you??

Keenan: She loved me. Big fucking mistake there.

Tanya Lock: Keep it in your bloody pants. Then you wouldn't keep getting yourself in trouble.

Keenan: If only I knew this sooner! ;-)

Sammi Darby: I would tell him to not lose sight of himself just because he's hurt and angry.

Keenan: Damn, girl. That's deep.

Feena Don: Put Keiran on please!

Keenan: Sorry, he's busy sniffing Lake's ass.

Lisa P. Kane: WTF is your problem? Suck it up and move on.

Keenan: Damn it, Lisa. I'm marrying her, aren't I?

Heather Marie: Do you really love Sheldon?

Keenan: If I didn't, then proposing was a big mistake!

Eve Nesselrotte: Find your dad and make him pay!!

Keenan: Looks like someone already did... Did you read the book or were you dozing? LOL

Jenifer Robare: Why didn't you just tell her you had feelings for her, good ones and bad ones—at least as you guys started getting older.

Keenan: You mean, every time I put out, I wasn't expressing my feelings? Son of a bitch!

ACKNOWLEDGMENTS

First to my loving, stubborn FAMILY, who puts up with my absence and never finding the time to come home. Thank you for all the support and encouragement. Although I found out the hard way that none of you could keep a secret, I still appreciate the pride you have for me.

DEVEN: You are both the person holding the gun to my head to get the book done and the one keeping me from getting anything done. Thank you for putting up with side effects of dating an author.

TIERA & KANESHA: Thank you for listening to me talk endlessly about writing and my books and the encouragement.

My COLLEAGUES AT C.R.: Thank you as well for putting up with the days I come in half-motivated and half-asleep. Albert, you're still the best boss ever.

1ST PLATOON: I am not Fifty Shades.

MASTERS: Without you ladies, who would know about me? Ladies, you're either up at the crack of dawn pimping or up before me. Thank you for all your laughter, support, and love. I'd be lost without you.

ROGENA & AMI: Thank you so much for the flexibility and putting up with my insecurities. Most importantly, thank you for treating me like a friend and not just a client.

TWISTED SISTERS, CRAZYBOOK_LOVERS, THREE CHICKS, and every blog/book group who ever gave me the time day: A big thank you for all the features, teasers, and promotions. You name it, you did it.

LYDIA, ADRIENNE, TIFFANY, & KATIE: I can always count on you guys for a laugh or helping hand when I need it. Love you guys.

DI: Thank you for being my inspiration for DI. Thank you for giving me the time of day. Thank you for being my confidante in everything dark. Thank you for being a friend.

JOSI, ASHLEIGH, MARY: Ladies, thank you for being a friend in this industry and for all the support. You ladies have shown that authors don't have to belittle one another if you just believe in your craft.

Also by B.B. Reid

Broken Love Series

Fear Me

Fear You

Fear Us

Breaking Love

Fearless

The Stolen Duet

The Bandit

Contact the Author

Join **Bebe's Reiders** on Facebook!

Twitter: _BBREID

Instagram: _BBREID

www.bbreid.com

About B.B. Reid

B.B., ALSO KNOWN as Bebe, found her passion for romance when she read her first romance novel by Susan Johnson at a young age. She would sneak into her mother's closet for books and even sometimes the attic. It soon became a hobby, and later an addiction. When she finally de-cided to pick up a metaphorical pen and start writing, she found a new way to embrace her passion.

She favors a romance that isn't always easy on the eyes or heart, and loves to see characters grow—characters who are seemingly doomed from the start but find love anyway.

Fear Me, her debut novel, is the first of many.